PENGUIN

The Eve

# The Eve Illusion

## GIOVANNA AND TOM FLETCHER

PENGUIN BOOKS

PENGUIN BOOKS

UK | USA | Canada | Ireland | Australia
India | New Zealand | South Africa

Penguin Books is part of the Penguin Random House group of companies
whose addresses can be found at global.penguinrandomhouse.com.

First published by Michael Joseph, 2020
This edition published by Penguin Books, 2021

001

Copyright © Giovanna and Tom Fletcher, 2020

The moral right of the author has been asserted

Printed and bound in Great Britain by Clays Ltd, Elcograf S.p.A.

The authorized representative in the EEA is Penguin Random House Ireland,
Morrison Chambers, 32 Nassau Street, Dublin D02 YH68

A CIP catalogue record for this book is available from the British Library

ISBN: 978–1–405–92716–1

For Buzz, Buddy and Max

# I

# Michael

Restricted duties.

Damn right they're restricted. I've barely received enough food to feed the rat that shares my quarters. I have to hand it to the fella: this place is meant to be impenetrable – an iron fortress – yet he's managed to find his way up nine hundred storeys and sought out one of the few humans in the Tower that wouldn't kill him instantly.

I assume it's a *him*. Or could this be the Eve of the rat population, kept locked away up here for her own 'protection'?

I throw him a scrap of bread, although I'm surprised they even call it bread, the artificial crap they created when all the wheat died out. He sniffs the crumbs but turns away without eating it.

'I don't blame you,' I scoff, chucking what's left into

my mouth. I wash it down with a swig of water and it still sticks in my throat.

After what I've done I'm lucky to be alive, let alone allowed to stay in this building *and* keep my job. We are the Final Guards, the highest level of security. We have one objective: protect Eve. Not only did I fail at it, but I put her in direct danger by taking her into that lift.

If the situation was different, if Ketch and half the team hadn't been caught in that blast at the sanctuary, I'd have been . . . Well, Ratty here wouldn't have a friend no more.

The fact is, though, the Extinction Prevention Organization need me right now. Security is thin and times are tenser than ever. Not that the EPO would ever admit that. It's not in line with the façade they present to Central, the barely beating heart of what's left of this world. Sometimes I think this place is all just one big show, an illusion. And I guess I've seen too much of the truth for them to let me go now.

The lab.

The blood.

The experiments.

Eve.

I clench both fists and dig my nails into my palms until all my knuckles click. Her face flashes in my mind again. It was the first time we'd properly met – I'd seen her countless times, of course, as one of her Final Guards, but we'd never made eye contact before. That was drilled into us all from our first day on the job.

She was terrified, I see that now. Trapped with me in the lift, like a metal prison.

Trapped with a *man*.

What the hell was I thinking?

*What are you going to do to me?*

I shake my head violently, trying to rattle away the thoughts. The thing that scares me most is that I don't know what I was going to do. There was no plan. I just knew I had to pull her from that room, from that maniac Potential. He'd already murdered Mother Nina, believing her to be Eve. I had to get her to safety.

Before I knew it, we were alone and . . .

The lights in my quarters burst into a blinding cold white, snapping me from my memory. Emergency sirens scream through the concrete corridors and punch my eardrums until I'm on my feet.

Ratty scampers away and my door swishes open.

'Turner!' booms Guard Ryan from the doorway, with a look of urgency. 'Final Guards, we're needed immediately.'

'But I'm Restricted!' I shout over the deafening sirens.

'Not any more.' He gestures at my bare torso and I follow his gaze down to my tag – the small circular implant sitting under the skin on the left side of my chest. The subtle red glow that I've seen for the last few days is now replaced with a refreshing blue. I'm back on full active duty with no explanation.

Something's happened.

I grab a vest and slip it over my head as I follow Guard Ryan out into the corridor, where the rest of my fellow Final Guards are gathering. They shoot me curious looks and I shrug. I'm as surprised as they are that I'm here, but I'm glad to be reunited with them.

The metal sphere opens. We climb inside and look to Ryan, our temporary commander.

'This is a real-world scenario. We have reason to believe the Tower has been breached,' Guard Ryan says, placing a matt black helmet on his shaved head. Eve's golden emblem catches in the light as the chin-strap self-fastens and automatically tightens. 'I know it's not ideal that I'm here instead of Ketch, but we've gotta work together now.'

The sphere closes and begins to glide.

'Wait, we're going up?' I blurt out. 'We're on the nine-hundredth floor. Where the hell's the breach?'

*YOU HAVE ARRIVED AT THE DOME*, the automated voice of the lift announces within a few seconds.

We all glance at each other.

The Dome?

A breach in the Dome?

That's impossible.

Ryan raises one eyebrow in confirmation as he backs out and heads to the Gate – the invisible barrier that separates the Tower and the Dome. I follow and instantly feel the tag in my chest vibrate as I pass through the transparent beam of energy, which scans for any unauthorized personnel and would induce instant paralysis. Temporary, of course, but I still wouldn't want to go anywhere near the Gate if my tag was still glowing red. Even my rat companion wouldn't get this far.

My heart skips at being back in action. Guard Ryan passes his hand over a plate on the wall and a hidden hatch slides open with a hiss. These hidden armouries are plotted all around the Tower. Only the commanding guard knows their location and can access them. For obvious reasons they can't have weapons fall into the wrong hands in here.

We suit up and arm ourselves in a matter of seconds. We've drilled these scenarios hundreds of times.

'Guards,' Guard Ryan barks.

'Ready, sir,' we chant in reply and fall in line.

I take second position behind Guard Ryan. Of course, I would be first if it weren't for the lift incident, but there's no time to dwell on that now.

Red strips of light suddenly illuminate along the metallic corridor, guiding us to the emergency.

'They must have located the intruder,' I say, and we all pick up the pace.

*EMERGENCY. ASSISTANCE REQUIRED IMMEDIATELY IN THE DOME*, a voice announces, making us all explode into a sprint, following the red hallways as all others have been blacked out.

'This can't be right,' Guard Ryan's voice mutters, through the earpiece inside our helmets.

We all know what he's talking about. The lighting is guiding us towards the garden zone.

The harshness of the concrete and steel softens as the doors unlock and slide open, allowing us into Eve's world.

Our weapons click gently as they automatically adjust to non-lethal mode.

Eve must be close.

We steal looks at each other. I know their hearts will be thudding, just not as hard as mine. They don't know Eve like I do. What she looks like up-close. What she feels like. What she . . .

'The Drop. Now,' commands a sharp voice we don't hear very often: Miss Vivian Silva's. I spot her ahead of us, radiating impatience.

'Yes, Miss Silva,' Guard Ryan replies instantly, and signals with his hands for us to follow at pace. Her sharp gaze studies us as we pass and I sense an undertow of anxiety that she can't hide behind her angular features.

Her eyes meet mine and the moment seems to linger.

I read the look.

This is my chance to redeem myself.

'Holy shit,' Guard Ryan's voice hisses in my ear. 'We have a situation.'

I sprint through the trees without a care for the endangered plant life that perishes under my boots.

The guards have gathered at the entrance to the Drop – Eve's favourite location in the Dome. The place she can look out at the world and philosophize, blissfully unaware that the entire thing is a sham. The most elaborate and expensive prison walls in history and she doesn't even know that's what they are.

RealiTV screens project an alternative view twenty-four-seven, controlled by the EPO or, more specifically, Miss Silva. Eve sees the world Miss Silva wants her to see – lingering sunsets that kiss the clouds for what feels like hours, eventually giving way to starlight bright enough to cast your shadow on the concrete. The perfect illusion for the illusion of perfection. And all this just to give Eve hope. To make her think the world's worth saving. No one else can do it, after all.

'What the hell is she doing?' Guard Ryan mutters.

'I can't see. Move.' I shove my way through the six guards huddled at the doorway as they fail to override the hacked system that's keeping them shut. My face is practically up against the glass doors by the time I see them.

Eve and Holly, the holographic projection she calls a friend.

'What are they doing?' I ask.

'I don't know, but she's got something in her hands,' Guard Ryan notices. 'I thought objects were banned on the Drop.'

'They are,' Miss Silva interrupts from behind. 'Now, stop gawping and get those doors open.'

'Yes, ma'am. Guard Turner, Guard Finn.' Guard Ryan steps aside and we set to work instantly. I pull the small plasma blade from my belt and begin slicing away at the seal between the doors but it's so secure I think it'll take hours to cut through.

'Why are these doors locked?' Guard Ryan calls, as Finn follows my lead and begins cutting too.

'The whole system has been compromised,' Miss Silva says, from her spot a few yards back from us.

'Compromised? How?' Guard Ryan asks. 'I thought this whole place was impenetrable from the outside, physically and digitally.'

'It is. This was done from inside,' Miss Silva says coolly, not taking her eyes from Eve.

'Sir . . .' Guard Finn says. He's stopped cutting at the sealed doors to point at the Drop.

We all look. We all see.

'No . . .' Miss Silva whispers.

Eve pulls back her arm and I catch a glimpse of a small multicoloured cube in her fist before she launches it into the air, over the Drop.

There is silence. Total stillness as we watch the cube rotate and glide gently through the air before disappearing from our line of sight. We all know what Eve would have seen next, though. That little cube will appear to be floating on a patch of sky as though some invisible force is holding it up.

She turns and yells at her projected companion with the widened eyes of someone woken abruptly from a dream. Or a nightmare.

The game is up.

Eve knows.

'Break the glass!' Miss Silva demands and we all jump into action. I remove my useless knife from the rubbery seal, pull back my gun and slam the butt against the thick glass doors.

Eve glances in our direction and my heart stops. I feel my face flush with embarrassment at the thought of her seeing me among this pack of wolves that are hunting her down.

'Turner!' Guard Ryan shouts, and I'm aware that I'm staring uselessly through the glass. 'Get back!'

I hear the high-pitched charge of a detonation device and my eyes instinctively find the source – two explosives stuck to the doors.

I leap for cover and feel the force of the blast knock the wind out of me as it blows the doors to pieces. Glass falls like rain from the artificial sky, and through the downpour I see Eve leap.

Chaos instantly follows.

Boots crunch on the broken glass as the Final Guard charge along the Drop, weapons drawn. I arrive at the edge first to find Holly's projection flickering as she grapples with an invisible foe. Whoever is piloting her has been found.

I climb over the circular railing and stare at the clouds below. Guard Ryan arrives at my side and we take a breath before jumping. My stomach lurches as we drop. The view looks so real, even though I know it's all a façade.

We crash on to the screens masquerading as the sky,

and they freeze and flicker. They were not designed to be walked on, let alone trampled by several adrenalin-fuelled guards. Guard Ryan is on his feet first and bolts after Eve as Guard Franklin crashes down next to me.

'I need backup.' Guard Ryan's voice crackles in my earpiece. I scan the horizon and find her – Eve, closely followed by . . . Eve?

There are two of her. The men chasing split up to follow them.

'They're both projections!' Miss Silva screams from the Drop above.

I scramble to my feet.

I have to do something.

I have to prove myself.

I raise my gun. It emits a soft green hue from the barrel. Eve, the real Eve, is still close – too close for me to be able to use my weapon.

'I've got her! I've done it!' Guard Ryan's voice rattles around my helmet.

I quickly flick the visor down.

'Locate Guard Ryan,' I command, and the display instantly highlights his body. He's a hundred feet or so away now, with Eve's foot in his grip but she crunches her heel into his face and he releases her.

Idiot. That's why he's not meant to be in command.

Now's my chance, though. The others are following the false Eves but I have the real one directly ahead of me.

She climbs. I sprint.

I sense Miss Silva's eyes on my back as I cross the sky. I steal a look but she's not on the Drop any longer. By the time I whip my head back Eve has vanished.

'Up there!' Miss Silva screeches. She's on the sky with us now. Man, she can move fast!

She points to a black hole where a panel of sky has been pushed in.

I'm the first guard to arrive at it and Miss Silva steps aside to let me through. It's dark and there's a ladder. I hear Eve's footsteps echo on the metal rungs above.

I begin to climb when BOOM!

The pressure in my head causes me to lose my grip and I fall, landing on Guard Matthews below.

Cool air rushes from behind me as it tries to escape the Dome with Eve. She's found the hatch.

I yawn, equalizing the pressure in my head. My eardrums pound, but there's no time for that now. I launch myself up the ladder but when I reach the top she's gone.

My helmet senses the change in oxygen levels as I step outside the Dome and into the chill of reality. I'm surrounded by clouds that loom with a threatening stillness, looking down on us as though awaiting a bloody battle. A narrow metal walkway wraps around the perimeter. My visor extends automatically and seals itself to the chinstrap. The pressure inside settles and fresh oxygen begins circulating.

*BREATHE NORMALLY*, the automated voice instructs.

'Locate Eve,' I command and translucent arrows direct which way I should turn my head.

There she is, further along the walkway, and she's not alone.

My heart stops.

It's *him*.

Dr Wells's son. The pilot she had a connection with. Bram.

But how could he be back? He'd already achieved the impossible once by escaping this place. Getting back inside? That's another story.

I run after them, feet clanging on the walkway. The fall below is impossible even to comprehend so it doesn't concern me.

'Target Bram Wells.' My visor highlights him.

I raise my gun, its primary function still locked as I'm so close to Eve. I aim at the glowing silhouette of Bram in my display and pull the trigger.

A non-lethal ball of energy pulses in his direction but misses.

'Drones deployed,' Guard Ryan's voice announces inside my ear, and I spot him coming from the opposite side of the walkway, cutting off Eve and Bram. 'They have nowhere to go now.'

He's interrupted by the voice of Miss Silva. It booms mightily through the air, causing everyone to stop.

My heart is pounding and my breathing is so heavy I can barely hear the words, but I catch the end.

'This is your home, Eve. Your world. It's yours and only yours. Perfection.'

Eve looks in my direction. My gun is raised at them.

'Weapons down!' Miss Silva orders, and the entire Final Guard drop their aim.

Suddenly I know what is about to happen. It flashes in front of me as a premonition.

I'm snapped back to the moment and see it unravel for real.

Bram pulls a Gauntlet from a yellow box, which is ready and waiting for him. He straps the harness around Eve and they climb over the safety rail together, all while Vivian Silva's voice blasts at them, followed by that of Dr Wells.

'What do we do, Turner?' Guard Ryan whispers into my earpiece, realizing he's no good in command, but it's too late.

We've already lost her.

'Just watch,' I reply.

They kiss.

They smile.

They jump.

They fall towards the broken clouds below, leaving an eerie silence in their wake, as though the whole world just gasped in unison.

The moment replays over and over in my mind, like a recording stuck on a loop.

Her lips pressed on his.

Her lips pressed on his.

Her lips pressed on . . .

I shake my head to clear the thought. I just saw the most important human in history leap from the tallest building in the world and all I can think about is that kiss.

I look at my fellow Final Guards. Their eyes finally rest on me, and I feel the weight of responsibility that comes with this uniform crash down on me, as though it wants me to follow them over the edge and through the clouds.

I know what I must do, what I'm trained to do . . . what I want to do.

I'm going to get Eve back.

## 2

# Eve

I'm falling with him through the air. Away from the world they built for me. Away from their prison and their lies. Away from their games and their manipulation.

I saw through some of it, of course I did, but how could I possibly have been aware of the depth of their deception? The thickness of the veil Vivian Silva has been holding in front of me all my life?

I knew Holly was a work of art, built for me to befriend so they could understand the workings of my mind. I knew she wasn't real in the traditional sense of the word, yet I was glad to have her.

Him.

Bram.

Unfortunately my gratitude was my downfall. It stopped me seeing my friend as a warning. Rather than being thrilled to have someone to talk to, I should've seen what Holly really was – an example of what they could do. I should have grasped that every sunrise and sunset, almost everything of beauty I ever loved, was a fabrication, built to keep me locked up in their pretty cage so I would do whatever they asked of me.

Until this point, my life has been a lie.

It's hard to accept. Was every part of it corrupt? Did the Mothers, the elderly women who raised me, taught me, dressed me every day, love me as they claimed? Were they all a part of the story? Or were their reasons for being there as pure as I believed them to be?

I think of the wrinkled face of Mother Nina, a beautiful soul who gave her life for mine, and I have to believe the Mothers were true. It's too agonizing to doubt them.

I feel a twinge of guilt as I think of them back up there in the Tower, and wonder what will become of them. They've dedicated more than a decade of their lives to me, only for me to run away.

*Am* I running away? Escaping? Or am I chasing the truth?

Was I right to take Bram's hand, and jump?

This is only our second meeting, yet I've known him – through *her* – for most of my life.

But do I really know him?

No time to ask questions.

Bram's grip around me tightens. Only then do I realize I've had my eyes closed since the moment I stepped away from what once was, and given myself to what is below. My face is buried in Bram's neck, my arms wrapped around his waist and over his broad shoulders. My legs tremble, locked around his.

The wind rushes past us at such an alarming speed that I'm scared to move. I force my eyes open. The monster of a building I once called home still rushes past us. Its appearance is oddly alien to me. I've never been this side of its walls. It's impossible to take it in now, though. It's nothing more than a blur.

We fall through storm clouds, one after another, blocking the view of what's at our feet, and showering us both with icy droplets. I'm drenched from the spray.

The world is loud, the wind thundering around us. Flashes of white and red flicker, the light dancing. It's like nothing I've ever known. It's mystical and terrifying all at once.

Dropping further still, we leave the clouds behind. And I see it.

The world below.

The ground we're heading towards seems to be alive. It moves and surges, dips and rises. It's only when I hear the voices calling, shouting, screaming and chanting, that I understand it's not the ground I'm seeing, but people. The outsiders, the public – the people whose saviour I've been told I am. The people who rejoiced at my birth. The people I've been warned will hurt me if I fail them. That's what Vivian wanted me to believe. Right now, as I'm hurtling towards the crowds, I have to believe she was wrong.

I've no idea why they're all here. Their eyes are fixed on what must be the entrance to the Tower – a hefty metallic structure, imposing and uninviting.

Bram jolts, and my grip on him tightens. I turn to find a black object flying beside us, projecting a red beam of light across Bram's face. He tries to turn, to shield us both, but it's no use. One hand grips whatever the contraption is that's allowing our descent, and the other holds on to me. We're circled by their technology. Wherever Bram goes, it goes. I've no idea whether it'll shoot, follow or protect us but, from Bram's reaction, I'm guessing it's not the latter.

Pushing through the air, fighting against the wind, I bring my leg up and over with as much force as I can muster. A swift roundhouse kick, and fragments of glass and metal split off in the blow. The object spins dizzily.

'Yes!' I scream at a surprised Bram, thankful that the hours of karate lessons they gave me have been of some use. The irony that it's to their disadvantage is not lost on me.

I go in for another kick. This one doesn't impact as smoothly. The fabric of my trousers is caught up in part of its flying mechanism, which is continuing to spin. It's stopped its erratic flight, but only because it's got a grip on my clothes.

Frantically I shake my leg, hoping it'll easily dislodge, but it doesn't budge. Instead it starts pulling at my trousers. It's surprisingly strong for something so small, causing my grip on Bram to slip.

I scream his name.

Another yank on my leg and we're pulled towards the Tower. My head whisks past the metal surface.

Another.

And another.

We're thrown around, like the ragdolls we used to play with when we were younger.

The next tug for freedom rips me from Bram. We scrabble for one another. Our eyes lock and I see my own fear echoed in his.

I drop.

But I'm not falling to my death. Instead I'm caught by the harness, and left dangling below him.

I grip the fabric and scramble to get my arms around Bram's leg. I breathe, trying to think logically. If I kick the whole thing off there's a chance it'll fly straight back into us, even if it's been designed to do me no harm, like the weapons Ketch and my guards use.

I raise my legs once more. With enough force to do some damage, but not enough to set it free, I start to jab repeatedly at the functioning propellers with my other foot. Eventually its lights die, its weight banging against my leg. It can stay there, where it's doing no more than giving me a few bruises.

Bram reaches down and pulls me up so that I'm back in his arms. My heart is hammering as I hold him close, my arms around his neck, my face buried in his short brown hair. It feels like we've been embracing in this way for hours. The world slows and fades away, cocooning us together.

Yet still we fall.

Bram pulls his head away, his dark brown eyes looking into mine so intensely, almost panicked. He starts shouting instructions at me, but I can't make them out. Now that we're closer to the ground the sounds from below are even louder. I think he's saying to be quick when we land, or maybe he's telling me not to be scared, but I can't be sure.

'I can't hear you!' I shout. Even my own voice is getting lost among the cries, explosions and sirens.

He tries again. He's worried.

'I know I'm safe with you!' I shout into his ear, hoping he can hear me.

I pull back to find him frowning at me, his lips pursing in a way I recognize.

Despite myself, I smile. Bram. *My* Bram. Just as she was once my Holly. He might look different now, but so much of him was entwined in her.

I remember the first time I met her, how thrilled I was to see someone of my own age running through the gardens of the Dome. And I can remember when I first met *him* – yanking that poor security guard Michael away from me, knocking him out cold.

I saw him and I knew he was her. Instantly.

I'm so lost in my thoughts that I'm shocked to find we're seconds from reaching the ground.

Suddenly we hit the crowd. The breath is knocked out of me, and something heavy is thrown over me, forcing me into darkness.

Hands grab me. Bram's are pulled away.

Voices are shouting, but I can't hear his.

'Bram!' I cry, reaching for him.

I fail. My grip slips. I'm ripped away.

I try to kick and scream, but it does no good. There are too many to fight off.

'Bram!' I scream.

I know I've lost him.

# 3

# Bram

*Eve!*

We hit the sea of people hard and hands tear us apart. The harness around us severs and we fall through the heaving bodies to the cold, wet ground.

I'm so desperate to call, to cling to her with all my strength and never let go, but I know I can't. I can't draw attention to us.

Not yet.

Stick to the plan.

I let myself get lost in the stampede.

When the waiting crowds saw us break through the cloud-base, the gasp of thousands of people hissed up through the air to greet us. We had done it – the impossible. There *she* was, falling from the sky, like an angel descending to answer their prayers.

Now we've landed, the real challenge begins.

'Where is she?' voices cry.

'I saw her!'

'It was Eve!'

'Let me see!'

'Is she alive?'

The crowd sways collectively as I disengage the Gauntlet, the device that slowed our descent, and shake my fist to regain feeling. With Eve now somewhere among the people, I am forgotten, no one. She may as well have fallen through the clouds alone for all they care.

With no one concerned about me, I scan the surrounding faces, searching for her. She has to be here. This has to have worked.

We are in the densest part of the gathering, between two cloudscrapers that stretch up towards the colossal Tower. Boxy, concrete structures with *WELLS INNOVATIONS* emblazoned in bold metallic lettering. No beauty, no design, just functionality. That's my father through and through.

This is the right spot. On the northern face of the Tower. That's what I'd written in my instructions to the Freevers – so where are they?

My eye catches something.

A flash of a familiar face through the heaving bodies. Helena.

She finds my gaze and nods. Her creased face is anxious but there's an unshakeable strength buried beneath. I knew she wouldn't fail.

She vanishes from sight, replaced by a heavy figure barrelling towards me, using his trunk-like arms to push through the masses.

Chubs.

I'm aware of more people approaching, more faces acknowledging me, more Freevers. They're all here, what's left of them.

For Eve.

Chubs finds me and turns his back, clearing a little breathing space for me to gather myself for what's about to happen.

'Are you ready for this?' he says, over the booming voices. 'They'll be here any second.'

At that moment hundreds of armed black drones identical to the one that targeted me and Eve drop from the clouds.

They pause, emitting a deep, tense hum as they hang overhead.

'Attention, citizens of Central.' Vivian Silva's voice pierces the air as her angular face appears on the walls of every surrounding building. 'We have experienced a catastrophic security breach. Eve, your precious saviour, is among you and her life is in severe danger.'

*Shit.*

Screams and cries erupt from the crowd.

'Our last hope for the human race cannot be harmed. She cannot be damaged. She cannot be allowed to escape . . .' Vivian pauses, then corrects herself '. . . to be *taken*. You are required to remain calm and still as we conduct our scan of the area. If you are aware of Eve's whereabouts, make yourself known immediately.'

I feel my face light up as though a searchlight has found me in the darkness. My pupils take a moment to adjust before I see the whole crowd is illuminated. Blinding white floodlights shine down from the drones above, sweeping the entire area.

I take a breath. 'This is it,' I whisper to Chubs.

'Are you sure?' he asks, not looking at me.

'. . . No,' I say honestly.

'I guess I'll see you back at the Deep,' he replies, turning to face me.

Pushing the surrounding people aside, Chubs ensures that I'm clearly visible, as is the girl now standing next to me.

*Eve.*

'THERE SHE IS!' Chubs roars at the top of his lungs.

Silence.

No screams.

No cries.

Just pure, stunned silence.

Heads turn, until the entire crowd is facing us. They all take her in. Her beauty. This is no realiTV screen. This is their Eve, standing among them.

We're in the eye of the storm and the only way out is to sail through it.

I raise my arm slowly and offer my hand to Eve,

keeping my eyes on the drones above. She takes it and my palm tingles at her touch, like an electric current surging through my veins, charging me for the escape. Giving me strength.

'Eve, run!' I shout.

The drones descend the second we move and chaos consumes the crowd. Chubs ploughs forward, clearing a path for us, heaving hysterical onlookers out of our way.

'Keep up!' he booms, and we try our best to follow but the crowd is starting to fight back.

'Let her go!' a voice demands to my right, a civilian with an image of Eve plastered all over his sweatshirt. I feel his arms grip mine and pull me, trying to separate me from Eve. I connect my knee with the man's ribs. There's a crack, he falls back, and we follow in Chubs's wake.

'They're coming! Interceptors, two of them,' he calls, signalling back to the EPO Tower.

I glance behind as two black vehicles appear over the pandemonium.

'I see them!' I shout. The EPO's armoured hovercrafts cover distance much faster than the watercraft of Central. Great for crowd control. Not so great for fugitives.

A blast erupts from the ground and a spark of light draws a streak of smoke across the sky. The Freever missile misses the Interceptor and hits one of the drones. Glowing embers from the explosion rain down, creating a tidal wave of panic that washes over the crowd.

'Time for phase two!' I call to Chubs, who immediately changes path.

I glance at Eve, who charges alongside me. Her face radiates determination. All around us people back off, as though an invisible forcefield pushes them away. Her power is contagious and I use it to battle through the crush of worshippers a few paces ahead of her.

'Nearly there!' Chubs shouts back. 'You'll be on your own from here.'

Up ahead the crowd starts to thin. We break through the outer wall and are forced to an abrupt halt.

I almost lose my footing. The edge of the walkway has no barrier. Where the concrete finishes, the water begins.

'Over here!' Chubs calls, pulling back a black cover from a sleek watercraft.

'Nice boat,' I say.

'It's not a boat; it's a hydrofoil. We've been saving this bad boy. Now get in!' he says, handing me a small earpiece.

The people surrounding us start to disperse as the Interceptors approach. No one dares defy the EPO.

*REMAIN CALM. YOU ARE BEING RESTRAINED*, the automated voice announces from above, as the Interceptor hovers towards us. Its rays cause temporary paralysis to those they touch while it searches the frozen crowd for us.

'Go, now!' Chubs demands, shoving me into the front of the craft. Eve jumps down into the seat behind me, wrapping her arms around my waist.

I twist the throttle and the engine erupts, catapulting us forward along the narrow canal faster than I anticipated.

'Jesus!' I cry, as a spurt of water launches into the air behind us.

It's fast, but it's not subtle. The Interceptor sees us and banks hard, releasing the crowd below from their suspended state as it accelerates after us.

The chase begins.

We break away at impossible speed, causing the hull of the hydrofoil to lift smoothly away from the surface of the water, more like flying than sailing. The faster we sail the higher we lift from the surface.

I steal a glance at Eve, whose determined gaze is fixed on the waterway ahead of us.

'Bram, are you getting this?' A voice crackles in my earpiece.

'I hear you! Saunders, is that you?' I scream over the wind.

'Yeah, I'll help guide you out. Just follow my directions.'

We zoom around the inner floodways of the Tower watched by thousands from the walkways above.

'Focus, Bram, these floodways weren't designed to be sailed down. There are obstacles everywhere,' Saunders says, as I clip the side wall.

'No shit!'

A drone appears to my right, tagging me with its targeting laser. Two more seconds and I'll be stunned.

I lean into a left turn that's almost ninety degrees, and send a wave of salty water over the concrete bank. It engulfs the drone, bringing it to the ground.

Saunders cheers. 'That's one less to worry about. We'll take care of the rest. You just steer that thing.'

'What about the Interceptors?' I ask. 'Where are they?'

'We lost one in the clouds; the other is gaining on you,' he says.

I take a look over my shoulder and see the red flashes of the Interceptor's lights. It's close on our tail.

'There's another left coming up,' Saunders says in my ear. 'Take it. It'll lead you to a tunnel.'

'Once we're through that we're in Central, right?' I ask.

'Right, but it's a tight squeeze.'

'How tight?'

There's no response.

I see the turn approaching and throw the hydrofoil into it at full throttle. This is no time for playing it safe.

The Interceptor turns hard, cutting the corner until it's flying alongside us. Through the window I see a Final Guard at the controls. He signals for me to stop.

Idiot.

He lurches the vehicle towards us, trying to ram us into the wall. I grip the brakes, slowing us down for the first time so that we sink back into the water.

'Don't slow down!' Saunders screams. 'They're on your back!'

I feel the presence of the drones looming behind us as I twist the throttle again. We accelerate hard and slip beneath the Interceptor.

I keep the hydrofoil darting from left to right, never giving them a still target. They won't fire lethals at us, not with Eve on my back, but there's plenty of weapons in their arsenal to incapacitate us without harming her.

A fizz of energy electrifies the water to our left.

It's a near miss. Very near.

'Bram, the entrance is coming up!' Saunders cries. 'Straight through there.'

'I see it. Shit, that *is* tight!' I shout.

The Interceptor rushes around for another pass. It's faster than we are and gaining on us. The drones move aside to give it room. The guard drops the hover vehicle down into the floodway, speeding inches over the surface.

'Watch your heads on the way in!' Saunders cries, as we approach the entrance.

I dip my head below the wind and Eve follows my lead. The Interceptor pulls up just in time as we glide into the narrow, pipe-like entrance. The sound of crashing drones echoes along the dark tunnel as they smash into the perimeter wall behind us.

'We made it!' I cheer into the blackness. Eve keeps a grip on me as we sail through the tiny water-outlet and I can't help but smile in the darkness.

Eventually the tunnel ends. We slip out of it into the river of Central, into the outside world. The hydrofoil bobs in the flowing waters as I glance up and down the river.

No one.

I glance back down the outlet and see nothing but black. Nothing followed us.

'Did you make it through?' Saunders crackles to life in my ear.

'Yeah, I'm out,' I reply.

'We lost connection for a moment in the tunnel.'

'Nothing followed us.'

'We're about half a mile from you, on our way,' he says.

'Okay, hurry.'

I see a small wooden jetty, the perfect place to ditch the hydrofoil and transfer into the Freever pod. I go to twist the throttle of the hydrofoil – but my arm won't move.

I lift with all my strength but I'm stuck, rigid.

Paralysed.

*REMAIN CALM*, the automated voice announces from above.

*YOU ARE BEING RESTRAINED.*

# 4

# Michael

I have her.

I don't believe it. She's right there in front of my eyes.

Eve.

This is my shot. My redemption. Bringing our saviour back to safety.

*REMAIN CALM*, the automated announcement booms from beneath the Interceptor. The instruction is meant for the fugitives below but I take it on board too. *Remain calm, Turner.*

I steady my breathing and grip the steering column as I hover over their heads.

I'm going to be a hero. *Michael Turner – the saviour of the saviour.*

*REMAIN CALM.*

. . . Right.

I glance at the rigid figures on my display, their red bodies glowing hot against the blue chill of the river.

'Facial recognition,' I command, and the onboard scanners emit a low hum. My thumb lingers over the talk-back, ready to call for backup, but I'm desperate for confirmation first. I can't screw this up. I have to be sure.

*ONE HUNDRED PER CENT MATCH – BRAM WELLS*, the onboard assistant says.

It pauses.

'And? What about *her*?' I ask, my heart pounding.

A piercing buzz erupts in the cabin. An alarm.

*UNREGISTERED VEHICLE APPROACHING FROM THE SOUTH.*

No, not now!

I swing the Interceptor around, still holding my prisoners in paralysis below. I slide my door open, raise my rifle with one hand and lower the Interceptor until I'm alongside them.

Her face is obscured by his at this angle, but her long hair flows out behind, frozen in a gust of wind that no longer exists.

I drift forward into *his* eyeline. My jaw tightens. I remember the last time we met.

He can see me.

This must be killing him.

An engine roars and the river rocks beneath us as a boat approaches. No, not a boat – some sort of glass craft, custom-built by the look of it. The front section reflects the water as it cuts through the current. The rear is covered by some sort of canopy, hiding whatever, or whoever, is aboard.

It's on top of us quicker than I realize and something explodes out of it before I can react. A shot. Something connects with the bonnet of the Interceptor and the reactor engine cuts out.

*WARNING. ENERGY LEVELS CRITICAL.*

The Interceptor loses power and my stomach is in my mouth as I plummet towards the river. My rifle falls to the floor as I use both hands to grip the lifeless steering column helplessly as the emergency system kicks in and I'm slammed into my seat. Air blasts from below, cushioning the fall and preventing me from crashing into the water.

The system steadies the Interceptor but it's a dead machine now, hovering a foot above the river on backup power.

I reach for my rifle.

'I wouldn't do that if I were you,' a voice calls from across the water.

I pause and slowly turn my head to see the glass pod bobbing up and down in the river next to Eve and Bram's hydrofoil. Eve and Bram are stretching, their paralysis lifted.

'Hands where we can see them, if you don't mind,' he says – one of Bram's accomplices, pointing a weapon at me. Not just any weapon, an EPO rifle like mine. Thieves. Two more men appear from under the camouflage canopy and join him on the hull. For a second I catch a glimpse of what's at the back of their glass pod: a man, strapped into some sort of harness, his face obscured by a strange mask. The canopy falls and I lose my line of sight.

'Who are you?' I ask.

No reply.

'Who do you work for? Freevers?'

'It appears that way, doesn't it?' the man says, with a smirk, nodding at Eve while keeping his finger on the trigger of the rifle aimed at my head.

'Where are you taking her?' I'm stalling for time rather than expecting answers.

Laughter bursts from within the pod.

'You still can't see it, huh?' The guffawing buffoon snorts from behind his rifle. 'Oh, please, can we show him, boss?'

Bram stands on the hydrofoil. Eve remains seated.

'Boss?' I say. '*You*'re in charge of this lot?'

Bram steps across to the pod with the help of his comrades. Three on the hull, plus Bram and the masked figure – too many to fight alone . . . *You should have called for backup first, you idiot.*

Suddenly I notice Eve is staring at me. Our eyes lock for a moment.

'Eve . . .' I call, my voice catching slightly in my throat. 'Eve, do you really trust these men?'

She doesn't reply. She just stares.

'Turner, right?' Bram says to me, as the hydrofoil ebbs and flows on the tide between us with Eve not saying a word. 'Who's she meant to trust?' he asks. 'The people who've kept her locked up her whole existence, or the people who just opened the door for her?'

'Well, I don't see her walking through it,' I reply. Eve is still sitting, staring at me. 'Eve, don't go with them,' I say to her. 'We can protect you.'

'Turner . . . Michael, isn't it?' Bram asks.

I nod.

'Michael, you are one of the few people in this world to have met Eve in person. To have spoken to her, face to face. But you went further than that, didn't you? Tell us, Michael, did Eve ask you to put your hands on her when you dragged her, screaming for her life, into that lift? Is that what you call protection?' he says.

'It was a mistake, the biggest of my life, and I'm trying to make amends for it now. I would never harm *you*, Eve, and that's the truth.' I'm still speaking to Eve, not Bram, and I mean it.

But it's Bram who replies. 'Mistake or not, it happened, and I know more than anyone the effect Eve has on you once you meet, once you've seen her . . . *touched* her. You've not stopped thinking about her, have you?' he says, shaking his head in pity. 'Obsessed, like all the hundreds who came before you and failed at protecting her.'

36

'It's not like that,' I say, through clenched teeth. I glance at my rifle, just a few feet from my hands.

'You'd be dead before you felt the metal,' snarls Bram's accomplice with the gun, following my eyes.

One of his men leans in and speaks into Bram's ear. Bram nods in response.

'Time to go. Say goodbye to Eve and forget her. She's not yours to protect any more.'

The pod's engine growls to life. They loop around and sail away along the river in the direction they came from . . .

Leaving Eve sitting alone on the hydrofoil.

What the hell?

'Eve?' I say, struggling to understand what just happened.

They left. Without Eve.

'Eve!' I call, as the hydrofoil she's sitting on rocks in the wake of the departing pod.

I lunge for my rifle. Something's going on. I scan the area quickly. The river is dead.

Just the two of us.

Me.

And.

Eve.

My heart begins to race. *Remain calm*, I order myself.

Eve suddenly moves.

'Are you okay?' I ask, lifting one foot from the dead Interceptor and taking a look at the murky water between us. The gap to the hydrofoil is big but, with the surge of adrenalin tingling in my veins, I know I can make it.

'Stay there, I'm coming over.'

But then I see her smiling.

It grows into a laugh. Not a happy laugh, a mocking one.

I hold on to the doorframe, heart pounding.

Eve disappears before my eyes. Then she flickers back into existence. My mind connects the dots and I realize I've been fooled. We all have.

She's not the real Eve.

She's a damn projection.

The man in the back of the pod wasn't wearing a mask. It was a visor, a pilot's visor. That thing must have been broadcasting her projection inside the EPO perimeter wall.

Eve begins to flicker again, her signal dying as the pod sails out of range.

Before she fades completely she blows me a kiss with one hand and gives me the finger with the other.

Then she's gone.

# 5

# Eve

I'm over someone's shoulder now. Still covered, still in darkness. Yet their handling of me has softened. They have me. I'm theirs. They must know I'm not going anywhere.

My body bobs up and down as my grunting captor moves, seemingly through water. With each movement there's a splash as they dart left and right.

My heart thumps – adrenalin getting me ready to fight, to run, to do *something*. But I'm clueless. I'm unsure whether to continue to kick and scream as before, breaking free so that I'm out in public where it might be safer, or whether it's best to submit to their will. I don't know who I'm with. I don't know what their intentions are. I also don't know what the reaction of the crowd around us would be if I showed myself now.

I am lost.

I'm unequipped to be here.

'Attention, citizens of Central,' a voice booms.

I snatch a quick breath while we come to a stop. Even though the material around me muffles the sound, I recognize the voice instantly. Vivian Silva. It's hardly surprising that her presence is felt down here too. I doubt I'll ever be free of her.

The crowd around me are silenced.

'We have experienced a catastrophic security breach,' she states, her voice as cold as ever. 'Eve, your precious saviour, is among you and her life is in severe danger.'

The screams of anguish, despair and disbelief startle me.

Vivian continues to speak, silencing them.

'Our last hope for the human race cannot be harmed,' she tells them. 'She cannot be damaged. She cannot be allowed to escape. To be taken.'

I feel the body of my captor stiffen.

For a moment I wonder what will happen, but the answer depends on why I'm in this position in the first place. Was I spotted and taken on a whim? Is this part of a plan? Is it my security team who've managed to get hold of me and are subtly trying to take me back – returned like a piece of stolen property?

The hold on my body becomes tighter as tensions spike around us. Voices murmur words of suspicion. Theories start to circulate.

Without warning my foot is grabbed and pulled,

and I yelp with fear. There's a scuffle around me, pushing and shoving, before my foot is released and I hear the brutal sound of flesh impacting on flesh, followed by a groan and a heavy splash.

From far away I hear shouting, the declaration that someone has spotted me.

I take a deep breath as I hear more of the flying objects from before pass overhead, waiting for them to make my whereabouts known and for the crowd to discover me properly.

But the pandemonium doesn't come, at least not to where I am being held. Instead I hear voices in the distance. I can't distinguish exactly what's being said, but it seems it's the distraction needed. I'm moved from one shoulder to the other, my capturer preparing to continue moving, and I don't fight against it. I'm not sure I could even if I wanted to. We start moving away from whatever seems to have gripped everyone. Dodging through crowds, marching through what sounds like water.

I do not fight, kick, scream or protest. I play my part. I tell myself that, whatever this is, it has to be better than being unprepared in front of thousands of people. In reality, I'm terrified.

'We're nearly there,' the voice mutters, presumably to me.

I'm shocked — not at the reassuring nature of the words, but at the voice itself. It's female. Even though I've spent my life surrounded by the Mothers, the sound of a female voice here is a surprise, and a strange comfort. Over the years, the Mothers shared glimpses of their lives out here and hints of what had led them to join me in the Dome. Vivian's descriptions of what life would be like for them if she were to expel them into the world below were horrific. Yet here is a woman, a strong and capable one, leading me away from my previous 'care'.

My body is turned and lowered.

'Have you got her?' she asks someone, as new hands find me. My cover billows enough for me to see the corner of the boat I'm being lowered into, along with three pairs of sturdy black boots, all soaked. 'Steady now,' she instructs. 'Straight to Ben!'

I sit, the floor beneath me rocking from side to side as they work quickly, darting across the deck. An engine revs into action, my body lurching forward with it as it moves. Eventually the pace becomes steady. We chug along calmly, water rolling in our wake.

I've never seen a boat in real life, much less been on one – although even if I thought I had, I'd be questioning the experience after recent events.

A boat.

I've read about them in books, seen clips of them in action. Yet the feeling of the wind pushing against me as we go, the rush to the senses, it's nothing like I imagined. Even hidden, unable to see clearly, I'm aware of the beauty in it.

'Eve,' the woman calls loudly, so I can hear her

over the wind, the engine and the water. She places a hand on my knee and crouches lower so I can see her creased, freckled face peering below the bottom of the veil. Not kind and soft, like Mother Nina's, but strong and likeable all the same. As our eyes meet for the first time she sighs, relief flooding her features. 'We won't be long now.'

'Where are we going?' I ask.

'Somewhere they can't find you,' she replies, her eyes darting up to the Tower we're moving further away from.

'Who are you?'

'All will become clear,' she mutters. 'But I need you to stay under there a little longer. Eyes are watching and we don't want to arouse suspicion.'

'But why have you helped me?' I ask. 'What do you want from me?'

'We want nothing,' she says, one side of her mouth curling into a smile. 'We wanted only to give you your freedom . . . You're free, Eve.'

Free. This is freedom.

For now, I'll take it.

# 6

# Eve

'We're clear,' someone calls, as the boat comes to a stop after what feels like eternity.

Hands find me. I'm guided on to my feet, picked up and moved from the boat to solid ground.

'Tell them we're here, then leave us. Travel back later when it's dark,' she orders.

The engine gives a little rev before moving off again, leaving us. Before I can allow myself to panic over the silence that ensues, I hear something bubbling beneath us. Water giving way as something emerges from the depths. A stone staircase.

'Come. Tread carefully,' she says, her hand on my wrist as she guides me on to the top step of the staircase that leads us back down towards the water.

'You can take that off now, Eve. We won't be seen

here,' she says quietly, gently removing the fabric that's been keeping me hidden.

I've been under the thick, dark veil for so long that the light seems harsh and bright. My eyes take a moment to adjust, but when they do I get a brief glimpse of the intricately beautiful structure around us. Made from a mixture of iron and stone, the materials work together to create something solid and formidable. It's a building drenched in historic importance to a world far away from this one.

Ben – Big Ben. Of course. A memory stirs: I'd asked Mother Nina what she did as a child – I was forever asking about her life before the Tower.

'There was always something to do or somewhere to see. We'd wander through parks, museums, galleries, or sometimes we'd walk up the river, taking in the sights – the London Eye, the Houses of Parliament and Big Ben.'

I remember laughing at the name as she explained the clock in more detail.

Now here I am, inside it.

Beside us, bobbing in the water, is another transportation device, a ball of some kind. I take a deep breath, instantly aware of how different the air is here. It isn't pumped in through air vents. It's real, damp and thick.

She's watching me, I see, her eyes absorbing me in the same way I've been soaking up the view around us.

I look at her, really taking her in. I've never met a woman like her before. She's rugged, her hair cropped short, her hands rough and chapped, her muscles rounded and strong. It's only now that I realize how similar all the Mothers were: feminine, delicate. Did they have to fit certain criteria to be given their roles? Not one of them was anything like the woman before me.

Well, except Vivian. There was nothing delicate about her. She was a Trojan, steely and cold.

Thankfully the woman before me is nothing like Vivian either. She looks stern and direct, but her face breaks into a warm smile when she notices me studying her. Her shoulders lower, her body relaxes. I'm here. Clearly her plan worked – and I'm sure now that this *was* all part of a plan, carefully orchestrated. Nothing about this woman's behaviour suggests she grabbed me on a whim.

She looks relieved. I imagine it's quite a big deal to kidnap the first girl born in fifty years.

'What's your name?' I ask. There are so many questions in my head, and finding out who she is seems a good place to start.

'We should carry on,' she urges, turning to go down to the awaiting vessel.

'Wait. Tell me your name.' My voice is firmer than I intend it to be, but it has the desired effect. She hesitates, her foot hovering as she decides whether to turn back to me or continue down the steps.

'Helena,' she shoots back, her foot resting on the ground.

I'm hit with a memory of an English class back in my old life, one with Holly at my side. Books splayed open as we read Shakespeare's play of star-crossed lovers: *A Midsummer Night's Dream*. Helena. I can't help but feel bitter that they filled my head with fiction – and provided me with no clue as to what the real world is actually like.

Helena reaches down and presses something on the wall of the sphere, causing a door to hiss open. I spot a man inside, although he doesn't come out to say hello.

'I'll help you in,' Helena declares, placing a hand on my waist and practically picking me up to get me safely across from the stairs. She joins me with a thud, and the vehicle wobbles. The door shuts and the man next to us goes about what is clearly the familiar routine of checking we're secure, ensuring the door is sealed and confirming our arrival through some sort of handheld speaker. We're sucked back below the water – which I can vaguely make out through a thick, murky window as bubbles engulf us.

I'm aware of Helena's eyes on me again.

'It's worth you catching your breath before we go inside,' she tells me. 'People will be excited to see you down there. Expect it to feel overwhelming. Even though we've warned them to be calm, it's an exciting day for us all. We've worked hard to make this happen.'

'Where are we?' I ask, trying to ignore the nerves I'm hit with.

'The Deep. Our base. Where we work, sleep and live.'

'Is it safe?'

'We've called it home since just after you were born and they've never once got near to tracking us down. Doesn't mean they can't, of course, but they've had no such luck so far. Either we're doing something right or they're doing something wrong.'

I nod.

'The Deep is your home too now, if you want it to be. You'll always have a place with us. You can be sure of that.'

'And who are you? Why are you helping me?' I ask.

'We're your people. Your supporters, campaigners . . . your loyal subjects,' she tells me, smiling. 'We're Freevers. Free–Eve–ers. I came up with that, a long time ago,' she adds proudly. 'We've just wanted you to have a choice. The only way you can do that is by knowing the facts, and there was no way you were getting those in there.' She makes no attempt to hide the contempt in her voice.

'Yes, I started to see that,' I admit, wondering how much she knows.

'Finding Bram was the best thing that's happened to all of us.'

'You found Bram?' I shriek, surprising us both. 'He's a part of this?'

'You didn't know?' She frowns at me. 'You really have no idea who we are?'

'None,' I say, feeling stupid. I think back to the moment before we touched the ground after our jump. Bram was shouting something at me, but I couldn't make it out. Was he trying to prepare me?

'So Bram knows I'm here?' I ask.

'Of course . . . It was his idea.'

'So he'll be here soon too?'

Her face twists before she replies. 'I hope so. Depending on how it's gone up there. Getting you out was the most important thing. That was the start of putting things right.'

'But . . .' I'm unsure what to say. I lost him before, and now my heart has already begun to ache at the thought of losing him again.

'I think it's time we went in and answered some of your questions,' Helena says.

I realize we've stopped. 'Okay.' I nod, trying to focus. This has always been about so much more than one person. More than him, more than me.

I jump to my feet with a wobble. It's time to find out what's going on.

This place is like nothing I've ever seen before. I'm used to large open spaces with trees and bushes – albeit fabricated. I was living high in my pretty Tower, and now I'm down in the depths beneath the city, walking along dimly lit passageways, where everything is hot, close and sticky. The air is moist, the walls lined with beads of sweat. My wet clothes cling to my body as though they're glued in place.

Helena stops in front of a door. Looking up at me, her mouth opens to speak, but she appears to stop herself. Instead she purses her lips tightly, bows her head, presses the handle down and pushes forward.

I see a couple of hundred people in a vast, high-ceilinged chamber, all silenced. They are holding each other tightly, clearly in disbelief. Men take comfort from other men or older women scattered throughout the crowd. They're not clumped together or frightened, just leaning on each other for support. All are looking at me with deep curiosity. I take in their scruffy clothes, heavy boots, and grubby faces.

'She's free!' a deep voice yells, from somewhere in the crowd, and the room erupts with cheers and laughter.

The room feels authoritative, as though it's seen many monumental events in the past. I wonder if any have been quite as big as this one.

'Let Eve speak!' calls another voice, through the chaos. 'We want to hear what she has to say.'

'Don't put her on the spot like that!' someone else cries, as the crowd hushes expectantly.

'She probably doesn't know half of what's been going on yet,' I hear one woman shout.

'I bet she knows they took her for their own gain, not for anyone else's. Not for her own good.'

'They stripped her of her rights. Forced her to live in there with them.'

'She's been that organization's pawn her whole life!'

'Who knows what she knows?'

Voices are yelling over each other. Anger flares. Not at me, but at the EPO. The invisible people I didn't get to see or meet, but who dictated my upbringing.

I feel a flush of shame. I've been so ignorant, my whole life. I never questioned anything I was told. I won't make that mistake again. From now on, my actions and decisions will reflect only on me.

Helena stands beside me, her arms raised in the air. The crowd quietens into a respectful silence.

'Tonight is for celebrating what we have achieved today. Tomorrow is for understanding.'

There are murmurs and nods as the crowd take on board her words. It's strange watching a woman harness such regard and power from so many without the need to spread fear, like I watched Vivian do so many times.

A cheer rises as people look past me. I turn to see a group of young men walking through the door, arms raised in victory, all turning to me with nods of recognition. One guy breaks through the crowd and starts walking towards me, his long face breaking into a relieved smile as he opens his arms wide and envelops me in a hug.

'Oh,' I say, caught off guard.

'I'm so sorry. I'm Saunders.' He laughs, blushing as

he realizes his mistake. 'We know each other. I know you,' he stammers awkwardly. 'I was . . . a couple of years ago . . .'

It takes me only a moment to understand the connection and fit the pieces of this crazy puzzle together. As I look closely at his eyes I see a shape I recognize.

'You were one of my Hollys,' I say, and he grins with pleasure. But my attention is caught by someone new walking through the door.

A huge smile spreads across my face. He sees me, and as our eyes lock everything around us falls away.

# 7

# Bram

It's deafening. My back is pounded with congratu-
latory slaps and I'm engulfed with hugs from every
direction. Tiny soundbites of conversation find my
ears – *We did it. She's free. It's over. It's just the beginning.*

*What next?*

I push through the crowd, deeper into our cavernous chamber beneath the flood. I don't need to
ask where she is: it's obvious. She's in the centre of
the room, her presence pulling people in, like the
sun holding the planets in orbit.

She has found her place in the centre of our uni-
verse.

'Let the poor boy through!' Helena booms, as she
marches through the crowd and takes my hand.

Without thinking I wrap my arms around her and
feel a wave of tension release. 'We did it.'

'*You* did it, young Bram,' she whispers.

'I like the new hair,' I say, admiring her shaved head.

'Well, I didn't want to draw any more attention to myself out there. It's not every day you see a six-foot woman in her early seventies who could kick your arse wandering the streets of Central.'

'Can't argue with that.' I smile.

'Now you'd better save her from this lot before she begs us to take her back to the EPO.'

I glance up and see Saunders pulling Eve in for a hug.

Idiot.

'Okay, okay, let's give Eve some space,' I say, making my way towards her. 'You too, Saunders.'

'Oh, right, sorry!' He fumbles nervously and moves out of the way, leaving Eve and me standing face to face.

Her eyes look into mine. I know what she's doing. She's searching for *her*, the eyes of the one person she trusts – Holly.

'I'm here,' I say.

She nods.

The moment lingers, and there's a strange awkwardness in the air between us that's never existed before. Not when I'm Holly. I'm suddenly aware of the noise settling, the eyes around us focusing, the attention, the expectations.

Shit. I'm going to have to say something.

I take a deep breath.

'What do we do now, Bram?' a voice calls from the balcony.

'Er . . . I . . . don't know.'

*Brilliant. Great leadership skills, Bram.*

I try again.

'We know the EPO will respond with full force. They will be searching Central, leaving no stone unturned. Staying beneath the flood is our safest option. I want our surface movements totally locked down. We have all we need down here for now so Central is off-limits until further notice. Eve is safe here and, until we have more information, I want us all to lie low.'

That was a little better.

'It's not about what we want,' Helena calls, turning to face Eve.

I look at Eve. She takes in the room and steps forward.

'My name is Eve,' she announces with a slight tremor in her voice. The room erupts into cheers and laughter.

'Why are they laughing?' she whispers to me.

'I don't think you needed to introduce yourself, Eve,' I reply with a smile. I raise my hands and the room calms.

'I'm not sure who you are. I'm not sure where we are. I'm not sure of anything any more . . .'

The room is silent.

'. . . but something about you, about this place, just feels right.'

They cheer again. Eve has captivated them.

More questions are hurled at her, and I see the panic flare in her eyes.

'All right, calm down, you lot!' Helena cries, calling the room to order. 'Eve needs to rest. We all do! There will be plenty of time to share stories and discuss the historic events of today, but right now we must give her space to adjust to being down here with us.'

The room bursts into life instantly, everyone trying to be heard.

'You two had better scram or you'll never get away,' Helena mutters to us, as she tries to calm the room.

I nod and reach for Eve's hand. She pulls it away from me instinctively.

'Sorry!' we say in unison, then laugh awkwardly.

'I should be the one to apologize. This is a new world for you, Eve. I get that,' I say, glancing at the excited chaos around us.

She smiles.

'Follow me.' I turn . . . and feel her fingers grip mine. My chest tightens a little, as though she's taken hold of my heart rather than my hand. 'This way.'

I lead us out of the hot chaos of the main chamber and into the sealed hallways of this sunken hideout. Chubs follows, his large frame blocking us from sight as we go. 'Just making sure you get there with no more hassle,' he says.

'Thanks.'

'Chubs, by the way.' He bows his head at Eve.

'I'm Eve,' she replies.

'Yes, you are.' He smiles, studying her face as though she were a work of art.

'Ahem!' I clear my throat. 'Shall we?'

I lead the way, and Chubs falls behind, making sure no one follows.

'Where are we?' Eve asks, taking in the damp surroundings.

'We're in a building in the old city. Beneath the flood. Most of it is only used as the foundations of Central above, but there are a few hidden gems, like this one,' I explain. 'I'm just thankful the Freevers managed to find it before anyone else.'

I twist through the network of tunnels, stepping over tubes and pumps that keep the flood out.

I glance back and see Eve taking it all in. 'I know it's different down here. Hot, damp, dark . . .'

'Real.' She adds, 'I love it.'

We walk on.

'How do you remember where you are down here? It's a maze,' she whispers.

'The pipes,' I say, pointing out the thin blue one over our heads that I'm currently following. 'It's the only way to navigate the Deep. I had to figure that out pretty quickly but I still don't know the whole place.'

'Where are we going now?' she asks.

'They've had a room prepared for you for a very long time,' I explain, ducking through a clear plastic divider.

'I see,' Eve says softly. I've not seen her like this before. Uncertain. Nervous. Even a little scared.

'Almost there.' I open a door into an enormous chamber. The ceilings shoot up dramatically over our heads. Faces glare at us from the rotting paintings on the walls, and the cold floodlights create eerie pools of deep shadow around the cavernous space.

'Oh!' Eve gasps.

'Don't worry, it's not this room,' Chubs says, as he steps into the chamber. 'It's through there.' He points. 'This is as far as I'll come, though.'

'Thank you,' Eve says to him.

I walk on, Eve following, and we cross the hall together.

'What was this place?' she asks.

'They called it Parliament. This was where the fate of the people was decided.'

'Like the EPO Tower of a time gone by,' Eve notes.

'Yes. Now reduced to a sunken wreck, inhabited by rebels who fight the people trying to decide our fate.'

'I like that.' She smiles.

'Me too.'

I open the door for her and let her enter before me. She glances at a small sign on the door – *Robing Room*.

Inside, it's smaller than the chamber we walked through but by no means less grand.

'Is that a . . . ?'

'Throne? Yes. I forgot to mention that this place was originally a palace. Bit much?' I laugh.

'A bit.'

'Well, you never know, you might learn to love it.'

'Hmmm, Queen Eve has a nice ring to it, right, Hols?' She pauses. 'Sorry, Bram.'

'It's okay. It'll take time. This is new for *us*.'

As I say it, I realize how weird that sounds – *us* – as in me and the most important person on the planet.

'This might be a silly question but how do you turn the lights on?' Eve asks. 'Are there lights?'

I walk to the wall and point to a small bronze switch. I flick it and the glow of bulbs warms the room.

'Wow.' She grins at the ancient technology.

'Vintage lighting. Original period features. Comes complete with its own water feature.' I gesture to the leaking ceiling as a few drops fall into a bucket.

'I'll take it.' Eve laughs.

She studies the room, notes the small but perfectly made bed in the far corner protruding from a hospital curtain.

'This isn't for ever,' I say. 'I know what it feels like to leave that place behind for this one. It's a shock. At least, it was for me when I first came down here.'

'I have so many questions.'

'I know. There'll be time for that, but right now you need rest.'

'Where will you be?' she asks, sounding a little concerned.

'I'll be in the next room if you need me. Not far. Chubs is guarding the only entrance, so you're safe now,' I reassure her.

She nods and takes a few steps towards the bedroom as I return to the doorway.

'Bram?' she calls softly.

I pause, already knowing what she's about to say.

'Stay with me?' she whispers, looking hopefully at me.

I can't not give her what she needs. Not tonight.

'Okay,' I whisper, as I close the door.

# 8

# Eve

Walls. Tall, regal, oppressive walls stand proudly around me. The room is beautiful – even though the plastic sheets that hang to protect it from flooding are clearly visible. They make me feel small, scared and nervous. I'm used to being surrounded by nature – a luscious green garden full of blooms and colour, and a never-ending view of the sky. Perfect sunrises and sunsets. At least, images of them.

I'd laugh if the truth weren't so demoralizing.

I want someone to strip it all back. To tell me simply what's going on and what I should be feeling.

'What was true?' I hear myself ask Bram. My voice surprises me. I sound so vulnerable. But, of course, I can be vulnerable around him. I trust him. He has earned my trust time and time again. He came back for me, putting himself in danger in the process. He has already seen me at my lowest, albeit always through her eyes. If I can't voice my insecurities to him, then I'll never be able to do so with anyone.

'True?' he asks.

'In there. My life. Was any of it real?'

Suddenly I feel weak and tired. How long have I been awake? It must be the middle of the night, at least. It's impossible to know in the darkness in which they live down here below ground. But, as exhausted as I am, I need to know this. Everyone wants me to wait until tomorrow before trying to make sense of it all, but it's torturous not knowing whether I can look back at anything fondly, or whether I should turn my back on the lot of it.

'I know there have been lies and my life has been guided by their manipulation. But were there some elements of truth within all of that?' I ask. 'Or do I need to grieve a complete life I never really had?'

'Your relationships were real,' he tells me.

'Even though everyone else knew I was just a pawn?'

'We were all pawns, Eve. Not just you,' he says.

'At least you were aware of it,' I say. 'But everything I did and said and felt – I just don't know how much of that was really me, and how much of it was them.'

Bram inhales deeply, looking around the room as though it'll provide him with answers.

'I believe it was really you,' he answers. 'I believe you really felt those things. I have to, because if you didn't then I didn't. And I don't want that to be the case.'

I watch his lips, and move my gaze up to his dark eyes. My cheeks flush.

'I don't think there's ever just one truth, Eve,' he says, breaking away and standing up. 'Even with my dad, I can say what I want about him and question his motives as much as I like, but I'm sure he has his own reasons for doing what he does. I'm sure he must believe there's good in it.'

I look beyond Bram to the rest of the room they've prepared for me. Alien textures, patterns and fabrics, an unpleasant smell in the air. The uncertainty it's layered with. Despite what Helena said, this isn't my home. Not yet. It's so different. So cold. So uninviting. 'Have I done the right thing?' I ask. I bite my lip and tears spring to my eyes.

'Yes,' he says without hesitation.

'Then why do I feel so unsure? Why am I aching for something that never was?' My chest tightens.

'Do you really wish you were back up there? Ignorant of what really exists?' he asks softly.

'No.' I'm shaking my head. 'No, I don't. There's just a lot to make sense of.'

'Trust me, I'm still learning. There's lots to wade through, but we'll get there,' he says. 'Together.'

I'm unsure whether he means together with the Freevers, or just us as a pair. The word sends a flush of excitement through me, but then I think of Holly, and I understand what I really want right now.

'Can't you just be her?' I ask. 'Can you be my Holly?

63

I need my friend. I need something I know to anchor me so I don't drown in all of this.'

'Don't be scared of the people out there, Eve,' he says softly, gesturing to the door behind him. 'They just want to give you your life back.'

'A life I didn't even know I should have.' I'm aware of the bitterness in my voice. 'Just sit with me,' I plead, sliding off the bed on to the floor, crossing my legs.

Bram drops to my side, his arm gently brushing against my own. I ignore the butterflies in my stomach. That's not what I need now.

I inhale, taking deep breaths to centre myself. I close my eyes and allow a calmness to work its way through me.

*Through the darkness I see where I want to be.*

*Suddenly I'm back on the Drop. A breeze washes over me as I hold my chin up and bask in the warmth of the glorious sun. There's a smile on my lips. My feet dangle over the edge, flexing and pointing in my black laced-up boots, the way I love doing in ballet. The fabric of my dress flutters and curls in the wind.*

*She shifts beside me, making sure I know she's there, but, then, I know she always is when I'm out here.*

*I turn to her with a grin. She returns it.*

*'Good day?' she asks.*

*'You would know.' I smirk, and so does she. We know it's cheeky of us to talk in such a way, to allude to the fact I've not seen this Holly all day even though technically I've been with Holly in classes, but we do it anyway. I like getting that reaction*

from her, and I can tell she enjoys knowing she's special. She always has done.

'What are you doing back here?' she asks.

'What do you mean?'

'You left me,' she says, matter-of-fact.

'No, I –'

'Come on, Eve. I wasn't enough. This place wasn't enough.'

'You were,' I say, scrambling for the words to tell her how important she is to me.

'Are you doubting yourself? Doubting them?' she asks slowly, squinting as she tries to read my face. 'Why else would you want to come back here? You dreamt of escaping this place, and now you have you're running back. Silly, Eve.'

'You don't know what you're talking about.'

'Don't I? I know you, Eve. I know all about you.'

'What do you mean?'

'Go back to them, Eve.' She shrugs indifferently, as though the thought of me leaving means nothing to her. 'You left us once, now leave us again.'

'Holly, no,' I say, my head shaking furiously.

'Do you love us?' I hear her say, although the sound is coming from over my shoulder. I turn to see another Holly. She's pouting, although not with real sadness. She looks menacing. Demonic.

'Yes,' I whisper.

'I don't think she means it,' comes a third voice from behind.

I go to protest, but I'm stopped by a force whacking into my back. I feel my body lurching forward. I reach out to stop myself, to grab on to something, but I can't.

*I land with a crunch as my body hits the screens displaying the idyllic view they've given me. They flicker from sky blue to black. From something, to nothing.*

*'Don't let us stop you, Eve,' says the third Holly. She stands above me, raising her foot high. I screw my eyes shut, fully expecting the weight of it to come down on me. Instead a thud echoes all around me as her boot makes contact with the ground by my head.*

*A crack appears, running from the tips of my fingers to under my chin. I try to scramble back to my feet and make a run for it, but it's too quick. Too sudden.*

*The sky beneath me falls away, taking me with it.*

*'No! No! NO!' I scream, trying to hold on to something, my arms and feet flailing through the air.*

*I fall.*

*As I succumb to my fate I look up and see their faces. Dozens of Hollys, all looking at me with the same satisfied look.*

*They're glad I've gone.*

# 9

# Michael

The rain drums on my shoulders as I walk towards the solid pane of glass. Voices call from beyond the perimeter.

*'SCUM! TRAITOR! MURDERER!'* Those are just a few of the nicer labels to hit my back as I leave the outside behind.

*'HELL, NO, EPO!'* they chant, as my retinas are scanned. There's a small beep followed by a hiss of clean air escaping as the entrance to the Tower is revealed. I step inside, dwarfed by the doorway that supports three colossal letters – **EPO**. Illuminated, of course. No subtlety. We own this town and, boy, do we like to remind people.

The glass reseals itself behind me, silencing the mob outside and I lean against the wall for a moment, finding the cold concrete oddly comforting.

'Weapons on the tray,' huffs Grudge, the security guard. That's not his actual name, we just call him Grudge because, well, I guess that's self-explanatory. Needless to say, he makes life difficult. Today there's a tiny hint of a chuckle in his voice.

He knows about my downed Interceptor.

'It wasn't my fault.' I roll my eyes.

'It never is, Turner. It never is.' He smiles and it looks weirdly unnatural.

I proceed through the body scanner. All clear. I clip my gun and cuffs back on my belt and begin to notice the whispers that are echoing around the cavernous entrance to the EPO Tower. Indecipherable, all but one word that repeatedly lands in my ears – *ESCAPE*.

'She's gone, then?' Grudge mumbles, with zero emotion. He's not permitted to have an opinion but his obvious lack of concern for this world event feels genuine.

I nod.

My chest buzzes. My tag is vibrating beneath my skin. I glance under my wet uniform and an amber glow illuminates my chest – it's an order.

'She's waiting for you all up top,' Grudge explains, taking pleasure in breaking this news.

I tap my tag once.

*ALL FINAL GUARDS REPORT TO THE DOME UPON ARRIVAL AND AWAIT MISS SILVA*, the voice instructs, via my earpiece. They might as well make it a permanent implant. The floor directly beneath my feet immediately changes appearance. An amber strip, matching my tag, draws a line from my feet to the lift. It is the path I must take, and now that I have opened the message I must obey.

'Follow the Yellow Brick Road.' Grudge waves an imaginary magic wand with his fat hands in the direction of my path.

'I'll be sure to ask Silva for a brain for you,' I say, and make a swift exit along the glowing line.

My tag emits a gentle, satisfying click on my chest with each step I take in the correct direction. If I were to veer off course, the tag would warn me with some firmer alerts. Go totally off-track and the little piece of bio-tech sends a warning to the EPO before hitting you with a whopping charge of power that even the toughest bastards on the squad couldn't defy. Basically, once you've been given your order, you stick to your path.

I wait for the lift to arrive.

'Crashed another one?' Guard Ryan says, shaking his shaved head as he arrives at my side. Beneath his dig at my piloting skills, I sense his nerves. I feel the same churning sensation in my gut.

'No. Not *crashed*,' I say defensively. 'Okay, so my track record for crashing Interceptors isn't great, but we only take them out in high-risk situations. It's what they're designed for. It was disabled by Freevers this time.'

'Right. Freevers!' He raises his eyebrows.

'Yes. *Freevers.* I thought I had her, Ryan. I was this close!'

'What happened?'

'She was –' Our conversation is cut short by the arrival of the lift. This is the express ride to the top. One thousand floors in under ten seconds.

Our eyes are scanned again. Clearance for the Dome is highly restricted. Or, at least, it was when Eve was there. Things might be about to change. Big-time.

The door begins to close but a gloved hand suddenly stops it. It reopens instantly and two heavily armed men step inside.

Soldiers.

'Who the hell are you?' Ryan says, his hand reaching for the gun on his belt. Only Final Guards are permitted to carry weapons inside the Dome.

Whoever these men are, they must have some sort of clearance I've never heard of or they would never have made it into the building armed like this.

'Silence,' the soldier on the right commands. 'Hands where I can see them.'

Ryan shoots me a look, but before either of us can do anything the soldier closest to me pulls out a small flat disc.

'Keep still,' he barks, as he holds it in front of my face and the black plate flashes a blinding hot light into my eyes.

Another retina scan?

'What the hell is this?' I say, shielding my face with my hands.

'Emergency protocol,' the other robot-like a-hole barks.

*FLASH!*

He does the same to Ryan.

The soldiers' faces are hidden behind partially frosted visors. No doubt they're seeing all kinds of information in front of them right now.

'All clear,' the armed mystery men say with a nod. 'Would you rather we travel alone, sir?' one asks, directing his question to someone standing outside the lift.

'No, it's fine,' mutters a voice I recognize in an instant. It's the Wonderful Wizard himself: Dr Wells.

He steps inside the lift and positions himself between the two soldiers and I realize who they are: Dr Wells's personal security. Ever since his son's dramatic departure from our world inside the Tower he has upped his own security to rival Eve's. The general opinion was that it was a tad on the excessive side and that our master was getting a little paranoid, but, considering the current state of affairs, I'm starting to think he may have a point.

'Sir.' Ryan and I nod sheepishly.

He ignores us but as he settles in the lift his eyes dart in our direction. In that briefest of flashes, he seems to absorb everything he needs to know about us. It's as though he studied our innermost thoughts with just a casual flick of his eyes.

*THE LIFT WILL NOW ASCEND. PLEASE HOLD ON*, a calm female voice instructs, as the door seals itself.

We are immediately launched vertically, slicing up the core of this mighty building.

I stare at Wells's face. The creases in his skin carve deep canyons across his forehead, signs of a face that has worn many frowns. Not surprising: carrying the weight of this place on your shoulders and having to deal with Miss Silva as a boss can't be easy. I can't imagine what it must be like to have the fate of our species depend on the success of your work.

I glimpse a familiar expression. One I saw just a little earlier on another anxious face. His son's – Bram. There's a similarity, the kind you can't quite put your finger on. It could be the eyes, the way they dip slightly at the outer edges giving off major melancholy vibes. Or perhaps the way the muscles protrude from his cheeks as he clenches and relaxes his jaw.

I wonder if he's thinking about his son. I realize I'm not just looking at a man, I'm looking at a father whose son is out there, in a violent world, and he doesn't even know if he's alive.

But I do.

'Sir.' The word comes out of my mouth before I've thought it through. Shit, what am I doing?

His guards instantly face me.

'It's okay.' Dr Wells calms them. 'Yes, Turner?' he says without looking in my direction.

'You know my name?'

'It's written on your uniform,' he explains, though I hadn't seen him read it.

'Oh, right.' Idiot.

'Although I never forget a face, and since your infamous encounter with Eve, I have watched you closely,' Wells says, still not looking in my direction, as though each word he utters is a distraction from his thoughts. 'Did you want something?'

'It's . . . er . . . it's just . . .' I catch eyes with Ryan, who is mouthing *ABORT! ABORT!* at me from the other side of the lift.

'I just wanted to . . . It's just that outside, I saw Bram, your son.'

Silence.

The lift arrives at the Dome.

'I have no son,' Wells says calmly and exits the lift, followed by his guards.

Ryan and I are alone.

'You. Are. An. Idiot,' he says, nice and slow so I understand.

'Yep.' I sigh. 'I am.'

We step out of the lift, which closes behind us and descends in a few seconds.

'You gotta start playing things a little safer, you know,' Ryan says, under his breath, as we follow our illuminated paths along the concrete outer corridors of the Dome.

'I know. I know!' I say, and I do. I've been on thin ice for a while.

'Look, we all wish Ketch was back here, and the whole team knows that you're meant to be leading us right now.'

'Yeah, well, I'm no Ketch. Plus, those are pretty big boots to fill. I don't envy you right now.'

Ryan sighs.

'What?' I ask.

'Do you really have to ask? Someone managed to break into the Dome, kidnap the most important person on the planet, get her down to the ground and escape with her. I'm the acting commanding officer of the Final Guard, the unit that is specifically trained to stop that exact thing happening,' he says, rubbing his temple. 'I'm in big shit.'

'Oh,' is all I manage to say. He's right. He is in big shit. We follow our illuminated path through the greenery of the Dome. It's busy with people who usually have no business here, people who should be in their hiding places, creating this illusion, the orchestrators of Eve's reality. Now they're out in the open, studying the disturbed soil, analysing the escape route in fine detail.

Ryan raises his eyebrows as we pass the shattered doors that lead to the Drop, the crunch of glass under our boots alerting a few white-coats to our presence.

They say nothing.

We say nothing.

I get the feeling I'm not the only one who feels like an intruder in here. This is Eve's home, real or not, and this seems like breaking and entering.

Our paths eventually cross with those of my Final Guard comrades, glowing from underneath the soil and leading us to the upper garden zone.

'Welcome back, Captain.' Hernandez nods and the whole squad turns to greet me.

'Yeah, and what a day to return,' Reynolds adds.

The Final Guard pauses for a moment. What a day indeed. We've all dedicated years to protecting something that isn't here now. We failed and we all feel it, the anxiety.

'It's good to be back. I just wish it were under different circumstances,' I say to them.

'Don't we all?' Ryan mutters, and my six teammates nod in agreement.

We are like a family. The Final Guards: Ryan, Franklin, Reynolds, Hernandez and the Murphy twins, Finn and Ewan. Of course, there are guards no longer with us, those who gave their lives for the good of life itself.

'How's your brother?' Franklin asks me.

'He's been better,' I say honestly. Images flash in my head from my first visit with Ketch on the Med Level half a mile below us, where the smell of his burnt flesh and raw wounds made me physically sick. 'But he's alive.'

'We didn't expect anything less. Tell him the new

management hasn't a clue what he's doing,' Reynolds jokes.

'Watch it! I can suspend you now, you know,' Ryan threatens.

A nervous silence falls unexpectedly between us and I'm tuned in to the collective anxiety about why we've been called here.

'Look –' I take a breath – 'before we go in and hear whatever Miss Silva has to say, I just want to apologize to you all.'

'Don't be soft, man,' Finn says.

'You did nothing wrong by us,' his twin adds.

'Well, you say that but when I . . . when Eve and I had our encounter, it was at a time when she was fragile and unsure of her future. I can't help but think that what happened between us might have had an influence on the thoughts that eventually led to her leaving this place.'

'Don't flatter yourself, Mr Turner.' Miss Silva's voice cuts through the air like a sword. 'The door is open, when you're quite ready, gentlemen.'

*Shit.*

The guards widen their eyes in a you're-screwed kind of way and my stomach lurches.

'Why can't I keep my mouth shut?' I whisper to Ryan, as we head into the upper garden zone.

The UGZ is the largest space within the Dome and usually home to thousands of plants, birds and other wildlife. Most endangered, some totally extinct in the wild after the climate shift wiped out their habitats. We would often locate Eve in here, enjoying the flowers, feeding the birds.

Now, though, it's empty. No fluttering of wings, apart from the butterflies in our bellies.

'Enter, line up and don't utter a word,' Miss Silva instructs. No, orders.

She stands perfectly still in the deep shadows of towering plant life. Her straight shoulders rise and fall slowly as she takes a deep breath.

'*I hereby solemnly promise to devote my body, mind and being to fully serve and fulfil the requirements of the position within the Final Guard,*' Miss Silva recites from memory. 'Do you remember those words?'

'YES, MISS SILVA,' we bark in unison.

Of course we all remember the oath we took when we were accepted into the Extinction Prevention Organization. It was a life-changing moment for us. Joining the Final Guard was everything I'd ever dreamt of.

'We have experienced a catastrophe of unthinkable proportions,' she says, with unnerving calm, 'and you failed to fulfil your oath in every possible way.'

We don't move. We don't dare even glance at one another.

'You did not fail the EPO. You did not fail me. You failed Eve,' she says, almost in a whisper. 'She trusted you all to keep her safe. To protect her. To prevent the exact events of the last twelve hours. Commander Ryan, would you care to say anything on behalf of the

Final Guard? Is there any explanation for their sheer incompetence under your command?'

Ryan steps forward immediately, without hesitation, his fingers visibly shaking as he clasps them behind his back.

'Miss Silva, the escape was planned and executed with precision. We were –'

Ryan is interrupted by Miss Silva raising a hand, using her palm to silence him.

'Escape?' she says, tilting her head. 'This was no escape. This was a kidnapping. An abduction. We have provided every technological tool necessary to keep her safe, to keep her from being taken, and still you allowed a single person to penetrate our defences and take the most important human on the planet from right under your noses. Eve's safety was your responsibility.'

'YES, MISS SILVA,' we all bark.

'NO!' she screams. A few strands of her platinum hair fall over her face. 'Not you.' She addresses the collective. '*You.*' Miss Silva points a long, thin finger at Ryan.

'My apologies, Miss Silva. I won't fail you again.' Ryan gulps.

'You are correct about that, Ryan.' Miss Silva snaps her fingers and two armed soldiers step forward from the shadows beside her, weapons raised and aimed at Ryan.

We all instinctively twitch. The sight of unidentified

armed men in the Dome makes us want to reach for our own weapons. It's our training, second nature.

Vivian Silva doesn't flinch. She stares with her cold eyes into Ryan's, cutting through the tears forming as he falls to his knees in front of us.

'Please, we tried everything we could,' he begs, but it's too late. The armed soldiers march forward and I recognize them through the partially frosted visors: the same two who escorted Dr Wells in the lift.

'Commander Ryan, you are under arrest for suspected treason, purposefully neglecting your responsibilities in order to allow the saviour to be forcefully removed from the EPO Tower.' The soldier places two thick cuffs around Ryan's wrists that click into place.

The second soldier pulls out a small black sphere and swipes his thumb across it. Ryan is instantly pulled up from his knees by the cuffs.

The soldier takes out a second, larger, set of silver restraints and secures them around Ryan's ankles.

'Miss Silva, I swear, I'm no traitor. I'll make it up to you. Please. Please!'

The soldier swipes his thumb over the sphere again and the restraints drag Ryan's body away from us.

'Please! Turner, don't let them do this. Please!' he screams, as the soldiers escort him away.

Adrenalin rages through my body and it takes every ounce of my self-control not to pull the gun from my belt and eliminate the soldiers dragging him away.

But I don't.

We all stand rigid watching our comrade dragged towards an unknown fate until he disappears. Fighting it would achieve nothing. Not in here. This is Vivian Silva's world.

I force some deep breaths through my clenched teeth.

Miss Silva lets the screams fade all the way into the distance. We listen to him for what feels like eternity until they must finally have entered the lift to descend.

'Obviously there's going to be another shift in command,' she says plainly. 'Turner, you will now step up to commanding officer of the Final Guard. Is that clear?'

I'm speechless.

'I do not repeat myself.'

'Yes, Miss Silva.' My voice shakes as I try to force a confidence that doesn't exist. 'I will lead the search to find them and return the saviour to her home.' That sounds like what I think I'm *meant* to say.

'There will be no need to search for them, Commander Turner,' Miss Silva says, her lips showing a glimmer of a smirk.

'I'm sorry, Miss Silva, I don't understand,' I say honestly.

She tuts, frustrated by my stupidity.

'You will not need to *search* for them because we have people here, traitors, who already know where she is,' Miss Silva says with a simple sigh. 'Extracting that information will be far easier than searching an entire city, don't you agree?'

She lets the words settle on us for a moment.

*Extracting information.* Sounds a lot like torture to me.

'You are dismissed, gentlemen.'

'YES, MISS SILVA!' we shout, and fall out in shock.

# 10

# Eve

A knock on my door wakes me.

I didn't fall asleep easily. I lay awake for ages, obsessing about what I might see when I closed my eyes – people reaching for me, viciously pulling me in different directions, or Vivian dragging me back to the Tower, locking me up and banishing me to solitary confinement for ever. No lies. Just silence and no one. No Holly. None of the Mothers.

Anxiety threatened to take hold of me but, thankfully, my mind went quiet and allowed the sleep to come. It crept up on me, soothing my aching body and busy mind.

It helped that he was here, of course. Bram sat beside me and held my hand the whole night. Anchoring me so that my mind couldn't trick me into thinking I was elsewhere. Pinning me to this room. Planting me with him. Keeping me safe. Or, at the very least, making me feel it.

There's another knock at the door before it's slowly opened. Bram sleepily peers from behind it, carrying two bowls. His face is grubby, with lines of dirt contouring his features. Despite everything, my stomach performs a little flip as he glances at me.

'Morning,' he croaks.

'Morning.' I smile, sweeping my hair away from my face. The sight of Bram looking dishevelled in the same clothes as last night makes me aware that I've not seen myself in a mirror since we jumped. I've never been so self-aware, which is ridiculous given the circumstances.

'Okay, I have to be honest with you,' he starts. 'I should've warned you before.'

'What?'

'The food,' he says apologetically. 'It might make you wish you'd never jumped. Breakfast?'

I laugh and take the bowl. It's full of green slop. I gag as the stench rises up and hits the back of my throat.

'Yeah . . . my reaction was similar,' he admits.

'Are you joking? You actually expect me to eat this?'

'That's all there is down here . . .' This time the smirk is gone.

'What is it?'

'Floodweed,' he says matter-of-factly. 'It's awful. Truly disgusting.'

'And there's really nothing else?' I ask, hoping this might be some sort of joke.

'We're not in the Tower any more, Eve. There are no banana trees down here,' Bram says. 'Not quite the right environment for them to flourish.'

'Very funny.' I pick up the metal spoon and stir it through the thick green lumpy sludge. 'I should march up to those gates and demand to be let back in just for the bananas.'

'It's best to get as much as you can in there in one go. Eat it all in as few mouthfuls as possible!'

'Thanks for the advice . . .' I say, as Bram gulps down the lot, even using his spoon to scoop up the leaves that have stuck to the sides of the bowl. Nothing has gone to waste.

My tummy grumbles as I look down at my own bowl of slop. 'Great. When I'm given actual food in the Dome I'm not hungry. Now I'm faced with this I feel ravenous.'

'Sod's law.'

'I've been thinking,' I start, putting the bowl on my lap. 'My father. I want to find him.'

Just saying those words makes my desire stronger. The last time I saw him I was three years old. I don't recall the episode clearly, but it left me with a moon-shaped scar on my wrist, a rough patch of skin that my thumb traces over as I speak.

Although he was cut out of my life as a result, I still dream of him most nights. Sometimes I'm back in that room on the last night, being dragged away from him. Other times we're walking through a field with my mother, the two of them laughing. I've always wondered what parts of him I've inherited. Whether I look like him or if we share any personality traits, even though I've grown up without him – the ultimate test of nature or nurture.

The thought of finding him fills me with excitement, although Bram is looking less fired up by my plan.

'I know he's out there and that they lied to me, Bram.'

'That's true, but –'

'I know your relationship with your dad isn't great –'

'Non-existent,' he cuts in.

'Right . . .' I say apologetically. 'But I need to find mine.'

Bram takes a deep breath, plucks my full bowl from my hands and places it on top of his. He rests them on the bedside table before sitting next to me on the bed. 'Eve . . .' he says, looking into his hands.

'I need to try, Bram. This is what I want to do.'

'I'm so sorry. I should've told you this last night.' He runs his fingers through his short dark hair. 'It was the first thing I did when I got out of there. Not only was it important to you, it became the only way of making sure we knew the truth.'

'What are you saying?' I ask.

'We found him, Eve. But he's not here now.'

'Where's he gone? What happened? Where is he?' I ask, the questions tumbling out. 'Did he not want to see me?'

'He did. Very much so,' Bram says, glancing up at me with a pained expression. 'It's just . . . he's back in there. In the Tower.'

The words knock the air out of me.

'What?' I whisper.

'Eve, it was his idea.' His voice is low. 'We knew we had to create a diversion. Do something that would pull their attention and their resources away from you. Your dad was adamant. You should've seen what they did to keep him from you, Eve.' He shakes his head. 'After they dragged him away all those years ago, they told the world he was mad, banishing him so that he couldn't persuade anyone otherwise or stop what they were doing. Ernie took his voice back. He walked straight back inside the Tower, and their cage was rattled. Their guard was down as they focused on how they could break him once more, and that was when we got you out. Eve, your dad sacrificed himself so that you could escape and have the freedom you deserve.'

'I don't understand why he'd do that,' I say, as my fingers brush the scar on my wrist.

'Because you're his daughter and he loves you. He felt like he'd failed you the last time he tried to get you out of there. He didn't want to make the same mistake twice,' he says.

'He didn't need to seek redemption or forgiveness. He just needed to be here.'

'You wouldn't be here if he was.'

Silence fills the room. I can't argue with my dad's reasons for doing what he has. He's acted as a loving father. I might not be a mother yet – I might never be one – but I'd like to think I'd experience a bond like no other, and put my child's needs before my own.

'What was he like?' I ask.

'Kind. He's everything I'd want my dad to be,' he says.

'Do you think he blames me for her death?' The question comes out quickly, but it's one I need to ask.

'Categorically no,' is Bram's reply. 'He's devastated that you've been led to think that.'

I believe him.

'He went back in there,' I say. 'It's crazy that after all this time, he'd do that for me . . .'

'He did what so many of us would do without a second thought,' says Bram. 'It's what so many of us have and will continue to do for you. It's what you do for those you love.'

'My life is no more important than anyone else's,' I tell him, trying to ignore the way my heart thumps.

'Says the saviour of mankind.'

'Don't call me that,' I say, glaring at him. I suddenly feel angry at the label. All it's ever made me feel is other, isolated and alone. Not special, just burdened.

'Eve, come on,' he starts.

'No, Bram. No!' I get to my feet, my arms flying wildly to articulate my point. 'I'm only here because others have given their lives for me. How can the "saviour of mankind" be happy *taking* lives? Where's the logic in it?'

'You know there's more to it than that.'

'No, there isn't. It's simple. My mum died because I was *born*,' I remind him. 'I don't want my father to die to keep me alive.'

'He made his choice.'

'And I wasn't given one.' My voice is rising. 'You know me better than anyone. You know I would never have left if I had been told he was in there. If *you* had told me,' I add, remembering that Bram had urged me to jump, knowing full well my dad was in the Tower.

His head dips as he sighs into his lap.

'I have to go and get him.'

His eyes shoot up at me, a look of incredulity on his face. He opens his mouth to speak but stops himself and takes a breath. 'We all risked our lives to get you out,' he says slowly. 'Ernie knew what he was doing. You aren't going back.'

'Says who? You? My commander? Have I just gone from one prison into another?' I ask. 'At least this looks like one, I suppose.'

'Eve! You're not alone in having someone in there.'

'I'm going back.'

'Your life is too important.'

'What is the point of a life if you don't do anything

with it? And surely the whole point of me having my freedom is to decide my own future, right?'

Something flashes across his face. For a second I see her, and I know he understands.

He understands, but that doesn't mean he's happy.

# 11

# Bram

She's got to be kidding.

'We risked everything. Breaking in and rescuing you wasn't easy, you know.' I try to explain the obvious.

'*Rescue?*' she says, cocking her head to one side. 'I'm sorry, did you ever hear me say I needed rescuing? Is that how you see me, like some pathetic fairy-tale princess? A feeble girl who needs someone to save her?'

I stare at her and swallow a lump of floodweed that lingered in my throat. 'Have you finished?' I ask.

'No,' she snaps.

I sigh, feeling like we're back on the Drop and she's venting her frustrations at me via Holly. I need to let her get it out. I know her. I wait for her to fill the silence, as Holly would on the Drop.

'We're not on the Drop now,' she says accusingly.

*Shit.*

'That's right. You think you know me, *Bram*, but you forget that *I* know you just as well.'

We stare at each other for a moment but I know she has more to say.

'You can't hide behind Holly any more. There's no EPO to hold responsible for the things you do now. What happens down here, what these *Freevers* do, it's all you.'

I open my mouth to speak but nothing comes out. I suddenly see how right she is.

'Eve, everything you just said, it's true,' I say, as earnestly as I can but it still sounds like a lie.

She raises an eyebrow.

'No, I mean it! It's my fault and I'm sorry. I didn't realize it until just now, but it wasn't you I was rescuing from that Tower . . . it was me,' I say, more to myself than to her. It somehow hits me harder saying it out loud.

She takes my hand, and it's like electricity connecting us. I used to think that the pilot suits and kinetic gloves gave a true representation of reality, but the truth is, they are nothing like feeling the power of the physical presence of another person.

'We both jumped. Together. We freed ourselves,' I say.

'We freed each other.' She smiles.

A sudden thud rattles the hinges on the door to the Robing Room.

'Yes?' I shout.

'It's Chubs,' calls a voice from beyond.

I roll my eyes at Eve. She smiles.

'Can I –'

'Yes, yes, come in!' She cuts him off.

Chubs enters, sees us standing together and averts his eyes awkwardly as though he's caught us in the middle of an intimate moment. 'Sorry,' he says, staring at the floor.

'It's fine, Chubs. What is it?' I ask.

'The drones have returned to the Tower. Word on the water is all search-craft are heading back too. Looks like we're clear, for now.' He shrugs, with a smile.

'They've called off the search?' I ask, my brain switching from the euphoria of Eve to the worrying reality of an unexpected move by the EPO.

'Yeah!' Chubs laughs. 'Pretty great, right? I guess we can relax for a while, give the Water Watchers a rest and call in our scouts at the Tower.'

'No,' Eve says instinctively.

Chubs's eyes move from me to her, then back to me.

'No?' Chubs repeats.

'This isn't right. They're up to something.' Eve frowns at me, as though searching for something we've all missed.

Chubs looks to me for the answer.

'I think Eve's right. Calling off the search sounds

too good to be true. It's got to be a tactical move,' I agree.

'Or maybe they're just resigned to the fact that she actually got away.'

'She?' I say. '*SHE?*'

Chubs frowns at me, confused.

'Are you referring to the most important human on the planet? Is *she, the saviour of mankind, the answer to our extinction*, someone you think the EPO would just let go? Is *SHE* someone whom Vivian Silva would just accept has escaped?' I say, trying to express how much of a curve ball the EPO have just thrown.

'Bram,' Eve says quietly.

Chubs is staring at the floor, deflated.

'Chubs,' I say, 'I'm sorry. It's been a long few days.'

'No, it's okay. You're right.' He sighs. 'It is strange that they'd call the search off now. I'll go up and tell the scouts and Water Watchers to stay in position and continue until further notice.'

'No,' Eve announces.

Chubs and I stare at her.

'No?' I ask.

'I'll tell them,' Eve says to Chubs, without even a glance to see what my reaction is to this.

'Bram?' Chubs asks, the confusion obvious in his voice.

'It's okay, Chubs. It is Chubs, isn't it?' Eve asks.

'Yes . . . erm . . . Miss Eve . . .' he mumbles nervously.

'It's Eve, just Eve. Chubs, take me to the surface. I'll deliver the orders myself.'

'Absolutely not,' I interject, unable to hold back any longer.

'Excuse me?' Eve says.

'Are you actually insane?' I ask. 'The surface? You want to go up there after everything we went through to bring you safely down here?'

'I want to see the world. It's been hidden from me for too long.'

'No, Eve. Not yet,' I say.

'Then I really have left one prison for another.' She's staring deep into my eyes.

I hold my gaze firm and don't break. I can't let her go up there, it's too dangerous, but I can't keep her locked up, like the EPO did.

'You can't stop me, can you?' she says.

I hesitate. It's all she needs.

'Chubs, lead the way.' She stands and marches to the door with purpose.

'Eve, wait!' I call, but it's too late.

She's out of the door in a flash. Chubs can barely stay ahead of her to guide her. I follow in their wake.

'What the hell is this?' Saunders says, pulling his big nose out of a vintage, water-damaged book while sitting at his post outside the entrance to the submerged sphere that leads to the surface.

I catch Chubs widening his eyes at Saunders, warning him.

'Eve, shit!' Saunders says, dropping his book into the foot of water he's standing in.

'Just plain Eve will do,' Eve replies, with a smile, trying to soften him. As if she needed to. 'I want to go up now, please.'

Saunders immediately looks at me for clarification.

'You don't need to look at him. I'm not your prisoner, am I?' Eve asks, and I can hear the fire inside her, the one I helped ignite.

'. . . No, Eve,' he replies.

'No?' she repeats.

'No. You're not our prisoner,' Saunders says slowly, trying to buy time to think of what to do.

'Look, Eve. All we want is to do what's best for you,' I say. It sounds pathetic.

'What you *think* is best for me. I guess Vivian was just doing what *she* thought was best for me too, was she?' Eve replies.

I've got nothing.

None of us has.

'I think it's time that *I* start deciding what's best for me, don't you?' Eve says, stepping forward towards the brass door to the spherical pod that goes to the surface.

Saunders steps aside, throwing me a what-the-hell look.

'Well, are you coming or am I going to have to figure out how to do this on my own?' she says from inside the cramped sphere.

'No, we're all coming,' I say, following her inside with Chubs and Saunders.

We take our seats in the cramped vessel.

'Are you sure?' Saunders asks Eve, his hand hovering over the brass lever that is currently positioned over the word 'Descend'.

Without saying a word she reaches out and lifts the lever up until it clicks into the 'Ascend' position. The spherical underwater lift jolts to life. Gallons of water fill the chamber outside and our pod begins to float.

As we rise through the excavated interior of the clock tower, which was once one of this ancient city's most iconic landmarks, I notice Chubs and Saunders exchange subtle looks. They sense it as well as I do. The roles have shifted in the Deep.

I am no longer in command.

The Freevers have a new leader.

'Are you armed?' I ask Chubs.

He nods and pulls back his overcoat to reveal a selection of weapons. Far more than necessary but, for once, I'm glad of the arsenal he's carrying.

Without me asking, he reaches into his gun belt, unstraps a small blaster and hands it to me.

'Thanks,' I say, taking the weapon and arming it.

'Do you think you'll need that?' Eve asks, looking back at me from the small porthole.

'If the EPO are there, we'll need a hell of a lot more than a few hand-blasters,' Saunders chips in.

'Don't worry, we've got eyes all around the area,' Chubs says, comforting her.

'You know it's not too late to go back down?' I say hopefully.

But Eve just smiles.

I'd known it was useless.

# 12

# Eve

I'm shocked at the rush I'm feeling. I spoke and I was heard. Of course, I've always had this stupid title, but it carried no weight. I was only ever someone floating around in her own world above the clouds. I never really felt important. This is so different.

It was only as I started speaking, when I watched Chubs, Saunders and a bemused Bram listen and act accordingly, that I started to grasp the reality of the situation I'm in.

I have the power.

I've empowered myself.

What a rush.

Bram is scared. He's never had reason to express fear to me before, and now I know why: there was nothing at stake up there. Out here, the danger is real and that worries him. I knew it from the way his eyes darted around as he tried to make sense of the situation. How his voice rose when he spoke to Chubs. This means something to him.

That said, it doesn't mean I'm going to follow him or anyone else blindly. I have to figure out what's going on down here for myself, then make an informed decision on what's best to do. I shouldn't have snapped at him, but I'm sick of people gaining authority over me. I'm sure I'll find myself being short with him numerous times as we learn to live side by side – *properly* side by side. It's not going to be easy when there's so much else to think about, and our views seem to be pulling us in opposite directions.

We stop floating upwards as we reach the surface. The vessel bobs up and down.

'You'll need to –'

'Stop,' I cut across Bram, watching as Saunders releases the door and cold air bursts in. My body tenses. My shoulders ping up to my ears.

'– wear a coat,' Bram finishes, with an eye roll, chucking a bundle of fabric in my direction.

He doesn't wait for my response. He starts pulling on his own coat.

'Are you trying to mother her?' mutters Chubs, kicking Bram's foot as he stands up.

Bram's cheeks redden.

'Lead the way,' I say, following Saunders out of the

sphere and back on to the stone staircase I walked down behind Helena yesterday. From the top of the steps I see what I didn't have time to take in before.

The world outside.

The *real* one.

Murky brown water surrounds us, vast and uninviting. Buildings poke out – bricks growing thick green algae, glass panels smashed through to bring the outdoors in and let the inside out. Debris floats this way and that – items lost, discarded and useless, knocking their way along the river. Bumping into anything in their way.

Here anything is salvageable. Just take the way their headquarters have been botched together and saved from erosion. Outside items have been strapped together, united to create boats or rafts. Floating homes anchored by ropes and chains.

I think of my paradise in the sky – the garden they grew for me. Out here the only green is that on the brick. No trees, plants or shrubbery grow, painting the view with colour. It's grey and bleak, without the promise of life. It's become as barren as its inhabitants, who crouch in the shadows. But it's raw, real and damningly beautiful.

I follow the others back on to the small boat that brought me here. Chubs steers into the open river. More buildings protrude from below. Strewn fabric hangs, like flags or washing, billowing in the breeze – perhaps to declare ownership of whatever building someone has inhabited. The river ahead seems to dance with light, thanks to the huge screens suspended on the sides of buildings.

'What are they for?' I ask, gesturing at them.

'Pumping out whatever bullshit the EPO wants us to believe,' Chubs grumbles.

I turn to Bram. He shrugs in agreement, his eyes moving from mine and scanning the darkness around us. It's clear he's on edge.

'Can we go and look?' I ask, wanting to see for myself.

'It's not safe,' insists Bram.

'Is anything?' I challenge. I'm even more determined to seek out the extent of the EPO's lies.

'People are going to be looking for you even if *they* aren't.'

'Let's make sure our teams are still on the look-out first. Then we can get a bit closer,' Saunders interrupts, his eyes flicking between Bram and me.

Bram's face twists in annoyance while I nod in thanks.

We veer off the main channel, sailing under a huge steel archway, then into a tunnel. It's quiet. The sound of our boat as it pushes through the water echoes around us. We hug the wall to our left, disappearing under fabric hanging overhead. Approaching a clearing, someone steps out from behind the shadows, holding out their hand for us to stop. The dim lighting reflects off the weapon in his grasp that is pointing directly at us.

My body stiffens as my heart pounds in my chest.

'What the –' mutters Bram.

'For Eve,' Chubs calls, his voice hardened and full of authority as he holds out his arm and blocks Bram trying to raise his gun.

The man before us nods in acknowledgement.

'Rodriguez,' Saunders says, firing out the information to me and Bram – he's clearly never been down here either. I feel oddly satisfied to be somewhere neither of us has ventured.

'Our teams are still out there trying to decipher what's going on, but it's gone cold,' he says, holding his arm over his eyes to stop the lights from our boat blinding him. 'The team out east thought they had someone trailing them, but it turned out to be nothing.'

'How can you be sure?' I ask.

If my voice and presence are surprising to him, he doesn't let on. He's unwavering as he continues.

'It was just a couple of kids playing around. Ground teams who were in situ when you left say they've seen a lot of activity of troops arriving back at their base, but none leaving.'

'They're up to something,' Saunders says.

'Or they have something they know we'll be heading back for,' mutters Bram, rubbing his face over his hands.

'How many teams do you have out there?' I ask.

'Two in each quarter, four on the ground.'

'Right. Well, have them continue with their

surveillance,' I say, resisting the urge to say 'please'. Pleasantries seem out of place here. 'It's still early days. Who knows what they might throw at us?' The words seem laughable coming from my lips. I'm well aware that I have no idea what Vivian is capable of. Thankfully no one highlights this point to me as we say our goodbyes and make our way back to the larger expanse of water.

'Still want to go up there?' Saunders checks.

'Yes.'

We turn towards the lights, the boat travelling slowly. Bram chucks a wet blanket at me. 'We're already being stupid, so let's not be insane.'

Reluctantly I pick it up and drape it around me, covering my head so that just my eyes show.

The water around us becomes more populated, just as the buildings around us show signs of life. Groups of people gather in the shadows, shuffling through the darkness. Others shout profanities at each other from different types of watercraft – angry and mean. Burning sticks are thrown, and bangs are heard, along with screams of agony.

'They've been rebelling for so long it's become the only way some know how to communicate,' Saunders explains, ducking as something flies overhead.

I flinch, instinctively lowering my head to conceal myself further.

'Can we just get back?' hisses Bram. 'This is stupid. You being here right now is stupid.'

I'd be inclined to agree if it weren't for the melodic tones suddenly making their way into my ears.

As we drift closer, I see them. Underneath the glare of the dancing bright lights and the giant screens, basking in their brilliant white, a large gathering of people is singing as they look up at the images being shown. Their makeshift boats have been tied together, and they float as one united front. Their earnest faces sing out passionately – words about being found, being safe and staying hopeful. There's joyfulness in the moment, as though it's an occasion to come together. I spot one man, draped in colourful grubby fabric, singing with his arms open wide as his body sways, feeling the words with every fibre of his being. His faith is spellbinding to watch.

'Are they always here like this?' I ask.

'No. They're here because you're not in *there*,' replies Saunders, holding my gaze. 'There have always been pockets of hope, hidden among the chaos. You getting out – it's brought them out of the darkness.'

I turn back to the crowd and see more boats steering from the shadows. Arms reaching out, ready to join those already gathered.

'Oh, shit.' Chubs groans.

I follow his eyes up to the screens I'd been insistent on seeing. My heart drops into my gut as the words 'Traitors of Eve' flash before us in bold red writing, with four pictures of their chosen 'rebels' displayed below. Bram's body stiffens next to mine as his image is shown next to one of Mother Kadi. The third picture is of a boy who must be around my age. Floppy dark brown hair falls around his face. In a split second I recognize him. He was with Bram the day we first met. Clearly meeting Bram had stopped me giving him much thought until now, but that's definitely him.

The remaining man is older. His familiar eyes, so much like my own, reveal exactly who he is.

Dad.

The three images of those we know are still in the Tower fade, making way for the picture of Bram to expand across the screen. More words flash up. He's a fugitive on the run. Wanted for capturing me against my will. It's the story they're sticking with, their chosen narrative.

'Best make some room under that blanket, Eve,' says Chubs, gravely, nodding towards Bram, who sits a little closer, his head dipped, sorrow, pain and guilt dripping from his fallen face.

'I'm so sorry,' I whisper.

He shakes his head, and I long to drape my arms around him and hold him close.

'We should go back to the Deep,' I say to Saunders.

His eyes flit between Bram and me before he acts on my request. His hands fumble as he starts the boat again. He can't get out of there quickly enough. The mood is sombre as we retreat.

'Your friend,' I say to Bram, once the noise around us has died down and we're far enough away from the mayhem.

'Hartman.' He nods, rubbing his eyes.

'My last Holly.' I think back to the companion I didn't know who appeared before me in my room, giving me the final nudge to shatter their illusion.

'My best mate.' Bram nods again. 'I shared everything with him.'

'You had a tight bond?'

'The tightest.'

'I saw him,' I say, remembering. 'Before I left. He was . . . in pain. But he did all he could to get me out safely.'

'That sounds like him.' Bram sighs into his hands, his head turning away from me.

'He didn't just do that for me. He did it for you.'

'I know.'

'It was your plan.'

He nods.

'And do you really want your best friend, the guy who'd do anything for you, to suffer the consequences of your plan while we go off gallivanting into a new life?' I ask. 'Would you really be able to live with yourself if you didn't at least try to help him in return?'

I see my words working, just as I'd known they would.

The world out here isn't what I thought it would be – but what else could it be when so much has been stripped from its inhabitants? My birth was the symbol of hope they'd been looking for. Only I was taken from them. Claimed and paraded. Separated. Despite that, some found a way to show their support. These traitors, as the EPO have called them, these people who helped me escape and who show their love even though I appear to have deserted them, they're not traitors at all. They're truly loyal, and they're worth fighting for.

'What would you do if your dad was up there?' I ask, giving Bram one final nudge to fully understanding and supporting my decision.

'He is.' He laughs drily. 'And this whole thing has his name written all over it.' He sighs. 'I'm not going to stop you, am I?'

'No.'

'You know you'll start a war. It'll be them against the people. Are you prepared for that?'

'The war began decades ago. The difference is that now we know we're in one.'

# 13

# Michael

The Med Level stinks of disinfectant. It stings my nose as I exit the lift but I'm used to the sensation now. I walk the only route I was permitted to take while on detention. Visiting time with family or friends who have potentially life-threatening injuries is one of the few things that'll get you out of your dorm and I took full advantage of that.

Not that I didn't want to see my brother anyway.

I pass hundreds of empty cubicles, their only occupants the state-of-the-art medical equipment hanging unused and lifeless on the walls. Stuff exists in here that doctors in the outside world could only ever dream of.

That's the thing about disasters – war, disease, the climate shift: they bring about the fastest acceleration in technological developments. You've just got to survive long enough to benefit from it. Facing extinction is no exception. And living in the same building as the most precious human of our species gives us access to the very best medical equipment in history.

Handy when you get the sniffles.

Although the best tech couldn't do anything for most of Ketch's team, who were caught in that blast. There wasn't anything left to save. Ketch got off lightly in comparison.

As I turn the corner I'm greeted with a warm orange glow. I hear voices, which means the doctors are with him.

'You're healing well,' Dr Chaudhury notes.

'Not well enough,' Ketch grunts, with a slight rattle in his raspy voice.

'Your injuries were severe. You're lucky to be alive, Commander Turner.'

'It's not *Commander* any more,' my brother snaps.

'It's not *Turner* either, right, Ketch?' I make my presence known.

'The medical team have been wondering about this mysterious nickname you go by. If you don't mind me asking, why *Ketch*?' the doctor asks.

Before my brother can answer, I reach into my pockets and pull out the stash of contraband I've smuggled in for him and drop the dozen red sachets on to the bed.

'Ketchup?' The doctor laughs. 'I'm not sure your nutritionist will approve.'

'Laugh all you want. It's my guilty pleasure.' Ketch shrugs.

'Eve wasn't allowed to know his real name, as a security measure, so Ketch was born,' I announce, in my best mock-regal voice. I bow my head as my brother tears the corner of a sachet with his teeth and squeezes the contents into his blistered mouth, gulping it down like he's not eaten in years. So gross.

'Well, I'm sorry to say that your brother should go easy on the sugar intake. His number-one priority needs to be his recovery, Mr Turner.'

'*He*'s Commander Turner now.' Ketch sulks.

I give the doctor a look. *I'll talk to him.*

'Well, I'll leave you both to it. Don't stay too long, though. Your brother needs rest, not ketchup.' Dr Chaudhury shakes his head with a smile, as he leaves the cubicle.

Ketch lies back slowly on the bed, groaning in pain as his burns connect with the bedding.

'Healing well? Sounds promising,' I say, trying not to stare too hard at the blistered flesh around the dressing that covers his left eye.

'Yeah, yeah, "full recovery", whatever. Doesn't make any difference.' He sighs. 'Silva wants me off the Final Guard for good.'

His shoulders sink. I can see how much this is hurting him.

'I don't know what to say. I'm sorry.' The words sound sincere but there's an awkward silence between us as I sit on the end of his bed. I'm suddenly very aware of my uniform. The subtle letters *FG* embroidered in gold on my black jumpsuit now feel so glaringly obvious they're practically screaming, 'LOOK AT ME, KETCH!'

'I hear you were promoted.' He breaks the silence.

'Yeah.'

'Congratulations. Mum would have been proud of you.'

We both know that's a lie. 'No, she would have been proud of you. Always you, and you know it. I'd still be living down in the flood if you hadn't got me this gig,' I reply. I feel his uncovered eye staring at me. 'Don't look at me like that. It's creepy.'

'You're worried.' He reads from my face.

'No shit! I just watched their new private soldiers drag the last commander away after failing to meet Miss Silva's expectations,' I explain.

'Yes, I heard.'

'Well, I've already got a target on my back. Silva thinks I'm an idiot. I don't know why she gave the position to me.' Now that I'm venting, it all just spews out. 'Actually, I do. Of course I do. *You.* You're the only reason I'm still here. The untouchable *Ketch.* Exceeding bloody expectations your whole life. You know how annoying that was growing up?'

'Would you have preferred me to let them put you in the cells with the traitors? Because that was on the cards for you,' he says, keeping his cool.

'Course not,' I snap, sounding like a spoiled child. I hate myself.

111

'Well, then, you have some serious work ahead of you so it's time to stop acting like you did when you were ten years old and get the job done. You know how hard I had to fight to get you on the team.'

'I know.' And I do. He pulled some serious strings to get me through the door for the assessment. Of course he'd prepped me on what to do, how to stand, how to impress Miss Silva.

'I'm sorry. It's just been a stressful return from suspension,' I say truthfully. 'It's not every day the worst-case scenario comes true.'

'What's the latest? Any news on Eve's location?' he asks.

'Sorry, that's classified,' I say.

He kicks me and I fall off the bed on to the sterile floor. 'Okay, okay! It was a joke!' I say, as I sit back on the bed and sigh. 'We still don't know where she is. Miss Silva thinks we can *extract information* on her location from the traitors.'

'Extract information? Sounds painful,' my brother says. 'But Eve wasn't kidnapped by one person and if people know things, people will say things. If you push the right buttons, of course.'

I don't say anything.

'Sometimes doing the right thing means doing the wrong thing,' Ketch says, sensing my concern about how we will be acquiring this information.

'It's not just that. It's . . .' I pause and double-check we're alone. 'This wasn't a kidnapping.'

Ketch stares at me. 'Careful. We won't be alone for long,' he warns, using his good eye to indicate the open cubicle door.

I get up, check the corridor is clear and press my palm on the glass panel. The door closes. Privacy.

'I've seen footage from the drones,' Ketch says.

'Then you've seen them jump, her and Bram, together. It didn't look like she needed much persuading to leave, from where I was standing.'

I see Ketch's brain working as he thinks about it for a moment.

'She's been here so long, it's only natural that she'd want to know what's out there once the truth was revealed to her.'

I nod, hesitate.

'What is it?' he asks.

'Ketch, we're brothers and I trust you with my life,' I say.

'Mikey, calm down. What's up?'

'You've worked for the EPO longer than anyone. How did you know that your loyalty was in the right place?' I ask.

'My loyalty to the EPO?' he repeats, seeming almost amused.

I nod.

'My loyalty was never with the EPO, and it never will be. My loyalty is to Eve. That's where everyone's loyalty should be.'

'What about Miss Silva? She's a loose cannon!'

'It's not Vivian you should be concerned about. It's Wells.'

'Dr Wells? Really?' I ask.

Ketch adjusts himself in his bed to lean a little closer. 'Vivian was never like this when I started,' he says quickly and quietly, as though someone could walk in at any moment. 'She was kind and compassionate. She changed when he came here.'

'Why?'

'Times were different then. The EPO played a different role in all this. It was about Eve, that was all, protecting her, giving her and us the best chance at a future,' he whispers.

'And it's not any more?' I ask.

He doesn't reply. Then he says, 'You want my advice?'

I shrug.

'Listen to your gut and do what's right for Eve. Forget everything else.'

'What about you? What will you do next? Once you recover?' I ask, getting back to my feet.

'Don't you worry about me. I've got things lined up,' Ketch says, with a nonchalance I instantly see through.

'What are you up to?'

'It's nothing, and if you know what's good for you you'll leave it there.'

'Oh, c'mon, I'm your brother!'

'Let's just say with every door that closes, another one opens and –' He stops himself.

'And what?'

He sighs, frustrated with himself for saying too much. 'And I didn't even know this door was there.'

I blink slowly. 'O-kay . . . I'm not sure what that means,' I say. 'Seriously, what's the new job?'

Ketch just stares at me.

'It's like that, is it?' I ask. My own brother. Keeping secrets. This has got to be big.

He just nods.

'What the hell are you up to?'

'Look, it's a dull job but he needed someone he could trust, someone who'd been here for ever and understood how things work,' Ketch says, trying to sound casual, like I'm going to let this slide.

'He?' I say.

'Huh?'

'You said *he needed someone*. Who's *he*?'

My brother suddenly lunges forward, grabs the collar of my jumpsuit and pulls my head down until I'm face-to-face with him.

'Listen, Michael, this isn't a game. This shit is real and it's messed up but we're in too deep now. Okay? I wish I'd never brought you into the EPO, into this damn place. Sometimes I think we'd have been better wasting away down in the flood instead of being part of all this.'

I push him away and free myself. He winces at my touch.

'Just don't ask any more questions, okay, Mikey? I

can't lie to you, you know that, and you're better off not knowing this.'

I look him in the eye and try to find my brother in it, the brother I grew up with. He's there somewhere, hidden beneath the burns, bandages and secrets.

'All right,' I reply. 'Just don't get yourself wrapped up in anything stupid.'

He laughs, and the laughter turns into racking coughs.

I dim the lights as I leave the room. He needs some rest.

As I walk back towards the lift the echoes of approaching footsteps find their way to my ears. Instinct makes me study them. It's what I'm trained to do.

Boots. Heavy duty. Military issue.

Two . . . no, three men.

As they get closer their noise paints a clearer picture.

Only two wear boots. The third is wearing something lighter with rubber soles.

The regular click on every other step indicates a weapon on his belt connecting with the metal zip of his cargo trousers.

They're armed.

I slip inside one of the unoccupied cubicles on the Med Level, only a hundred yards from Ketch's room.

I have no reason to hide, but something is telling me I'm better not being seen.

*Listen to your gut . . .*

Ketch's words bounce around in my brain.

Silhouettes appear on the frosted-glass walls of the cubicle as the men turn into the corridor. Their footsteps are loud but they aren't talking.

I silently find a spot in the darkest part of the rear wall, hidden in the shadows.

Suddenly a figure walks past, dressed all in black, armed with multiple weapons. He's quickly followed by the mysterious light-footed man, and another armed soldier brings up the rear.

I might have guessed it would be Wells and his new henchmen, the bastards that dragged Ryan away.

A few moments later I hear them stop. I head to the door and peer into the corridor where I see the three men disappear inside my brother's cubicle.

So, that's the *he* Ketch was talking about. Oh, brother, what have you got yourself into?

# 14

# Eve

All eyes are on me as I stand in the chamber from the previous night with Helena, Bram and the team from earlier by my side. The last time I was in here it was full of excitement as they celebrated my arrival. This time they're more controlled with their emotions. They stand tall, eager and alert. They're completely silent as they wait for me to speak.

I haven't been caught off guard. I called this meeting. I asked for everyone to be gathered so that I could share my plan, yet I'm surprised by the weight of expectation I feel while they're standing before me. People aren't whispering to each other. I have their full attention. It's always been like this, of course. Back in the Tower, rooms and corridors would fall silent whenever I entered. The guards were forbidden to look at me – but I was just a tool then. I was just an object to worship, rather than a person to understand. I wasn't given a voice. They were just following Vivian's orders.

Standing here, in this vast room, I feel more like Vivian than myself. As though some part of me is channelling her confidence and authority rather than relying on my own.

'Thank you, all, for everything you've done so far and for the support you've given,' I say, with only the slightest tremor in my voice. 'It's been an interesting twenty-four hours, and I know it's going to take longer than that for all of this to sink in. It's hard to believe I knew nothing of your existence only a day ago, yet you've been fighting for me relentlessly – even before I was born. I cannot thank you enough.

'There's one thing for which I'll be eternally grateful, that you found my father. From my understanding, it wasn't easy to do so but you did. I've spent hours on the Drop thinking about what he and my mother must've been like. Thanks to you I'm a little closer to feeling what it is to have a real family.'

I glance at Bram for encouragement, but his eyes are fixed towards the crowd, a steely expression on his face. This is my decision. If it's something I truly want, I have to get it on my own.

I continue: 'I know he, like so many of you, risked his life for mine by going back into that building.'

The crowd shifts, relaxes as they understand that I know this particular piece of the puzzle – that my only living parent handed himself over to our enemy for me.

'Now I must go back for him.'

There's silence, then whispers of disbelief.

'After everything we've done for her?'

'Do all those who've died for her mean nothing?'

'How many more of us have to die for her freedom?'

I try again. 'It's just not fair that I should –'

'We fought for your justice,' interrupts one man, angry and bewildered as he speaks. 'Now it's time to topple the EPO and fight for our justice, and for the justice of every single person out here who has been pushed into poverty by their power. Don't talk to us about fair!'

'I didn't mean –'

'He's right!' shouts another voice. 'They've grown stronger while we've grown weaker. By freeing you we could start claiming back our rights. You going back in there would risk everything.'

'Freedom doesn't mean she has to do exactly what you want her to, though, does it?' argues a female voice to my left.

More words are shouted as the crowd becomes angry, and arguments break out. The noise builds. A scuffle starts in one corner of the room with the man who spoke of justice. I see arms in the air as punches are thrown in his direction.

Adrenalin surges through me and I find myself striding off the platform and through the crowd. I fight my way to the men throwing their weight around. As soon as I reach them I grab the first I see – a man who's at least a foot taller than me and twice as wide – and get him into a lock hold before swinging him over my shoulder and on to the ground. It's a move I was taught in one of my many lessons with the Mothers, but never had the opportunity to carry out – it didn't seem right to tackle a woman in her sixties to the ground so that I could learn a skill we all assumed I'd never need, and I wasn't allowed near the security guards to test it on them.

The way this man's weight shifts and rolls is surprising. The thump as he lands on the floor is so loud it vibrates beneath my feet. It interrupts the chaos, and we're left with what I was hoping for – silence.

The fighting ceases. They all look at me agog. Mouths wide open. They appear even more startled than they did when I walked in last night. I won't kid myself that I'm the strongest or most capable here, but they have certainly underestimated me. A lifetime in the Tower has given me an abundance of skills that I thought were redundant. I no longer feel that way. The boxing and martial-arts classes have paid off.

Thanks, Vivian.

'I take it we're all done?' I ask, pacing the small circle the ruckus was taking place in.

The defeated man scrambles to his feet, throwing me an embarrassed glance, then holding out a hand to the man he'd initially punched. Standing side by side, they fall back in line with their fellows, their disagreement forgotten.

It's unnerving being among the crowd like this, with the tension in the air tangible enough to grab. But I know I can't back away now.

I stay where I am, my body buzzing, and continue addressing them from here. This time I don't need to channel Vivian to do so. I'm set for fight or flight – and, right now, flight is not an option.

'When I arrived last night I learned your collective name. Freevers. You have dedicated your life to my freedom. But I have been wondering what that freedom means if I now find myself imprisoned yet again. Were you fighting for my physical freedom? So that I could walk among you? Was it my mental freedom? Was it the freedom to love whoever I wished? To make and learn from my mistakes? Was it freedom to act on my impulses and live life in the way I wished? What exactly were you fighting for?'

I give them time to reply.

No one does.

I stop pacing and root myself to the spot, noticing that Bram has moved closer, along with Helena, Chubs and Saunders. His eyes bore into mine.

'I never asked anyone to sacrifice their life for mine,' I remind them, slamming my hand into my chest. 'Yet so many of you did. Just like my father did, not once, but twice. I should be allowed the privilege of doing the same for someone I love, because that is my right. That is my freedom.'

A few heads drop.

'I don't expect any of you to join me. So many of you have given so much already. I can't ask that of you,' I say. 'I don't want anyone to feel pressured into helping me. But I owe it to you to tell you *my* plan while you move forward with yours. Somehow I will be going back to that building, and I will be leaving with the man who gave me life. Or I won't be leaving at all.'

Mouths open to speak, yet nothing comes out. Heads are tilted. Lips are licked and feet are shuffled. I can understand their hesitation and confusion. They've been waiting for me to arrive for so long, hoping I'd be able to offer them the answers they've been searching for. They longed for me to come, made it their life's work to get me out of the Tower in the hope that would sort out the mess the EPO had created of their lives, but perhaps they never really thought they could. Everything until this point has been hypothetical, but now it's time for them to shift their focus on what comes next.

I wish I could offer them more than the desire to be reunited with my dad.

'We're not leaving you either, Eve.' It's Bram's voice cutting through the silence. Heads turn to face him. 'Not now. Not ever.'

'The fate of the future lies with you. Yes, we want

to see them pay, but you are our saviour,' adds Helena. 'It's our duty to serve and stand with you, Eve.'

'I'm not changing my mind. I'm going back,' I tell her.

'I'm old enough to remember your mum and dad,' Helena says, stepping towards me so that she, too, is in the circle that's been created. 'They were good people, Eve. You and your father were meant to be together. They shouldn't be allowed to keep you separated any longer.'

I find myself nodding at her, as passion flares within me. There is no doubt in my mind that this is the right thing to do.

And I'm not alone. The whispers of disapproval have gone. Now there's a buzz in the air. The buzz of change. The buzz of people who do not want to be restrained any longer.

'We go in there,' I shout, looking around the crowd to include every single person standing before me. 'We go in there, we get my father, and we will make sure those bastards realize our lives are NOT to be played with! We are not pawns in their game, and we will not let them cheat us out of life. We will topple them, and we will enjoy watching them fall.'

The cheer is instantaneous.

'For Eve,' booms Bram, leaping forward and punching the air. He marches around me, his feet stamping a rhythm as he repeats the words again and again. Helena raises her foot and pushes it into the floor as the rest of the crowd starts to respond, matching their enthusiasm.

The rising sound causes vibration beneath our feet. People clap in time to the beat, drumming on their chests to help build the rhythm. 'For Eve,' they chant.

But it's not for me. That's a twisted illusion. This is for them, for us, for every single person in existence or who has come before us. Life is not to be won or taken. It's not to be played with. It is to be respected.

A voice sounds, low like a hum, rising and falling in a beautiful melody. Then a song begins, with dozens of voices joining in while everyone else continues to stomp and clap.

> *When the sky went dark,*
> *They took our heart,*
> *Left us bleeding*
> *Ripped our world apart.*
>
> *Gone was our hope*
> *When the days were long,*
> *But they ain't ever*
> *Gonna take our song.*

As I feel the energy build in the room, I realize that, like before, I am a symbol. But before I was a representation of hope.

Now I stand for defiance.

## 15

# Eve

The Freevers are still as impassioned when I leave the room a short while later. They all agree with my reasoning for going back into the Tower or, at least, understand it, but we haven't yet discussed how we go about executing my plan and theirs. It'll need careful consideration, yet there's no time to waste. Who knows what they might be doing in there to the people they've deemed traitors – my father, Mother Kadi, Hartman?

We agree to reconvene tomorrow, once we've had time to think through anything and everything we know about the Tower. They've done this so many times before when plotting to get me out, but now I join Bram and Saunders with insider knowledge on how the place runs – although some of that might be out of date already. I don't suppose the Mothers are still going about their days in the same way, for example – not without me there to tend.

In many ways I know less than anyone about what goes on up there. The world I thought had been beneath my feet while I was out on the Drop was nothing more than thousands of screens wired up to trick me. But it's possible I'll be able to see something the others have missed so far. That's what I'm hoping, and I'm feeling more charged than ever.

'That went better than I thought it would,' Bram says quietly, as we're walking through the corridors and getting out of earshot.

Once the meeting was over, he offered to show me back to my room, which I was glad of as I don't know my way around. It did make me wonder if I'll ever stop being chaperoned.

'It might only be the beginning.' I shrug. 'But it felt like a promising start.'

'The beginning is the bit that matters most.' Bram nods, and I notice his cheeks are pink. 'Take us.'

Us . . . The word causes a flutter in my chest.

'We've had years to get to this point. The foundations are so strong we can, you know . . .' He breaks eye contact and looks down at his boots as they stomp across the damp floor.

'I'm not sure I follow,' I say, something making me want to laugh.

'I'm just saying, sometimes taking things at a slower

pace can give better results than rushing in without thinking things through.'

'Oh, yes. I know that.' I nod, feeling myself blush.

We arrive at my door and I'm disappointed that we've reached it so quickly. I take the key Bram gave me earlier and insert it into the lock, but it jams as I'm turning it. Earlier he said there was a knack – a tilt of the key when at ninety degrees – but I can't seem to make it work. I wiggle it, to no avail.

'Here . . .' Bram says, slipping his hand under mine. My breath catches in my throat. I feel giddy.

He unlocks the door swiftly, yet we both linger, our hands still cupping the handle and key.

I gently prise his away so that they're resting in mine. I want to take in every detail – every wrinkle, scar and freckle. I glance up to see him smiling at our hands.

He doesn't make to leave, and I don't break away, so we stand there, soaking up the moment. I realize that he's seeing me, *really* seeing me, with his own eyes rather than hers. It hasn't occurred to me before and I'm left wondering if I look different to him up close. Whether I meet his expectations. The awe on his face makes me think I do. Watching him take me in makes me feel like I'm discovering parts of myself I've overlooked before. The sparkle of his eyes is intoxicating.

I don't want him to go. I want him to stay with me again, to take in more of me and for me to take in all of him.

I peer through the open door beside me, into my new bedroom, and back up to Bram's face. Our eyes lock and heat burns its way through my body.

'There you are!' booms Chubs's voice as he makes his way up the corridor, stampeding through the atmosphere that's been building between us. 'I was wondering if you fancied a nightcap, Bram. Morris has made some "vodka". Tastes like shit, no doubt – but it can't be worse than the floodweed.'

By the time he's at my door we've dropped our hands.

'Erm,' starts Bram, looking at his friend as though he hasn't understood a word of what he's said.

'Oh, and that was brilliant, Eve,' says Chubs, his face creasing with laughter. 'The way you took down Hobbs was mind-blowing. Seriously!' He pretends to flip some- one over his own shoulder and adds a karate chop. 'You must be buzzing.'

'Yes.' I laugh politely.

Chubs's eyebrows knit as he glances between Bram and me. We're hardly hiding the fact that he's interrupted something. Bram's become mute, I'm monosyllabic, and our bodies are stiff and awkward. 'You coming?' he asks Bram, unperturbed.

I see Bram's reluctance as he nods and turns to leave.

'Night, Eve,' he croaks, giving a little cough, unable to look up at me.

'We'll see you first thing!' Chubs says, with a wink,

as he slaps his mate on the back, then grabs him in a headlock as they wander off.

'Yeah . . . Night,' I say.

I walk into my room and shut the door behind me. I'm alone and the silence is deafening. I'm alone and feel lost. I'm alone and all I want is for Bram to be with me.

Things have escalated in my mind. The friendship has always been there, but since I arrived here the energy between us has been sizzling away. Now it feels tangible, and I want to hold on to that sensation and see what we can do with it. I can't be alone in these thoughts.

I spot a pile of fresh clothes resting on top of a cabinet to my left, alongside a small bowl of greenish water and a cloth. My body feels heavy with disappointment as I skulk over to it, take off my dirty clothes and begin to wash. The cool water is refreshing, and the new clothes aren't as damp as the ones I was wearing, but I feel more restless and frustrated than ever when I'm done.

I've spent for ever sitting at the top of a Tower waiting for someone else to decide my fate, and now it's my turn to take control. I'm not going to sit here in this room waiting yet again. I'm not going to let my chance of real life dwindle now that I have it. I have to act. Where's the sense in holding back and leaving words unsaid or urges suppressed?

I must remember who I am and be bold. I

commanded that room tonight, took it over and made people listen.

I can do this.

Feeling empowered, I march towards the door with determination. I swing it open and I'm face to face with Bram. His hand is in the air, about to knock.

My eyes widen, as do his. For a second or two I forget to breathe. There's so much I want to say, but it strikes me that the very fact he's come back speaks volumes. Besides, we've done enough talking already.

I reach forward and grasp his jacket, pulling him across the threshold and shutting the door behind him.

We fall into each other, our lips meeting, our bodies colliding. It's clumsy and new, but what else can I expect when I've never done this before, only rehearsed it in my mind? I nip his tongue, and he jolts in surprise, but he smiles and continues, slowing the pace.

I can't get enough. I want him. My whole body wants him. My hands run across his shoulders and down his back, skimming over his bum and along his thighs. I pause, lost in his kisses as his mouth finds its way to my ear and down my neck, every hair on my body standing on end, my brain seeming to swell in my head as he takes over every little cell and tiny atom of my being.

He has me.

My hands shake. The yearning inside me is so powerful, so electric and overwhelming. My body is overcome with passion for him, but I'm scared too.

This moment, this act, has been discussed so much. It was going to be an event for millions to rejoice over, and now it's just for us. The intimacy somehow makes it feel bigger, even more important.

'You okay?' he asks, moving his mouth from my neck and wrapping his arms around me while his eyes look into mine.

I hesitate.

'Eve,' he says, kissing the tip of my nose. 'There is absolutely no rush. We don't have to do this now. We have the foundations, remember?' His lips curl into a smile as his eyes soften – I feel my own follow suit.

'Bram?'

'Yes?'

'We're doing this!' I whisper, as I place my mouth on his while simultaneously pulling him to the bed.

'You're sure?' he says, his voice wobbling.

I reach for his belt and slowly pull the leather through the metal loop. My breath catches in my throat as it unbuckles and I start undoing buttons.

# 16

# Bram

My eyes open slowly. It's dark. It's always dark down here.

I blink a few times to wake myself fully but the sensation of rousing from a restful sleep feels totally alien. I haven't slept that well in . . . Who am I kidding? I've never slept like that!

The chiming of a clock winds its way through the hallways of the Deep and finds my ears, these ancient timekeepers still loyally carrying out their duty after all these years.

It chimes only once. One in the morning? Jesus, it feels like I've slept all night.

I close my eyes again and try to roll over but something stops me. Something is holding me in place. My mouth opens to call out when suddenly a soft voice groans sleepily next to me.

*Eve.*

I know her voice instantly. My heart settles as I feel her arm around my waist, pulling down with the weight of her dreams. I reach out and power up the small electric lamp on the table. It flickers into feeble existence and I look around the room. In its dim glow I see the ornate gold-leaf on the walls, the carved wooden panels and it comes back to me. I'm in the Robing Room . . . Eve's room.

Suddenly I remember.

My heart picks up again as I replay the events prior to my deep sleep and I can't stop the smile that spreads across my face. I lie awake, reliving the way we were together. Clumsy, nervous, happy, euphoric.

The event the world had been waiting for was definitely not how anyone had expected it. Least of all me!

Shit . . . My hands are shaking. Adrenalin is coursing around my body and I feel beyond awake suddenly as the memories flash around my head. Skin. Lips. Legs. Sweat. I want to save them all, keep them clear and fresh so they never fade away, but they are already diluted versions of the real event. I guess nothing could ever compare to that.

Ever.

I breathe in slowly and count to ten.

*Chill the hell out, Bram.*

Finally I settle. My hands are calm and I sigh, feeling the excited tension ease. Eve rolls over in her sleep, turning her naked body away from me. I catch the corners of her lips in the lamplight and see that she's dreaming. Content. Happy. As am I.

She used to sleep like that. A long time ago. Before all the talk of Potentials and repopulation. Lying next to her in the silence of night I'm reminded of her room in the Dome on the nights when I would stay with her, as Holly, for sleepovers. Sitting up until the 'sunrise', which was whenever the EPO decided it was. Sharing secrets, making new ones. For Vivian and my father, these were the most insightful sessions, giving them glimpses into Eve's mind that they would eventually use to manipulate her. For us it was forming an unbreakable bond, deeper than she had with the Mothers, more real than she had with the other Hollys.

Eve sighs and her hair catches on her breath. My mind recalls the night we first touched.

'Can we hold hands?' she asked, so seemingly innocent although we both felt the rush of rebellion as our hearts fluttered at this new sensation. The charge of static that leaped from our fingertips as the energy beams of Holly's projection were disturbed.

After that our sleepovers ended. Eve's sleep patterns changed, though, with nightmares, night terrors, sleepwalking. Her door was locked at night during those phases.

Eve tucks the thin sheet between her legs, hugging it to her bare chest and revealing her naked back.

The sight brings a light flutter of laughter to me. I can't help it.

I look away, trying to compose myself but . . .

The laugh needs to break free.

The more I hold it in the harder it tries to escape.

Shit. Shit. Shit.

I can't laugh!

But I must.

I do!

It hisses out as a suppressed snort or perhaps a muffled sneeze and my body convulses as I try to keep it back.

'What was that?' Eve croaks, half turning her head to look at me.

'Nothing,' I whisper.

She turns fully and sees my watering eyes. 'Are you crying?'

I blast out a throaty laugh that echoes around the wooden room. 'No! No! Not crying . . . I'm sorry. I just . . . I don't even know why I'm laughing,' I say, covering my face. I'm a mess.

She must think I'm nuts.

Through the gaps in my fingers I see Eve notice that she's showing a little more flesh than she realized and cover herself.

'Is it me?' she asks, becoming self-aware and shy.

*Pull it together, Bram!*

'Absolutely not!' I say. No laugh. Dead straight. 'I just realized where I was. This situation. *Us!* I just understood how absurd life is.'

'Absurd?' she repeats.

'Yeah, you know. Like, what happened last night. It was . . .'

'Absurd . . .'

'You know what I meant.'

'Well, I would have said a few things before *absurd*! Magical, perhaps. Wonderful? Amazing –'

'Special,' I interrupt. 'It was special, Eve.'

'*You*'re absurd,' she gibes, and relaxes a little under the sheet. 'And you're naked too, by the way.'

I glance down and see, yes, I am. 'Is there room over there for two?' I tease, trying to find a way inside the cocoon she's created around herself.

'No!' She smirks, tucking the sheet around her so that I have to fight to cover my modesty as she watches, giggling.

'So now who's laughing?' I say, as I roll over her, pulling her on top of me until we're face to face.

The faint lamp flickers and in the momentary darkness our lips find each other again.

Again?

As we kiss she loosens the sheet between us. It slips away and our warm, bare skin touches again.

Again . . .

This time less clumsy.

More intense.

Our eyes never breaking contact until it's over and we lie still in a world of our own beneath the world.

'Morning,' I say softly, handing her a mug as she wakes.

'Coffee?' she says hopefully.

'Not quite,' I reply.

She sits up and looks into the mug of lukewarm sugared water.

'Hey, at least it's not floodweed,' I say, taking a sip from my own mug.

'Were you watching me again?' She smiles.

'Yeah. You were dribbling in your sleep,' I say.

She throws the pillow at me as I fake disgust.

We laugh but silence quickly follows, falling over the room, and I'm very aware of how loud my swallowing is as I gulp the mildly sweet water. It seems to slosh down my throat, like a waterfall.

I stop drinking and put the mug down.

'You okay?' she asks.

'Me? Yeah! You?'

She nods, but I'm not sure she's telling the truth.

This feels new, not being able to read Eve. Years of experience in dealing with her emotions, studying her body language, learning to translate the nuances of her expressions. All that fails me now, as though she's changed overnight.

Perhaps we both have.

'There are fresh clothes for you. I mean, they're damp, obviously, everything is, but they're clean.' I point towards the small basket where a selection of outfits has been placed for her.

Eve wraps the sheet around herself, steps out of bed and walks towards the basket of clothes. The sheet catches on the bedpost and falls to the floor, leaving her naked in the middle of the room.

I quickly avert my eyes and hear her muttering as she tries to pull the sheet back around her. In the end, she resigns herself to crouching behind the throne.

I can't help but laugh.

'I'm not sure any queen has ever hidden behind her throne before,' I tease. 'Especially not naked!'

I hear her laughing. Genuinely laughing. It's the best sound ever.

'You can come out, I'm not looking,' I reassure her.

'You might as well. It's nothing you've not already seen now,' she says, stepping out into the room with flushed cheeks and the rebellious grin that only ever appeared when we were about to get into trouble on the Drop.

She goes towards the clothes but her hand lingers on the basket.

'What is it?' I ask.

'I guess a lot of people have seen me like this,' Eve says. She's staring at her naked body in one of the antique mirrors on the far wall.

'You were monitored your whole life, yes, but there was very strict protocol for your privacy,' I explain.

'Had you ever seen –'

'Seen you like this before? *Never.* Only the Mothers did, Eve, when they washed and clothed you,' I say, and it's true.

She puts her new clothes on. A grey jumpsuit and

a worn wool sweater. I see that she's thinking, but I can only guess at what.

'Should we talk about last night?' I ask. I don't know why I asked that. I'm hoping she doesn't want to talk! Talking about it means *thinking* about it, and if she thinks about it, she might decide she's made a colossal mistake.

'Do *you* want to talk about it?' she replies.

'Sure,' I say. Again, I don't know why the hell I said that.

There is silence.

I feel the unbearable urge to fill it. 'Look, if you're thinking last night was a big mistake and you want to forget about it then that's totally fine. I understand. It was a big day for everyone, but even more so for you, and so easy to get carried away in the excitement of the moment. I get it. Say no more. It never happened.' I seal my lips with an imaginary zip.

Eve stares at me and blinks slowly. 'You waffle when you're not hiding behind Holly,' she says.

She's right. Holly gave me the freedom to push boundaries that I, Bram, wouldn't.

'So . . . you don't want to forget it?' I ask.

She smiles. 'No. I want to remember last night for ever,' she says, walking over to me. She takes my mug and places it on the table next to the bed so our hands are free. 'It *was* special. Not for anyone other than us,' she says, taking my hands. 'But I think it's probably best that it stays between us.'

*Us.* She just called us *US*!

'That okay?' she asks.

'Of course!'

'There's a lot to focus on, and I don't want anything to distract us from what we have to do,' she says, squeezing my hands. 'You've done more for me than anyone else has. No one will ever understand what we've been through together. Only us.'

'Only us,' I repeat, as she nestles her head on my chest and we enjoy a moment of silence.

A heavy fist knocks on the door.

'Morning, lovers,' Chubs calls, through the wood.

Eve sighs. '"Only us" didn't last long.'

# 17

# Michael

The concrete corridor is quiet. The only sound is the barely audible murmur of four pilots talking among themselves within their dorms: they were dismissed earlier, and ordered to their rooms to await further instruction. Their particular skills are not currently required.

Without Eve, Holly is redundant.

Since her kidnapping – or escape, depending on which way you want to look at it – suspicion has hung thick in the air throughout the EPO Tower. A breach is near impossible, let alone actually getting her out. Were more people within the organization in on it? With Hartman and Bram confirmed traitors, both of them pilots from Squad H, it seems logical that Miss Silva and Dr Wells turn their attention to the four remaining pilots: Locke, Jackson, Kramer and Watts.

I won't lie, the thought of placing any of those men under arrest doesn't fill me with excitement. They are highly trained and know this place inside out. Since we lost Eve, tension has been high, trust in our security measures is low, and the last thing we want is a battle between two teams on the same side.

Could things get nasty?

It appears Dr Wells thinks it's a possibility, judging by our orders: *Arrest and detain all pilots for questioning. Use force if necessary. Non-lethal. No fatalities.*

Great.

As we approach their living quarters I unroll a thin square of transparent film and slap it against the wall.

*Three, two, one . . .*

The wall behind the square becomes transparent and we peer through into the room beyond, unnoticed by those on the other side.

'Jackson and Locke.' I speak into my visor.

'We have visual on Kramer and Watts,' Hernandez replies through my earpiece. A few hand signals are exchanged and we divide our squad, three on each door.

After a nod, confirming everyone is in position, I raise my arm in the air and clearly close my fist, the signal to 'go dark'. The Final Guard, under my command, simultaneously switch visors to night vision as the dorm and hallway lighting die.

My face is illuminated by the green glow from my visor, showing me the pitch-black world around me.

'What the hell?' comes a voice from inside. *Jackson.*

143

'Power cut?' asks his partner, Locke.

Outside the next doorway, the Murphy twins are in position with Hernandez. Franklin and Reynolds are with me.

'Check the hallway!' Jackson barks.

*This is it.* My heart is pounding and I can't help but wish Ketch was here overseeing this.

The door slides open and a head pokes out into the pitch-black hallway, inches away.

I see Locke as clear as day, his body heat radiating in night-vision. He can't see a thing, judging by his dilated pupils and wide eyes searching the darkness.

I don't hesitate and take full advantage of his blindness.

I simply place my fingertip on his temple. The charge of energy from my Pacify Glove on such a vulnerable spot renders him unconscious instantly and Franklin stops his limp body hitting the floor as he slumps.

'Well?' Jackson calls from inside. 'Where's the emergency lighting? I can't see a bloody thing!'

I slip inside. Silent and fast.

The last thing I want is for him to –

'Aaah, shit!' I scream in pain as blinding light explodes through my visor.

'Who the hell are you?' he growls.

I rip off my visor and see Jackson towering over me, a torch in his hand illuminating my face.

'You're under arrest. Remain where you are,' I say, but it sounds feeble. Pathetic.

'You're arresting us? Whose orders?'

'Miss Silva. On your knees, Jackson.'

'Where's Locke?' he asks.

I turn my head to the door.

WHAM!

His torch connects with my head. I spread my fingers wide, charging the Pacify Glove for a full stun. I raise my arm but he knocks it away and drives his other fist into my jaw with a crack.

'Back. Up,' I splutter, but Hernandez has already leaped into the dorm. He's equal in brute strength to Jackson and flattens him to the ground with a swift tackle.

I crouch down and place my finger on his spine, the charge making his body go rigid then limp, and he lies unconscious on the floor.

'Thanks!' I breathe. 'What about the other two?'

'They came quietly,' Murphy E. says from the doorway and I see the two silhouetted men facing the wall outside.

'Looks like you chose the wrong dorm,' Murphy F. laughs, and I nod in agreement while rubbing my throbbing chin.

'Let's get them down to Detention Level before this one wakes up,' I say, stepping over Jackson's body.

We step into the cool air of the Detention Level. None of the sleek design aesthetics from upstairs grace these walls. Just cold steel and rendered concrete. People who come in here rarely come back out.

The thought sends a shudder down my spine as I think of how close I was to being escorted here.

*Thanks, Ketch.* Our mother made him promise to take care of me when we signed up for the EPO and, boy, did he come good.

'Separate cells?' Hernandez asks, as we approach the glass prisons.

'No. Miss Silva wants them all together,' I reply.

Jackson groans as we drag his heavy arse across the concrete. 'Innocent,' he mumbles, as he slowly regains consciousness.

'Well, if you're all innocent, you'll be out and back up top in no time,' I say, as we come to a stop.

The wall beside us is made entirely of glass, revealing an empty cell. I remove the Pacify Glove and place my hand on the small frosted section. It instantly reacts to my presence, outlining my palm with harsh red light.

It blinks green.

*Clearance granted.*

The cell beyond the glass glows too, readying itself for prisoners.

A rectangle seam appears in the glass, revealing the only entrance as the now visible door opens.

'Inside,' Guard Murphy E. orders.

The pilots don't argue. There's no point. Even if they overpowered us there's nowhere to run to in here.

They trudge inside, the glass reseals itself and the frosted panel registers four prisoners.

'What happens now?' Locke asks through the glass.

'You are to be questioned,' Miss Silva says coolly.

We all spin around to see her walk towards us, sandwiched between the two security officers, their faces obscured by their frosted visors.

We salute.

'At ease. Good work, Final Guard.' She nods.

The team of pilots erupt into a chaotic protest of questions and accusations. Words crack and distort over the intercom.

'Mute cell,' Miss Silva calmly commands and the silent hallway returns in an instant. The prisoners within continue their animated defence but we hear nothing.

'Turner, fetch Hartman from his cell,' Miss Silva instructs, not even looking me in the eye.

'The traitor, Miss Silva?' I ask.

'You heard your order,' barks her guard.

Jesus!

I nod and signal for Reynolds to assist me and he follows me away from the cell.

Reynolds and I don't need to look at each other to know we're both thinking the same: shit is about to hit the fan.

Miss Silva doesn't show up on the Detention Level without reason, without an agenda. I mean, she just had her entire squad of pilots thrown into a high-security prison. Something's going on.

We march past the dark, empty cells towards the brighter end of the level, illuminated by harsh white light pouring out of the sealed rooms.

The first occupied cell approaches and we glance at the old man within.

The glass wall registers our presence and automatically displays his details.

*NAME: ERNIE WARREN*

*CRIME: TREASON. ATTEMPTED KIDNAPPING. FUGITIVE*

*SENTENCE: PENDING*

He winces in pain as he sits in the single chair in the centre of the cell. My stomach churns as he cradles his injury, the arm he lost on the same day that my brother was injured. A lot happened that day.

We walk on and white fluorescent light pours out again.

*NAME: MOTHER KADI*

*CRIME: TREASON. CONSPIRATOR. ASSISTED*

*KIDNAPPING*

*SENTENCE: PENDING*

The woman within doesn't deserve this. She devoted her life to Eve and this is how we repay her. My heart aches for her as she sits on the edge of her hard mattress, staring at the wall opposite. There's something calming about her. There's a wisdom behind her watery eyes, experience in her wrinkled face. She's a woman who is unafraid.

The next cell.

NAME: HARTMAN
CRIME: TREASON. CONSPIRATOR. ASSISTED
KIDNAPPING
SENTENCE: PENDING

'This is our man,' I say to Reynolds.

We look inside and see his chest rise and fall as he lies on his bed while I log into the cell by placing my hand on the glass. The door reveals itself and Reynolds and I step inside.

'Christ, it's hot!' Reynolds whispers, as the thick, stuffy air hits the back of his throat.

'Who are you?' Hartman groans, waking up suddenly.

'We are officers of the Final Guard. Your presence is required,' I inform him.

'Required? By whom?' Hartman asks, pushing his scruffy hair off his face. Reynolds and I hold out a set of handcuffs. He looks at them for a moment, then reluctantly slips his wrists inside and they click shut.

We hoist him up by his arms and carry him out of his cell. As we pass, Mother Kadi notices us and stands, her face emanating a kind, warm sense of safety.

Ernie Warren pays us no attention, focusing on massaging his wound, but I feel Hartman's gaze intensify as he stares at the man who disappeared.

'He's still alive!' Hartman whispers.

'He'll be okay,' I say under my breath.

Hartman snaps his head round to look at me, eyeing me suspiciously.

'For Eve?' he mouths, so only I see.

My heart races. I've never muttered those words, but after what Ketch said about loyalty, I'm starting to think differently of them. It's more than the motto of a rebellion. It's a promise to our future.

'There is fine.' Miss Silva's voice snaps me back to the moment.

We drop Hartman on the floor outside the cell holding his fellow pilots from Squad H.

'Locke! Jackson! What the hell are you doing in here?' Hartman says, with a note of panic in his voice.

The squad speak and point to their ears. They can't hear us and we can't hear them.

'What the hell are they doing in there? They're innocent. They had nothing to do with any of this,' he says firmly. Honestly.

'I believe you.' Miss Silva smiles. It's strained, as though her face hasn't used those muscles in some time.

'Then why have you arrested them?'

'Because not only were you a vital role in the kidnapping of Eve, Dr Wells informs me that you are also the person Bram trusted more than anyone else. I want information on these "Freevers" and if there's one person who can give it to me it will be you. And your team . . . Well, let's say their presence is going to help you do that,' Miss Silva says calmly.

Hartman stays silent.

I glance around at the Final Guard, who remain standing to attention beside the far wall. Their faces are blank, unreadable, but their minds must be working overtime, as is mine, splitting her words apart to read between the lines.

It's not good.

'Miss Silva, I can't tell you what I don't know,' Hartman says, his voice already trembling.

Miss Silva nods and her two armoured goons step forward. They remove the cuffs we placed on Hartman and replace them with a thick black cuff on each of his wrists and ankles, the same thick cuffs they used on Guard Ryan. They click into place and the guard pulls the small black sphere from his belt and swipes his thumb over it.

There's a light buzz as the cuffs send a current through Hartman's body, electrifying his muscles to gain control of them. With another swipe he's practically lifted off his feet by these restraints, hoisted up in front of the cell.

'I . . . can't . . . give you any information!' Hartman spits, through the obvious pain he's experiencing.

'That's disappointing but I think perhaps your ex-teammates might be able to help me change your mind,' Miss Silva says, hardly even looking at Hartman, as though she's monotonously reciting a script she's performed a hundred times.

The second guard unclips another device from his belt. He attaches it to the back of Hartman's head: his neck is suddenly rigid and his eyelids are pulled wide by an invisible force.

He screams in pain.

I step forward.

Shit. Why did I do that?

Her guards turn to me, alert.

'Stand down. Guard Turner was just eager for his next task. Isn't that right, Turner?' Miss Silva says. I know she's manipulating me but it's getting me off the hook so it's best not to argue.

'Of course, Miss Silva,' I say.

'Good. Then would you please authorize the cell to cease the oxygen supply to the prisoners.'

My chest vibrates and an orange glow appears at my feet, drawing a line to the glass wall of the cell.

My order.

So this is how information is extracted.

# 18

# Michael

Shit.

I feel the eyes of everyone on me.

I want to scream, *I HAVE NO CHOICE!* as I take the first steps along my illuminated path, but I must keep my face calm while my heart races.

Is she really asking me to torture her men? Her loyal employees who have helped her get so close to Eve for so many years?

'Whenever you're ready, Turner,' she adds, putting her hands behind her back.

'No! Please. They're innocent!' Hartman protests, as his eyes water from being held open so that he's forced to watch his friends suffer.

I wish time would pause for a moment and let me catch a thought, just figure things out, but it doesn't. If anything, time seems to be moving faster with everyone staring at me: Miss Silva is watching for me to do her bidding and prove my loyalty to the EPO; my fellow guards are watching for their leader to follow an order we all know is wrong.

I place my hand on the glass and the system unlocks, ready for my instruction.

I take a breath.

'Is there a problem?' the armoured guard snaps.

'There's no problem, is there, Turner?' Miss Silva says simply. 'He's going to reduce the oxygen supply now, aren't you?' She smiles. 'Whenever you're ready.'

I nod.

I turn and face the men within the cell. Though they cannot hear, their faces show that they know the situation isn't good.

I try to say *Sorry* with my eyes.

I try to express *I have no choice* with my thoughts.

I try but it's all pointless.

One way or another, I have to do what Miss Silva wants. I select the cell controls on the transparent display. The prisoners on the opposite side of the glass watch my commands in reverse, trying to make sense of the situation.

I swipe through the options for the internal configuration of the cell – temperature, lighting, humidity, audio, sensory: these prisons were built for every possible scenario and need. The next swipe reveals the oxygen-supply options and my heart stops.

I stab at the glass with my finger, making clear

what I'm about to do for the cell's occupants. Even seeing this in reverse on the opposite side of the display, there's no doubt of what's about to happen.

Locke realizes first. His eyes widen and flick up to meet mine. His lips move as he passes on the news to the others. Jackson steps up to the glass wall, making his body large and powerful.

He pounds his fists against the glass, but it doesn't even make a sound in the corridor.

His eyes are fixed on Miss Silva as he clenches his jaw.

Miss Silva sighs impatiently. 'Proceed, Turner,' she says, unfazed by the pilots' awareness of their fate.

I raise my shaking finger and drag the sliding bar down, reducing the oxygen supply to the cell.

'All the way, if you would,' she adds.

I hold my finger down and slide to the bottom. The display flashes red.

*WARNING. CELL OCCUPIED. OXYGEN SUPPLY NOT SUFFICIENT.*

I swipe away the warning.

'Now then, Hartman. When did you and Bram first plot to kidnap Eve?' Miss Silva begins her interrogation. She speaks slowly and purposefully.

'There was never a plan to kidnap Eve,' Hartman whines, his wide eyes darting around the faces of his friends. 'I – I was just trying to do the right thing for her. Bram told me nothing more than I needed to know!'

Miss Silva takes her time absorbing the answers while the panicked Squad H watch through the glass. Jackson paces the room, like a caged animal, while Locke speaks to him, trying to calm him to reserve oxygen.

'Your friends are scared. It's a funny thing, fear. It rapidly increases the heart rate, meaning the body requires more oxygen to feed the brain and the organs to stay alive. Ironic when the very thing causing the fear is the lack of oxygen,' Miss Silva says at a painfully slow pace.

'Please! Miss Silva, they're good men,' Hartman cries.

'Indeed they are, Hartman, which is why you should end their suffering now. Where have the Freevers taken Eve?'

Hartman shudders. 'I – I don't know!' He coughs.

Miss Silva sighs, exhaling slowly and allowing more time to pass.

'Did you know it's not me denying them oxygen that will kill them? It's the carbon dioxide they are breathing out that will eventually lead to their demise. They are, in that sense, killing themselves and each other. An average resting person in that cell could last perhaps forty-five minutes before irreversible brain damage occurs, eventually death. Four men of their body mass, under stressful conditions? I'd say they were already cutting it fine.'

Hartman twitches, trying to fight the restraints, but it's hopeless. The guard runs his thumb across the sphere and the cuffs pull him tighter.

'Hartman. These men, the pilots, are of very little use to me now. Eve's view of the world has been changed and when we get her back here, when she returns home, there will be no need for Holly,' Miss Silva explains. 'No one is going to question the disappearance of four irrelevant, potentially traitorous men, particularly when Eve is still at large. Their only hope, Hartman, is for you to tell me what you know.' Her angular features cast razor-sharp shadows on her pale skin in the harsh light.

Hartman says nothing. Doesn't he care about his men? *Tell her anything!* I think – but then I realize that Hartman is one of them, a Freever through and through. Not because he wanted to betray the EPO, or because he wants to see these men suffer, but because he believes in Eve. In the life she deserves and what that represents.

He's making it very clear where his loyalty lies while I stand here selfishly keeping my mouth shut.

I shake away these traitorous thoughts before Miss Silva reads them on my face.

*The EPO is where Eve is safest, where she needs to be*, I tell myself.

'If you think I'm bluffing, Hartman, you are sadly mistaken,' Miss Silva says calmly.

Suddenly one of the men inside sits on the floor, his back hunched.

It's beginning.

'Watts!' Hartman calls. 'No!'

The pilot raises a hand, shooing away his friends, reluctant to admit the first effects of asphyxia have set in.

'The first to fall. The faster one dies the longer the others will live. Every cloud,' Miss Silva says, with unnerving calm.

Tears are pouring from Hartman's unblinking, bloodshot eyes. I yearn to help him but I can't. I'd be killed just for the thoughts running through my head, let alone if I acted on them.

Hartman whimpers, and I can see he's torn in two. Stay silent and watch his friends die. Speak and kill the future.

The second man slumps to the floor, turning his back on the audience through the glass.

'Jackson. Yes, it takes a lot of oxygen to feed those muscles,' Miss Silva comments, as the block of a man struggles to remain on his knees.

How can she do this? How can she watch the men who have obeyed her orders for years suffocate in front of her? It's unbearable.

'I think it might be time for some audio, don't you, Turner?' Miss Silva suggests.

It's not a suggestion at all: it's an order I have no choice but to follow. I secretly take a deep breath, readying myself for the sound we're about to hear.

I place my hand on the screen again and unmute the cell.

Heavy breathing hisses around the corridor, followed by a cough and a splutter from Watts, who is now spread out across the cell floor.

'I can't tell you! I – I won't do it!' Hartman cries, as his friends struggle before him.

My heart sinks as I grasp what his words mean, what he has unintentionally confessed.

He *won't*. So, he does know.

I see Miss Silva's face flash with anger as she registers this.

Instead of exploding, though, she sighs. 'How unfortunate for your friends. Guards, you are dismissed.'

*What?*

We glance hesitantly at each other.

Dismissed? She wants us to leave? Now?

'You heard me, dismissed! Back to your dorms.' Miss Silva claps her hands as she leads the way to the lift, flanked by her personal guards.

We fall in line behind them and march away from the cells, leaving Hartman suspended in his cuffs in front of the cell, watching his friends slowly lose consciousness.

We fall into the lift under the watchful eye of Miss Silva's security to the soundtrack of Hartman's cries. The door swishes shut and we ascend rapidly with no more information than we had before, just four fewer souls.

I dare to look at Miss Silva, trying to gauge what's going on behind those piercing eyes. She is deep in thought, her lips silently mouthing words. Her eyes dart from left to right rapidly, as though she's looking through the window of a moving vehicle, before locking with mine.

'Is there something you wish to say, Turner?' she asks.

'No, Miss Silva. I'm just sorry it wasn't the result you were hoping for.'

A lie.

Miss Silva's lips slice into a smile. 'This was the expected outcome,' she explains flatly.

The lift reaches our dorm level and the door opens. The Final Guard are hesitant to move.

'Expected, Miss Silva?' I ask.

'Yes. This was the first stage, merely preparation for the next session. That is when he will talk. You are dismissed.'

I exit the lift in shock. She sent those men to their deaths. Jackson, Locke, Watts and Kramer were never coming out of that cell alive.

My mind flashes back to the arrest. The Final Guard sent to do Miss Silva's dirty work.

My brother's voice rings in my head . . .

*It's not Vivian you should be concerned about. It's Wells.*

I wonder how much Wells knows about this. Did

he agree to it? Surely not. The pilots were his team. Then where was he? Why didn't he try to stop it? Was he not present because he couldn't bear to see his innocent men murdered?

We walk back to the dorms in silence, all of us with the same thing on our minds: the next session.

# 19

# Eve

We've split into smaller groups to scratch our heads and come up with a solid plan. Every room, corner and hallway of the Deep is littered with people whispering and devising.

In a small, dimly lit meeting room, a floor plan of the Tower has been mapped out on the wooden table in front of Bram, Helena, Saunders, Chubs and myself. Helena has labelled its many floors and detailed what they're known to be used for – the upper garden zone and my sleeping quarters in the Dome are right at the top. Then, scattered around the page, there's my classrooms, studios, examining rooms and the laboratories – the thought of what goes on in there sends shivers down my spine. A few floors down is the room in which I met Connor and Diego, the two Potentials – encounters that went horrifically wrong.

It's strange seeing how few of the floors I've visited and how contained they kept me. I look further down the page to the places that weren't for me: the pilots' quarters, security, dining halls, training rooms and Cold Storage – an eerie place that I've learned stores people waiting for the next life. Not living, yet not quite dead. All waiting in limbo to be born again. It's absurd to think of the lengths people have gone to in the hope of living in happier times, yet this is the level that allowed Bram to break back into the Tower, so I'm thankful for it. I always knew that life was bubbling away beneath me, but I was naïve as to the extent of their operation. My life in the Dome was calm and tranquil. Below, it must've been chaotic as they kept Vivian's vision churning along.

As I study the floor plans, though, it's clear there are gaps in the Freevers' knowledge. Huge areas of the paper, the majority of the floors, in fact, have been left blank. When asked about them, Helena grunts, the sides of her mouth pulling downwards. 'We've yet to find a single informant left inside the Tower who knows,' she says, her head shaking. 'No one can get to them. It's as though they don't even exist. Lying low so they don't get caught, no doubt. Doesn't help us now but, hopefully, their silence will pay off in the long run.'

Could they be empty voids? Spaces waiting to evolve into whatever false freedom they would've been giving me next, had I still been there? I think back to my garden – the little piece of outside they used to take me to whenever I needed to be immersed in the wonder of nature – and then I remember how crushed I felt when I drove straight into their set, crushing their false reality and exposing their lies. It's highly likely more of those floors had been designed in that manner, or were going to be. Gigantic spaces dressed and used to give me the illusion of going outside, while keeping me caged and controlled. They would never have allowed me the opportunity to breathe real air or touch soil they hadn't planted. Where else were they planning on taking me and my clipped wings?

'We've also failed to find out where they're keeping your father and the others.' Helena sighs. 'We've been in situations like this before, where communication has been cut due to a breach in their security, but this is the longest period of radio silence from our team inside. It stands to reason that Vivian would put the place into lockdown mode, but it makes her moves difficult to predict.'

'Are we sure there's no way back in through the Dome?' I ask.

'Going in at the top, especially too soon, would be dangerous when we don't know where we're headed.'

'But she won't be expecting it, and it's a space I know.'

'You know what they wanted you to know,' Helena says, her voice soft.

'I know more than they thought!' I argue, remembering the times I tiptoed my way around up there, spying and listening. 'And the Dome –'

'We've said it's not possible,' a voice snaps. I'm surprised when I look up and see that Saunders is clearly exasperated. He seems exhausted. We all do.

'I know, but –'

'What?' he cuts in, his palms open to the ceiling. 'You think our stance is going to have miraculously changed and that your way will have opened up as an option?'

'No, it's just –'

'We can't get enough of us up there to make it safe. And, as Helena has repeated, it's unpredictable.'

I open my mouth to speak but no words find their way out of my mouth. I take in his fiery eyes and remember a time when they were kinder – when he was one of my Hollys. It was only in the last few years when each Holly had been given a role and time to be with me. 'I-concur' Holly was with me in academic classes, a buddy to learn with. 'Know-it-all' Holly was, more often than not, alongside me in physical activities, which gave me a buzz when I was better than her. Then Bram's Holly, *my* Holly, was there to take our friendship to the max. She unravelled my thoughts in a way no one else could. Even though I knew it was for them, I didn't mind. I liked letting her in.

When Saunders was part of the team, I never knew which Holly I'd be faced with at any time of day. It was more haphazard – maybe there were glitches in the control room back then or teething issues: it wasn't as smooth as it went on to become. I recall referring to Saunders's Holly as 'Emotional Holly', and I would know when she was with me not only because of the subtle roundness of her eye shape, but because of her nature. She cared more than the others and wore her heart on her sleeve. Now I wonder if that was why they stopped her visits. After all, the whole point of the Hollys was to give me company, extract information, then put their ideas into my head so that I was tricked into thinking I had free thoughts. Me having to attend to a Holly's needs got in the way of that.

The last time I saw that Holly, she had tears streaming down her cheeks because Vivian was reprimanding us for some minor misdemeanour. It wasn't a big deal, we'd been told off before – many times, in fact – but it was as though the world was caving in on her.

It's difficult to believe those tears came from the person in front of me. The shift in behaviour towards me stings.

'Saunders,' Bram hisses into his ear, giving him a little nudge in the ribs, 'calm it.'

They lock eyes. Saunders frowns.

'Bram, we're the lucky ones. We got out of that shit-show unscathed,' he says, giving me a tiny glimpse of the emotional girl I met years ago. 'Let's face it, they would rather we died than end up with Freevers, like we did. Others haven't been so lucky.'

'Lucky or not, you're one of us now. And, as Freevers, we support Eve,' says Helena, her voice deep and measured.

'I know that. I've risked my life for her, time and time again. But this would literally be a suicide mission for me and Bram,' he says, his voice cracking. 'We are wanted men. Eve should know that. To make sure she fully understands the impact her decision will be making on the two people she's known longer than anyone else here.'

'I do,' I say, my insides knotting at the thought of anything happening to Bram, or to him. 'As I said the other night, I'm not forcing anyone to join me.' I'm searching for any memory of Saunders at the last meeting. He must've been there, but I don't recall seeing his face or even him being part of the chanting. 'Saunders, you're both free to step away from this.'

'Step away? We are traitors to their cause,' Saunders states. 'You saw the propaganda they're putting out. People here might not believe their tripe, but their slaves in there will because they don't know any different. One step into that building and I'm toast for abandoning my duty. One glimpse of Bram and they'll shoot him dead for kidnapping their saviour.'

'I'm saving my father,' I remind him.

'Very noble of you. Very selfless. But at what cost? Am *I* the price you'll pay to be reunited with your dad? Is Bram? Eve, you've landed yourself in the best possible place and the best possible scenario. Sometimes you've just got to be thankful for what you have, rather than pig-headedly going for more.'

I clench my jaw to stop biting back and saying

something stupid, realizing that his outburst isn't like winning over the crowd, and that he's far more Emotional Holly than I've given him credit for.

'I'm sorry.' He sighs, shaking his head. 'I'm just feeling the pressure. You riled up an army out there, and while we sit in here desperately trying to hatch a plan, they're getting increasingly agitated. I don't want riots within the ranks.'

'Then don't go picking fights,' I say. 'I'm not asking anything of you.'

'You say that, but how can any of us possibly allow the girl we love to walk into that danger pit alone?'

His face darkens. With a quick intake of breath he turns and exits the room, leaving an uneasy feeling in his wake.

He's right. There's no way past Hollys would stand by and allow me to take on such a challenging mission on my own. I'm not asking them to join me, but I'm leaving them with little choice.

I can't bring myself even to look at Bram while I digest that thought.

## 20

# Michael

My chest vibrates.

I glance under my duvet and the orange glow spills out into the dorm. My tag. An order.

'Time?' I croak.

*THREE FIFTY-TWO A.M.*, replies an automated voice.

Something must be happening.

I yawn.

My chest buzzes again. Shit! I fell back to sleep.

'Okay, okay, I'm up,' I groan to nobody, as I swing my legs out of the covers and place my bare feet on the cold floor.

An orange line appears at my toes and leads out of the door, ready to guide me to my destination. I throw on my jumpsuit, slip into my boots and sleepily start to follow it.

I'm halfway out of the door before I remember my weapon belt and spin around to grab it. Gun. Knife. Pacify Glove.

Just in case.

I tap my chest.

'Collect Dr Chaudhury and escort him to Detention Level,' the voice instructs.

The doctor? Could Eve's dad be ill? I mean, the guy lost his arm. Losing a limb at any age is serious, but when you're that old? I'm surprised he's made it this far.

I guess he did have something pretty important to live for.

I think of her.

Eve.

Again.

Her face.

My betrayal in the lift.

I pick up the pace, shaking away the thoughts and focusing on the possibility of that old man, alone in that cell, in pain. He won't know that Eve made it out. His dramatic appearance at the Tower had to have been part of her escape, without a doubt, and it must break his heart not to know she's safe. Perhaps that's what keeps him fighting on.

As the lift doors glide open, Dr Chaudhury is already standing outside with a large medical case, ready to go.

'Good morning,' I say.

'Is it?' he replies, and joins me inside the spherical vehicle with a sour expression.

It's like that then. I don't say anything else on the descent, despite my eagerness to find out why we're being summoned in the middle of the night. A medical emergency? Or could it perhaps be something that is better done while the Tower occupants sleep?

*Okay, Michael, time to turn the paranoid conspiracy thoughts down a notch.*

We arrive and he takes the lead, assertive and sure, like he already knows where we're going and why we're here.

Why don't I know?

I quicken my pace to walk alongside him as we navigate the soulless Detention Level hallways, trying to wake my brain up and stay alert. I'm head of the Final Guard: if I've been ordered here it means something or someone needs guarding.

I feel the doctor's eyes on me as we walk.

'Everything okay?' I ask.

His eyes flick downwards subtly, but enough for me to catch, and I see I've had my hand subconsciously resting over the gun on my belt.

*Relax!*

Empty cells stare at us as we walk by. Cold rooms awaiting occupants who are yet to commit their crimes. We pass the cell that claimed the lives of the four pilots and I shudder at the memory.

As we approach the occupied cells I notice their glass walls have been set to privacy mode, preventing the prisoners from seeing out and us from seeing in.

Why?

Dr Chaudhury stops outside Hartman's cell, a red strip on the wall indicating that it's occupied.

'Please open the cell,' he asks.

'I'm sorry, Doctor, but I need authorization to allow you to visit the *traitor*,' I say but the label suddenly feels disconnected from Hartman. A traitor to whom?

'You're authorized.' A cutting voice behind us interrupts my wandering mind.

'Miss Silva.' I salute, turning to see her striding towards us with purpose, flanked by the two private soldiers who scan the hallway for potential threats, then nod at her.

*All clear.*

'Miss Silva, what's going on?' I ask.

'Miss Silva wants the information from the traitor immediately,' her soldier explains, as though she's too busy to speak for herself. 'Open the door,' he commands.

Miss Silva raises an eyebrow expectantly.

The breath catches in my throat.

The second session she spoke about, when Hartman would reveal what he knows: it's tonight. Right now.

Shit!

I think about Jackson, Locke, Watts and Kramer, and I hesitate.

'Is there a problem?' Miss Silva asks.

'No, Miss Silva,' I lie, and place my hand on the glass. It defrosts, giving us a clear view of Hartman.

My heart leaps as he comes into focus. He's standing, facing us, his arms rigid at his sides.

'How long has he been in those cuffs?' Dr Chaudhury asks.

'Over twenty-four hours,' I reply.

'For his own safety,' Miss Silva explains. 'The information in his mind is too valuable for us to risk him doing something . . . out of our control.'

I stare at Hartman's body being held in place by the metallic rings on his wrists and ankles. He wakes and looks back at us. At least they removed the device that kept his eyes open.

I instruct the cell to grant us entry and the seamless door in the glass opens. Miss Silva enters, followed by one of her two soldiers. The other takes position outside the cell.

'Join us, Commander Turner.' Miss Silva speaks from inside. It's a clear instruction and one I cannot decline. I step in and the glass reseals itself behind me.

'Mute cell,' Miss Silva commands.

The air is stale and hot. I see beads of sweat on Hartman's face. The doctor rests his case in the centre of the room and the soldier takes position by the frosted glass, mirroring the subtle silhouette of his partner on the other side.

'Good evening, Hartman. We are here to gather the information you have. I hope that now you've had some time to reflect on our last encounter you will be ready to make a more sensible decision.'

Hartman's mouth remains firmly closed. His eyes dart between Miss Silva, the soldier, the doctor and myself. They are scared eyes. Tired. Traumatized. The eyes of a man who has witnessed awful things.

'I think this time you'll find it easier to share your thoughts with us.'

An awful expectant silence hangs in the room.

He's not giving in yet.

*Good.*

I'm momentarily caught off guard by these thoughts, this unexpected support for someone who has betrayed the organization I'm a part of.

*He's betrayed them, not Eve.*

I try to convince myself that I simply don't want to see another man die, but buried beneath that is a glimpse of a truth I'm only starting to uncover . . .

*I'm with you, Hartman.*

Miss Silva nods to Dr Chaudhury and the light catches the sweat on his Adam's apple as he gulps.

The doctor kneels on the floor beside his case and opens it. I peer over his shoulder while Miss Silva slowly tours the perimeter of the cell, keeping her distance from us as though we're infected with some contagious disease and she might catch it simply by being in close proximity to us.

It's difficult to see inside the medical bag but placed on top, in the centre, is something I recognize. It's a visor, like the ones the pilots used to operate Holly in the Dome. I don't know a single person in this building who didn't wish they could put one on and experience life through Holly's eyes. Feel that connection with Eve.

'Obviously you recognize the hardware,' Miss Silva says, as Chaudhury prepares the headgear.

Hartman says nothing.

'But you'll soon notice Dr Wells has made some modifications,' Miss Silva says. 'Consider it an upgrade.'

Dr Chaudhury places the visor over Hartman's head of shaggy brown hair.

'Wells. I want to . . . speak to Wells,' Hartman croaks.

'If you think your former boss will sympathize with your current predicament, I'm afraid you're delusional, Mr Hartman. Dr Wells and I have fully aligned opinions on your future,' Miss Silva says, without even looking at him.

'This is going to be unlike anything you've experienced before,' Dr Chaudhury warns. 'The more you resist the worse it will be. I highly recommend that you reveal the information now to prevent this from happening.'

Hartman returns to his silent state, his lips trembling with resistance. I can't help but like him.

No, admire him.

We never had any conversations. Never even met, other than him standing over me in that lift as I clutched my throbbing face where Bram's fist had connected with it.

Shame. He seems like a good man.

I sigh. He's just a kid, really. We all are. But this is no game we're playing now.

'You may begin, Dr Chaudhury,' Miss Silva orders, and the doctor closes his eyes in disappointment.

'Please, Hartman, the alternative to giving Miss Silva what she wants is not worth it,' Dr Chaudhury practically begs, resisting the order to start the torture.

'Not worth it?' Hartman cracks. 'Not worth it? Do you think I want to be tortured? Do you think I wanted to see my friends killed? Do you think I wanted to risk my life and the lives of every person I've ever loved? No, Doctor. No. I did it because my friends needed me to. Because Eve needed me to. I did it because they believed it was the right thing, and for that reason I do too, and I will die before uttering a single word that might result in bringing Eve back to this place.'

Dr Chaudhury sighs.

'Die? Hartman, we don't want you to die. We want you to live as long as it takes to tell us what we need to know. Only then will we grant you the luxury of dying. Doctor, you may begin,' Miss Silva instructs firmly, taking position against the frosted glass, giving her a clear view of whatever is about to happen.

The state-of-the-art contraption is slipped over Hartman's head and the screen illuminates his face.

'So far not so different from the model you and Bram were running. Here's where it changes,' Miss

Silva says, nodding to Dr Chaudhury, who returns to his case and removes a long, metallic cannula.

'What's that for?' The words escape from my mouth.

'The transfusion,' Dr Chaudhury replies, nervously preparing the equipment.

'He's receiving blood?' I ask.

'Not blood, Mr Turner. Something far more exciting than that. Memories,' Miss Silva replies in her cold, emotionless, matter-of-fact tone.

'Memories?' Hartman utters from behind the visor.

'Yes,' she confirms, refusing to share any more details on this strange memory transfusion.

I'll just have to pay attention then.

'Hold still, please,' Dr Chaudhury says to Hartman.

'Well, I'm hardly fucking going anywhere,' he replies, stuck rigid in his invisible chains as the doctor connects the cannula to the rear of the visor. Two small needles automatically extend from within the visor and position themselves over Hartman's temples.

What the hell is that for?

Chaudhury follows the tube down to his medical case, which he opens fully, revealing the device inside.

'That's a datastore,' Hartman says, peering around the thin gap of his visor.

'Correct, Hartman. It is clear to me why you were the best at your job. Wells always said you had potential. It is a shame it will be wasted,' Miss Silva spits.

'I'm sorry, it's a what?' I interrupt.

'It's a box of information,' Hartman explains. 'Lots of information from the size of it. What's in it?' Hartman asks.

'I already told you, memories,' Miss Silva says, 'and not just any memories. You see, thanks to Dr Wells, we are now able to map the human mind better than we ever have before. It is a complex organic computer storing an unfathomable amount of information. Unlocking that information is –'

'Impossible. You can't store memories,' Hartman interrupts. 'Quit the bullshit scare-tactics and get this over with.'

'Not impossible, Hartman. Incredibly difficult, but not impossible. Let's not forget this organization has been built on the things people said were impossible, yet here we are.' Miss Silva grins. 'Not only is memory extraction possible but through this device you will not only visualize and see a memory, but feel it as though it were your own experience.'

'Memory transfusion,' I whisper.

Miss Silva shoots me a look and I straighten my back to attention.

'Why don't you just extract the memory from his head?' I blurt out. 'You know, just take out the information you want.'

The room is silent. Miss Silva, her soldier, Hartman and the doctor all look at me.

'Good question. For two reasons. First, because the

information he has been given is not his memory, it is Bram's or whoever has *told* him. If Hartman had been there himself, had he seen where they're hiding, it would burrow deep canyons into his synapses, but conversations are rarely significant enough, which leads to the second reason. A specific second-hand memory like that would take a painfully long time to locate,' Miss Silva explains.

I nod. It brings another question to my mind but I keep my mouth shut this time.

Why give Hartman someone else's experience of a memory? How is that going to get him to speak, unless . . .

I pause. The answer is obvious.

It depends what memory Hartman is going to receive.

In my moment of understanding, I glance at Miss Silva and find her cool eyes gazing at me. She raises a thin eyebrow. She knows I've figured it out.

'Death, on the other hand, is an extremely significant moment. It is crystal clear and, as it is the final memory ingrained on a mind, it is the easiest memory to locate. Not many people even contemplated the idea of a death memory. They're obviously not much use to the person who died, but extremely useful to us,' Miss Silva says, her blue eyes glistening as though she's loving every second of this.

'Whose memory am I getting?' Hartman trembles.

'Oh, we have a fantastic selection available tonight.'

Miss Silva nods and the doctor pulls a stack of files from his case and throws them on to the floor, all marked *DECEASED*.

They scatter at Hartman's feet and my heart freezes in my chest as I see the images now strewn across the cell floor.

**JACKSON   WATTS   KRAMER   LOCKE**

## 21

# Michael

Hartman tilts his head, trying to catch a glimpse of the files on the floor, desperate to see whose memory he'll soon be experiencing.

'No . . .' he whimpers, like a dog, at spotting the images of his friends. I can only imagine the horror going through his mind. It was unbearable to witness their deaths the first time, even for me, let alone if they were my colleagues, my friends, dying as the result of my decision.

'No?' Miss Silva repeats. 'You want this to be over? Fine! It can be. Simply tell me what you know.'

Hartman pauses. Is he actually considering it?

*No! You can't tell her now! You've come so far!* I want to scream.

*Shut the hell up, Turner!* My heart thuds as though I'm terrified Miss Silva can hear my thoughts. I glance at her but her piercing gaze is focused on Hartman. I flash a look at the soldier but he's standing to attention, staring into his visor like a robot.

My mind is betraying the EPO at every opportunity. I don't know Hartman. I don't know what they plan to do with Eve. My life is inside these EPO walls, walls that shelter me from the world beyond.

*A world we've turned our backs on.*

'I – I –' Hartman stammers, still craning his head to see the photos of his friends. 'I can't!'

Miss Silva sighs.

'Very well, Hartman. Your way it is,' Miss Silva says, giving Dr Chaudhury space as he follows the long silver wire from Hartman's head to the machine and connects the cannula to the memory-storage device. The moment the connection is made, Hartman lets out a shriek of pain.

'Had enough already? We've not even begun the transfusion yet!' Miss Silva shouts over Hartman, and I see that the two needles have pierced Hartman's temples causing two drops of deep red blood to trace lines down his cheeks, then meet in the middle under his chin. They are quickly joined by a single tear.

'It's ready, Miss Silva,' Dr Chaudhury mumbles.

'Very good. Hartman, you are about to feel something you've never felt before,' she says.

'What's happening?' Hartman sobs.

'A synthetic fluid is being injected inside your skull,'

Dr Chaudhury mutters, clearly hating every second of this.

The machine springs to life and the silver cannula jolts as liquid travels through it.

'Won't that kill him?' I ask.

'I hope not. Once complete, his mind will be physically connected to this "storage device", as you so labelled it, and he will be able to access not only his own complex network of memories but also, if instructed, those we have stored here.'

Hartman's body shakes as it tries to resist the substance filling his skull.

This is insane.

Miss Silva has lost the plot. Has Wells actually agreed to use his technology to torture his own men? Or has she gone rogue?

I've got so many questions going through my head right now.

'Try to relax, let the connections take hold.' Dr Chaudhury is rubbing the light stubble on his chin nervously.

A burst of adrenalin shoots around my veins, reacting with the anxiety in my stomach and igniting a fire there. I feel as though I have been abruptly woken from a dream and seen the nightmare of this reality. My fingers instinctively roll into fists, my nails digging into my sweating palms. I've taken a wrong turn on to the road of loyalty to the EPO: now that I see where it leads I want no part of it.

I want to grab the cable protruding from Hartman's head, rip off the visor and run.

But I don't.

I want to pull the gun from my belt, aim it at Miss Silva and pull the trigger.

But I don't.

I want to run as far away from this place as I can and join the fight out there.

But I won't.

What would be the point? I'd be just another so-called traitor and I've seen what happens to them. I'd be killed before I'd got anywhere near the streets. Whether I like it or not, I'm stuck on the inside.

*On the inside.*

My racing thoughts stop. If my loyalty is with Eve and I truly want to help her, then maybe I'm in the best place for it. Someone on the inside, a Freever who isn't in a cell. Or dead. Yet.

If I want to remain that way, I must play my part.

Hartman's body suddenly relaxes.

'His body has accepted the transfusion,' Dr Chaudhury breathes as Hartman's vital signs are displayed on the device's screen in front of him.

'Good. Let's begin with Jackson,' Miss Silva says to the soldier, who suddenly springs to life, reaches into the outer pocket of his armoured vest and pulls out a small leather pouch.

He hands it to the doctor who unzips it with trembling fingers to reveal four transparent discs secured inside. He slips one out and places the pouch on the datastore before holding the coin-sized disc to the light.

'No . . . please . . . no!' Hartman slurs, the effects of the procedure suddenly obvious.

Dr Chaudhury looks up at Miss Silva, his eyes pleading with her not to do this, but she stares back with a strong and clear message. Do it.

He has no choice and inserts it into a thin slot in the datastore.

The black box instantly comes to life with a mixture of clicks and beeps along with the faint glug of the liquid being pumped into Hartman's head. Blue light flickers from somewhere within the box, then suddenly becomes a solid red.

Hartman lets out a deafening scream.

His piercing voice echoes around the small chamber as though it were trying to escape.

Dr Chaudhury covers his ears, trying to detach himself from the horror of what he is being made to do.

'Hartman!' Hartman calls out his own name, as though speaking to himself. 'Hartman, you backstabbing piece of shit!'

'Jackson's final moments were full of hatred. Hatred towards one person, Hartman. *YOU.*' Miss Silva speaks as she paces around the edge of the cell.

He starts to cough.

'What's he seeing?' I whisper to the doctor as the lights from within the visor strapped to Hartman's head flicker and flash.

He looks me in the eye. 'You don't want to know,' he says quietly.

'No, no, show him, Doctor, show him,' Miss Silva commands, overhearing us, beaming with pride, as though this despicable invention of Dr Wells were some miraculous breakthrough.

Dr Chaudhury closes his eyes and releases a long sigh. He types something into the keypad of the data-store and a few seconds later a thin silver rod extends from inside it and throws a splash of light on to the concrete wall.

'Is that . . . in his head?' I ask, seeing Kramer, Watts and Locke standing around the cell.

'Yes. The device is sending Hartman's neurons down the synapses of Jackson's mind, the clear, trau-matic pathways that were carved into his brain as Hartman decided that the information in his head was more important than the lives of his friends. It seems your friends disagreed with you,' Miss Silva says to Hartman, as his arm twitches in perfect synchrony with the footage being projected of Jackson, grasping at the glass wall of the cell.

My stomach flips as I see my own face there.

I'm looking at myself through the eyes of a dying man as I stand by and do nothing to help him. Even though I know it's wrong, that they're innocent, I do nothing.

*BAM!*

He thuds on the glass. Hartman's fist punches the air.

*BAM!*

A second time.

He's becoming weaker.

Weaker.

His vision fades, colour disappears first as his eyes are starved of oxygen.

He blacks out.

Silence.

Hartman slumps in his restraints.

'Turner, be so kind as to wake him,' Miss Silva says to me.

I follow the wire that runs along the floor, then up into the top of the contraption on his head and give Hartman a gentle nudge.

'Hartman. You alive?' I ask, raising the visor to see his pale, sweaty face.

'I'm afraid you'll need to be a little more forceful than that. His mind has just relived death,' she says, as though this were something normal, something acceptable.

I look at the exhausted, beaten person in front of me and raise his chin.

'Hartman. Wake up,' I say, tapping him on the cheek.

'Harder,' Miss Silva demands.

I grit my teeth and slap him.

'HARDER!' she barks.

I pull back my hand for a fuller swing.

'JACKSON!' Hartman screams, waking from one nightmare into another.

I drop my hand.

'Are you ready to divulge?' Miss Silva asks. 'Or would you rather relive another death?'

'Kill me as many times as you want. I'll never betray Bram like you did,' Hartman spits.

'Locke,' Miss Silva instructs without a moment's hesitation.

Dr Chaudhury's shoulders drop and his eyes close as he opens the little leather wallet of death once again. He slides out the second disc and puts it into the machine before replacing the visor over Hartman's face.

The machine cycles through the same beeps and clicks, flickering blue lights, then a solid red.

'No!' Hartman winces, his body becoming rigid as though receiving an electric shock.

Then nothing.

He hangs in his restraints.

Slowly his mind finds the memory and his breathing becomes heavy.

'I . . . I . . . I can't breathe!' He panics, his chest rising and falling rapidly.

'My lungs. Help! Please, help!' he cries.

'You're killing him!' I shout over his screams.

'Not him. Locke,' Dr Chaudhury says, switching the projection on again, showing me what he sees.

He's back in the room, looking at Jackson on his knees beating at the glass. He glances at the terrified faces of Watts and Kramer, before finding me again through the window.

He slumps to the floor as Hartman tries to clutch at his throat though his restraints hold him back.

It's over.

He died faster than Jackson. Thank God.

Hartman blacks out again, hanging lifelessly in his chains.

'Turner, would you do the honours again?' Miss Silva asks, not that I have any choice in the matter. I'm here so she doesn't have to get her cold hands dirty. Like the doctor and the guards at either side of the door, we do her bidding, no questions asked.

I walk to the motionless heap of a person, suspended in front of me.

'Is he okay?' I whisper to the doctor.

'For now, yes. Physically he'll hold up but his brain cannot cope with much more or his mind will be permanently damaged. Our brains are not designed to take on the consciousness of someone else, let alone four.'

'Enough time-wasting. His is the mind of a traitor and it belongs to the EPO now, along with the information inside it. Wake him,' Miss Silva orders.

Brain damage? Permanent? I try to process the doctor's words.

If Hartman survives, he'll never be the same person.

*If he survives.* It sounds like he'd be better off dead.

Would he be better off dead?

I look at the broken human being in front of me.

'Wake him,' Miss Silva repeats. 'Now.'

Hartman groans.

He would be better off dead.

My heart races as I realize what I must do to help him. It's the only way to end his suffering and I'm the only one who can do it.

I must kill him.

For Eve's sake, and Bram, and all the Freevers out there, but mostly for Hartman himself.

My first duty as her inside man.

But how? I can't be seen. My eyes dart to the soldier, standing at the glass. I have to be discreet, invisible. All I have with me is my gun. Definitely not. Knife? Again, too obvious. And my Pacify Glove . . . That might work, but how? Even if I could get the Glove on my hand without being noticed I'd have to deliver a full charge to his head to kill him.

I feel Miss Silva's eyes on me so I step up to Hartman and lift the visor to reveal his face. His eyes are glazed, rolling to the back of his head. White foam bubbles at the corners of his mouth as he breathes.

I hear the high-pitched clink of the next glass disc as Dr Chaudhury removes it from the pouch. Miss Silva's head turns to oversee.

I have a moment, right now.

I whip my hand down to my belt and start to unclip the conductive Glove, lined with probes ready to give one hell of a charge to whatever they touch.

Enough to kill? In Hartman's condition, I suspect just a fingertip would push him over the edge.

'Is he ready?' Miss Silva snaps, and I let the Glove hang back at my belt. 'What's taking so long?'

I can't activate it without being noticed.

'No . . . more . . .' Hartman mutters.

'Ah, welcome back! You know how to make it end. Until then, we continue. Let's see how Kramer felt when you killed him.' Miss Silva nods to Chaudhury to start the system.

'Please . . . Please, Turner. Make them stop,' Hartman croaks.

'Turner?' Miss Silva hisses. 'You think *he*'d help you? He's lucky I didn't do to him what I did to your squad. Isn't that right, Guard Turner?' she asks.

'Yes . . . Yes, Miss Silva.' I wobble, feeling the Pacify Glove weighing heavy on my belt now.

Hartman manages to focus his vision momentarily and sees me. In the split second that our eyes meet I try desperately to project my plan to him, but I guess the last thing he needs right now is more thoughts from someone else's head.

Hartman contorts, and Miss Silva steps closer to me than she usually would.

'Lower his visor.' Her close proximity makes me shudder. I'm fighting every urge to run far away from this evil at my side.

But I complete her command, lowering the visor over his face once more, then step back, following the silver cannula to where it starts next to Dr Chaudhury.

The projection plasters the wall: Kramer is

remaining calm, conserving his air and trying to distract himself from his dying teammates.

I suddenly see that Miss Silva, her security soldier and Dr Chaudhury are watching, their attention on the images. Now is my only chance.

I plunge my hand into the Glove while it's still attached to my belt and activate the charge.

It emits a subtle high-pitched tone. The sounds coming from the machine drown it out as it pumps more synthetic brain juice into Hartman.

He gasps.

On the wall Kramer scratches his throat.

It's starting to happen.

I position myself next to the storage device, and let the Glove hang over where the silver wire begins its journey into Hartman's head.

'I – I – can't breathe!' Hartman whispers.

Kramer falls to the floor. Hartman jolts.

He thrashes his head from left to right, trying to get the air that will inevitably escape him.

In the flashing light from the projections I see Miss Silva's lips twitch, as though she's keeping a smile at bay.

As Kramer dies for the second time, Hartman's body responds as he is about to lose consciousness again.

I feel the adrenalin of rebellion soar around my body.

Can I do this?

He's an innocent man.

I must. For his sake.

For the future.

For Eve.

As he takes Kramer's final breath I carefully unclip the charged Glove and let it fall.

Silently.

Unnoticed.

It lands on the device and electrifies the cable, sending fifty thousand volts directly into Hartman's brain for less than a second.

As Kramer passes out, the projection cuts to black and Miss Silva fires a look of frustration at the doctor, which I don't hesitate to use to snatch back the Glove.

Hartman hangs lifelessly; only I know that this time he's not unconscious.

*Rest now, Hartman.*

*You're welcome.*

## 22

# Michael

'Turner.' Miss Silva snaps her fingers at the lifeless body hanging from the shackles.

I try to move but my feet seem rooted to the spot. I'm desperate not to be the one who breaks the news that currently only I know.

The news that I am responsible for.

'Well? Bring the traitor round. We have one memory left and if he still doesn't speak, we shall go around again,' Miss Silva snaps.

'Miss Silva . . . I'm not getting any response from the device,' Dr Chaudhury says.

It's starting.

'No response? What exactly does that mean? Can we proceed?' she barks, stepping impatiently towards the black box on the floor.

I see the doctor start to panic: he knows it's more

serious than just a little reboot. The classic switching off and on is not going to solve this.

'Miss Silva, the datastore appears to be dead,' Dr Chaudhury says nervously.

'Anything I can do to help?' I say, taking a glance at the machine I destroyed.

*Be natural, Mikey. Chill.*

'Why have you not brought him around yet?' Miss Silva snaps.

'What the . . .' Dr Chaudhury whispers, as he raises the shiny cannula in his palm. A wisp of smoke puffs from where it connects to the storage device.

The doctor's features drop as his head turns to Hartman. Miss Silva's cutting eyes aren't far behind and the doctor rushes to the motionless prisoner, ripping off the visor and checking his pulse.

'What have you done?' Miss Silva barks at Chaudhury, as he tears open Hartman's shirt, exposing his bare torso.

The doctor shoves a hand into his pocket, pulls out a transparent film and wraps it on Hartman's ribs. It instantly makes his skin appear invisible, revealing his heart, deep within his chest.

'It's not beating,' I note, trying to keep up my act.

'No shit,' Dr Chaudhury replies, as he puts on two kinetic gloves and gestures in the air. A hologram of Hartman's heart appears floating in the middle of the room and Chaudhury enlarges it as he takes a syringe from a red case inside his pocket. He plunges the needle straight into Hartman's chest, using the enlarged holo-gram to guide it between his ribs, narrowly missing bone and lungs as it approaches his heart.

'What are they?' I ask, as dozens of tiny insect-like creatures swarm around his heart.

'MIDs,' Chaudhury replies. 'Microscopic Internal Defibrillators.'

The minuscule lifesavers appear at Hartman's holo-graphic heart and, within seconds, align themselves perfectly, then –

*ZAP!*

Hartman's body jolts violently at being shocked from within.

'Again!' Miss Silva barks.

The doctor nods, and the tiny mechanical creatures charge for another blast at restarting Hartman's dead heart.

*Don't work. Please don't work!*

His body contorts again.

Nothing. Again.

'Miss Silva . . .' Dr Chaudhury says, looking at her feet.

'You assured me this machine would work,' Miss Silva rages, her pale face closer to flushing than I've ever seen it.

'Theoretically, Miss Silva, yes, but this is brand-new technology. There are so many risks.'

'Risks? How dare you blame the technology? This is nothing compared to what we have achieved below.

Nothing. *You* have failed me,' Miss Silva says, and the soldier at the glass stands to attention.

'You have failed Eve,' she adds, and as she turns I see her nod at her soldier. The order.

He launches into action, stepping through the floating hologram of Hartman's lifeless heart to rip the invisible film from his ribcage.

'No! Please!' the doctor cries, raising his hands in surrender as the masked soldier plasters the transparent material on to his chest, making his heart visible.

The soldier raises his rifle and points it directly at the seemingly open chest of Dr Chaudhury, giving him a clear aim at his beating target.

'Wait!' I shout, without thinking, but it's too late.

There's a deafening crack, like a bolt of lightning, in the cell as the bullet passes through the X-raying sheet, killing the image as it pierces Dr Chaudhury's heart.

He's dead before his body hits the floor.

'Shit!' I say, placing one hand on my gun instinctively – but who am I going to shoot? The soldier? Miss Silva? Then what? I can hardly step out into the corridor and casually walk past the other soldier who, at this moment, is totally oblivious to the chaos within this muted cell.

'At ease, soldier,' Miss Silva commands, and he returns to his post at the frosted glass, his breathing made faster by the thrill of the murder he just committed.

'I'd been growing tired of his failures for some time,' Miss Silva adds.

I feel a little dizzy. I thought I'd seen the darkest side of the EPO but this is beyond anything I could have imagined.

I slowly move my hand away from my weapon. I don't want to give him any reason to shoot me.

It's clear Miss Silva suspects nothing about Hartman's death, making the Pacify Glove, now back on my belt, feel heavy and obvious again.

She steps over the doctor's body to Hartman and leans close to his lifeless head. 'What did you know that was worth dying for?' she whispers, as though contemplating his next move.

'I guess we'll never find out now,' I say, feigning frustration.

Miss Silva shoots me a look I've not seen before. It's smug. Devious. She reaches into her pocket, pulls out a holo-pad and taps a command.

What the hell am I meant to do now?

What would Ketch do?

He was always the man with the answers. The man who'd make things happen. Got shit done. Maybe that was what he was to Miss Silva.

'Miss Silva, shall I have the bodies taken care of?' I say, trying to sound loyal and appear helpful, but mostly to get this night over with.

'You will do no such thing,' she says, then allows a silence to fall over the two dead bodies between us.

Now what?

She waits. Calmly.

Suddenly silhouettes of people appear through the frosted glass wall of the cell. Two people. One of them obviously Miss Silva's second soldier. The second?

I remove my gun.

The soldier raises his at me.

'At ease. I ordered him here,' Miss Silva explains. He waves his hand and the glass obeys, defrosting instantly.

The soldier doesn't lower his aim until I re-holster my weapon.

Through the glass I see the new person she summoned. He is dressed in an unusual pristine white lab coat that hangs like a robe over his square frame. He carries a leather case in one hand, which must be heavy, judging by the way he holds his shoulders unevenly.

'Who is he?' I ask.

'He is one of a small group of specially trained surgeons. Dr Wells calls them Cardinals,' Miss Silva says flatly.

*Them?* There's more? And what has Wells got to do with these surgeons?

Miss Silva motions with her hand and the door obeys, revealing the seams of the thick doorway for this *Cardinal*, allowing him inside. He is older, with a strip of grey hair that sits like a crown around the back of his bald head.

'I believe the one in restraints has some valuable information which he failed to reveal before his departure. Would you please retrieve it?' Miss Silva instructs. The Cardinal nods.

'Retrieve the information?' I ask, my heart sinking. Can he do that?

'No, Turner. His entire mind,' Miss Silva replies, stepping aside for the Cardinal to access Hartman.

I stare at Miss Silva for a moment, trying to figure out what the hell that even means. *His whole mind?* He can retrieve a mind?

The Cardinal reaches within his white lab robe and removes a silver sphere, a remote like the ones the security soldiers had. He swipes his hand over it and Hartman's restraints flip his body horizontally as though he is lying on an invisible stretcher.

'Cause of death?' the Cardinal asks, aiming the question at me, his voice flat and emotionless.

'Unknown, but he was connected to that datastore and midway through a memory transfusion,' I explain, trying to keep up with all their terminology so I sound like I know what the hell they're doing.

I see his eyes flash to Miss Silva at the mention of the torture device.

'It must have malfunctioned or something, I dunno. It all just cut out. I guess Hartman did too,' I add.

*Okay, chill out, big mouth, before you say something you shouldn't.*

'There is an operating theatre in the Dome. I can make it available to you immediately if . . .' Miss Silva suggests.

'There is no time. His mind is already decaying at this temperature. We must begin the removal here,' the surgeon says.

Miss Silva sighs.

*Remove what?*

'Very well. Do what you must,' she orders.

*What the hell?*

I step back as the Cardinal removes his surgical tools from within his white robe. He unrolls a small mat containing a selection of stainless-steel instruments perfectly tucked inside the compartments.

Inside his leather case I see an icebox beneath the wires of a surgical drill.

I try not to stare. I don't think my stomach can take seeing whatever he is about to do so I avert my eyes to the ceiling and listen instead. Still trying to take it all in.

I catch words between the piercing whines of the drill and the cracking of bone.

*Scanning. Connected. Analysing. Decoding.*

Words I've never heard in surgery before – not that I've ever been around an operation, let alone one on a dead guy.

'I need absolute silence,' the unorthodox surgeon demands. Miss Silva, her soldier and I reply with our cooperation.

I stand for the next twenty minutes, glancing intermittently at the brutal procedure.

'I have a clear map. Removing now . . .' the Cardinal says, finally breaking the silence.

'Good,' Miss Silva replies.

I've never seen a human brain before. I shudder as he places it in the icebox.

'Removal complete. The rest cannot be done here,' the Cardinal says.

Miss Silva nods to her soldier, who reaches into his armour pocket, pulls out another glass disc, identical to the ones the pilots' memories were on, and hands it to the Cardinal.

Soon he will have Hartman.

His mind, his thoughts . . . his secrets.

'I want it all. On there,' Miss Silva says.

The Cardinal nods.

'Turner.' His cold, calm voice jerks me back into the moment, and somehow the sight of the two corpses seems fresh, more shocking than it had just a few minutes before.

The way the Cardinal steps over Dr Chaudhury's body, as though it wasn't there, makes my blood boil. I kneel at his side and gently close his glassy, staring eyes.

'Miss Silva, are we to emulate this one too?' the cardinal asks, noticing me at the body.

'No,' she replies. 'I have no use for it.'

*It? IT?* Is she referring to the doctor? His body? His mind? It? Miss Silva is more malevolent than I'd ever imagined. Is this what power does to you?

'Turner, you are to escort the Cardinal. No one is to see or hear you,' she instructs.

'But, Miss –' the Cardinal objects, a frown creasing his smooth forehead.

'Do not interrupt me!' Miss Silva explodes. 'You cannot travel alone and unarmed carrying that information. I am satisfied with his loyalty now.'

I'm stunned.

'You are to escort the Cardinal and the information he is carrying. If anyone tries to stop you, shoot them on my authority. Do you understand?'

'Yes, Miss Silva,' I reply.

'Miss Silva,' the Cardinal interjects, 'you cannot mean him to go inside –'

She cuts him off with her raised hand.

'Turner is to escort you to the core. You are to leave them at the gate.' She directs the order at me.

I don't have a clue where that is or what she's talking about!

'Excuse me, Miss Silva, where am I to escort him exactly?' It comes out more apologetically than I intend.

I become aware of eyes on us. The Cardinal is staring at Miss Silva and me, waiting to find out what she will say.

'The Cardinal will lead the way, Turner,' she says. 'You wouldn't believe me if I told you.'

# 23

# Eve

There's a knock on my door. I roll over in bed – Bram isn't here.

'Bram?' I call through the dark.

'Eve? It's Saunders,' comes the unexpected reply, causing a heaviness to land on my chest. He's the first visitor I've had – where the hell are Chubs and Bram?

*Calm down, Eve*, I tell myself.

'I have something for you,' Saunders whispers, through the wooden door.

'Oh?' I say.

'I know it's early but I saw Chubs and Bram on their way to breakfast and thought . . . Well, I owe you an apology. For the other day.' I hear him take a deep breath. 'You'll like it,' he adds.

'How do you know I will?' I ask, sliding out of bed and throwing on yesterday's clothes – they're already damp.

'I know a lot about you.' He chuckles, 'Remember?'

'You *did*,' I remind him. He's irritating me. I instantly regret my bluntness when he doesn't reply. Our last encounter left me feeling sick with guilt. 'Thank you,' I mutter.

'You haven't seen it yet,' he calls.

'But you know I'll like it.' I'm deliberately kinder. The last thing I want is tension between us.

Saunders is so emotional. I remember that from when he was Holly, childlike and bashful, and the memory transports me back into the Dome. He was the most fun Holly. His heart was on her sleeve, which meant I knew just how invested she was in every moment with me. Someone like Saunders wouldn't be able to fake that delight.

'So . . . can I give it to you?' he asks.

'Of course!'

I open the door of my room to see Saunders wearing the beaming smile I'd predicted, a vast contrast to the cloud that had fallen on it the last time we were together. In his hands is a little box, his fingers cradling it against his chest.

Suddenly I'm nervous. Whatever he has must carry some sort of importance. I thought it was something silly – something to apologize for his crappy attitude towards me. Seeing him looking at me so expectantly, with a charged energy that zaps from his body, makes me think otherwise.

'Come on in,' I say. I step aside and open the door

wider. My own olive branch and attempt at an apology. Our conversation has bounced around my brain since our last meeting, leaving me to question my words and how they must've hurt him. It hasn't made me feel particularly good.

'Oh, I . . .' He hesitates. He glances down the corridor. Unlike Bram, Saunders is evidently more cautious about entering my room.

'Come on,' I say, managing not to laugh while grabbing hold of his arm and pulling him inside. 'Take a seat,' I say, pointing at the desk while pulling across an armchair so that I can sit next to him.

I see him glance at something across the room and cringe when I spot yesterday's bra hanging from a lampshade – I'd been trying to dry it out. Not an easy feat when everything here is permanently moist and soggy. 'It's just a bra,' I explain, as though he's asked a question.

He nods, his lips pursing. He coughs and shifts in his seat, then reaches out and brushes his fingers over the top of the box, which he's carefully placed on the table in front of us.

'So what is this?' I ask.

'Since your birth you have been observed.' He starts with a theatricality that tells me he's definitely practised. 'Even before that, when you were still cocooned in your mother, you were being transmitted for all to see. News of your arrival shattered the despair and gave a glimmer of hope to –'

'Saunders!' I laugh. You'd think I'd be used to people

206

talking about me in this way, but something about it makes me feel uncomfortable. Or maybe embarrassed.

'Too much?' he asks, stopping mid-speech.

'Yep.'

'I take your point,' he says, giving himself a shake as though he's trying to relax. 'Okay, the short version. From the moment the human race knew you were on your way, you've been talked about. As they watched whatever the EPO had to offer – your first tooth, first steps, first word – you became the star of the most intense realiTV show ever created. Those moments have been on repeat for as long as I can remember. We've all seen them, but they're highlights from your life, even if you don't necessarily remember them.'

'I don't want to see me in that Tower,' I say, the thought of watching my gullible self sitting up there making me feel sick.

'I understand that. With things the way they are I can understand how the Tower must seem to you now. But there was so much love. There still is. I want you to know that. It's so easy for things to get tainted . . .'

'Mother Nina and Mother Kadi.'

'Exactly. And others,' he says, sliding the box across the table so that it sits just inches away. He swipes a flat palm over the top, the motion causing light to fan out. A screen instantly appears. 'Ever since I was a little boy my dad had been recording and collecting whatever he could. Clips of you up there, interviews, pictures. All important moments of your life.'

'Is he down here?'

'He died six months before I made it out of the Tower,' he says, with surprisingly little emotion in his voice. 'They didn't tell me.'

'I'm sorry.'

'He was your biggest fan,' he says, as though he hasn't heard me. 'I'm pretty sure he would've been down here as a Freever, had it not been for his disability. I would have been his carer, but he gave me to the EPO. Knew I'd be useful to them, and you.'

I think back to how old we must've been when I first met his Holly. He was one of the originals, which would've made us incredibly young. How difficult must it have been for him, and the others, to leave their parents and live in a strange place? I didn't know any different, but they were plucked from their homes or offered up, like a sacrifice.

'I went to our old home,' Saunders says, his hand waving over the beam of light and making it flicker. 'It's a wreck now, but it was all still there piled in boxes. You. I wanted you to have it, so that you can see what the world has witnessed of your life. It might give you a greater understanding of how the world came to love you . . . and where you came from.'

The last few words ring in my ears.

'You mean . . . ?' I gasp.

'Your parents.' He nods.

'I've seen so little of them.'

'We can start with them, if you like,' Saunders

offers, clearly taking delight in my excitement. 'They were caught on a surveillance camera moments before they were told about you. It was routine practice to document visits. For research purposes. The footage is a bit grainy, but . . .'

I stop breathing as two faces appear on the screen. There they are, Corinne and Ernie Warren, gazing at each other. They don't appear to know they're being filmed as they sit on a bench in a hospital corridor. The light is stark and bright around them. They are completely lost in each other. Other people walk up and down, going about their business, and the two don't even notice.

I'm dizzy with excitement when someone knocks on the door, rooted to the spot, unable to look away. A split second later, I'm aware of Bram's head peering around the door.

'What's happening here?' he asks.

'Look,' I say breathlessly.

'You've given it to her!' He slaps Saunders on the back.

'You knew?' I ask.

'Of course I did,' he says, with a laugh, perching beside me on the armchair. 'It's Saunders's pride and joy.'

'Mine too now,' I admit. 'Look how affectionate they are. The intimacy is just . . .' My voice trails off when the figures on screen lean towards each other and kiss, their mouths slotting together perfectly.

Their lips part, but their heads stay close together. Their eyes might be closed, they might be sitting in silence, but there is total unity.

As we watch, Bram places a hand on my shoulder and rubs my collarbone with his thumb. I'm aware I should shake him off, with Saunders here, but it feels so soothing to have someone comfort me, the closeness mirroring what we're seeing on screen.

Corinne, my mother, takes an audible breath. 'I'm going to love our little boy so much. He's a miracle.'

'Could be a girl.' My father smiles, and she rolls her eyes.

'We'll scan you now, Mrs Warren,' says another voice.

The three walk towards a room, a bed and a screen.

'She's a midwife,' whispers Bram. 'They used to help mothers in pregnancy . . .'

'Right.' I nod.

'You've lost before?' the midwife asks.

I can see her face now. It's cautious, making me wonder how many women she'd scanned, how many times she'd had to give bad news, and how draining that must've been for her.

'Years ago,' Mum admits nervously, while my dad takes her hand and gives it a reassuring squeeze.

'Several times?'

'That's right,' Dad replies. Mum is visibly shaken at the memories. 'The last time was eight years ago.'

'And you're fifty-one and off the screening

programme for failure to carry?' She still directs the question at my mother, even though my father has taken over.

'So they said,' he replies. 'But look at us now.' He chuckles, attempting to soften the tension in the room.

'Hmm . . .' says the midwife. 'Lie back, please.'

My mum obediently does as she's told and blue jelly is squirted on her rounded stomach. Her face freezes with fear as the midwife picks up the probe.

The worry is now clear on both their faces. They don't appear to breathe while the midwife pulls the screen around to block their view and punches at buttons with her fingertips.

'I didn't know you had *this* moment, Saunders!' says Bram. 'This is rare footage . . .'

'Yeah. Really special,' I hear Saunders say. I try to block them out so I can fully absorb what I'm seeing.

'Oh,' says the midwife, looking from the screen to my mum's exposed bump, trying to marry the two.

'What is it?' my dad asks.

'Another loss?' asks my mum, the shake in her voice causing a lump to form in my throat.

'No, it's –' She stops and stands tall, taking a breath. 'I'm just going to get a second opinion.' With this she leaps out of the room, leaving the bewildered couple staring after her.

'Oh, my gosh,' I say, my eyes watering as I look up at Bram. I fight the urge to jump into his arms as tears fall down my cheeks on to his hand. He holds me a little tighter. I reach up and squeeze his arm in response.

'Look, I'm actually on duty,' Saunders says, slowly rising to his feet.

'But it's not finished, has it?' I say, my eyes going back to the screen, willing it not to end.

'No, it hasn't. I've just got to go. People will wonder where I am and . . . you two watch, I'll –' He breaks off and makes towards the door, just as the screen is invaded by half a dozen officials in white coats, making no attempt to reassure my mum, who stares at them in fright.

The door clicks shut and I'm aware I haven't thanked Saunders, but as the midwife picks up the probe and places it back on that beautiful bump, the professionals in the room gasp and mutter, and as the penny drops for the couple on the bed, who are now sobbing with relief and love, all thoughts of him disappear.

I was so loved. I was so wanted. And not in the grandeur of what my life became and what I symbolized to the world beyond, but within that couple. My family. They are why I'm here.

Suddenly I feel myself yearning to know more of the love and joy they had for me. With a pang, I long to be wedged between them, sitting side by side, like they were at the start of the footage. Oh, how I'd love to listen to them talk, knowing I was exactly where I belonged.

A moment with my mum is out of my reach now: that was snatched from me long ago. But there's still hope for me and my dad.

Hope.

I need more than hope.

I need to do everything I can to make it happen.

## 24

# Bram

Eve yelps with pain.

'You okay?' I stand instantly.

'Yes! Chill, I just bit my lip!' she says, pulling me back into my seat at the breakfast table. 'At ease, soldier, before you cause a scene!'

'Sorry.' I sit and notice the gossip-hungry eyes staring at us from around the dining hall.

She dabs her mouth with her finger and examines the few drops of blood.

'Should I fetch the doc?' Helena asks her quietly.

'For biting my lip?' Eve frowns.

'How bad is it?' I ask.

'For goodness' sake, you two! You were fine with me leaping off a building last week, and *you* bundled me into a bag! Now you're worried about me biting my lip.' She laughs. 'You need to get out more . . . We all do!'

I nod to Helena, who returns to her meal.

'You don't actually need to chew the floodweed, you know. I find the easiest way is to just neck the stuff.' I demonstrate by gulping down a mouthful without chewing and finish with a satisfied exhalation of floodweed-scented breath.

Eve rolls her eyes and nudges me in the ribs.

My heart leaps. I'm still not used to the feeling, the realness of it. The sensation of her touch versus the kinetic suit I used to wear that simulated it. Will this ever get old?

'I'm serious, though. It's like mass cabin fever down here,' Eve says, looking around at the room of sunlight-deficient soggy men. She decided to eat with the Freevers rather than in the privacy of her room.

'You've lived your whole life in a "cabin" and got along just fine,' I say, knowing full well this is a hell of a lot different from the EPO experience.

'But this time I actually know I'm in a "cabin",' she says. 'Plus we had the Drop. Real or not, that place was an escape.'

'I know. Despite everything, I miss it. We had some good times up there.'

'We're having better ones down here,' Eve says quietly, secretly placing her hand on my leg.

My stomach flips.

Floodweed sticks in my throat.

I choke.

Cough.

Green water comes out of my nose.

Eve laughs.

'Helena, maybe we do need the doctor after all,' she teases.

'Bram.' Saunders approaches our table, interrupting my embarrassment.

'Yes?' I swallow hard on the lump of food in my throat.

'A word, if you have some time?' he asks, and his unreadable expression suggests he doesn't want a casual chat.

'Sure, I'll just finish this,' I say, nodding at my almost empty cup of slosh.

Saunders heads back to his seat two tables away.

'I remember him. From inside. *His* Holly,' Eve says.

'You do?' I reply, surprised.

'I remember all of you. You were all different. Subtly, of course, but when you have only one friend you find yourself knowing every detail about them,' Eve explains.

'What about him, then?' I ask. 'What was his interpretation of Holly like?'

'Emotional,' she replies, with wide eyes, and I nod in agreement.

'That's what got him into trouble,' I explain.

'I assumed.'

I finish my food and stand.

'Don't be too long,' Eve says, as I leave the table. The implication sends electricity through my body.

I reply with a smile and reluctantly head to Saunders. Let's see what the hell he wants.

He leads me out of the dining hall in silence. We navigate the corridors of the Deep side by side, not saying a word until we're climbing into the brass capsule that leads up. Our only connection to Central . . . to the world.

'We're going out?' I ask.

'I think we could both do with a change in scenery,' he replies. 'It's okay. I've cleared it with the scouts. You're safe.'

He must have read my mind as I remembered the images of my own face plastered over the screens that decorate the city. He might be a little irritating but I trust Saunders.

'We were pilots once . . . Now look at us,' he says, as the submergible ascends.

'Squad H – brothers!' I reply.

'Brothers.' He laughs. 'Not many people know what it's like to live two lives, spending years delving into the weird world of Holly, figuring out who she was, becoming her, collectively appearing as a new person, a unique personality. It's a lot to leave behind.'

'You're not the only one who feels it. It's weird leaving her. Like leaving part of our personality in the Tower,' I say.

'It's impossible. She's part of all of us,' he replies, and the sphere jolts to a stop. He twists the circular handle 360 degrees and the sealed metallic door opens.

Grey shards of daylight pour in through the frosted glass of the half-flooded clock face, causing me to shield my eyes.

'So where are we going?' I ask.

'I want to show you something.' Saunders steps through the broken glass panel and out into the make-shift dock on our hidden part of the river.

I glance around nervously.

I hate being out here.

Exposed.

Not because I'm worried about being caught; I'm worried about revealing the Deep's location. About revealing Eve. It takes just one person with a keen eye and the game is up.

Central is rife with opportunists sniffing around for their golden ticket to an easier life, and who can blame them?

'Of course, Holly started with you, the first! The *originale*,' he jokes, as he gets into a black dinghy.

I climb in after him.

'Pretty crazy that those things you did instinctively as Holly, when you were just a kid, had to be analysed and replicated by us other pilots. We all adopted a little bit of you into our own thoughts,' he explains.

'I bloody hope not!' I joke.

He doesn't laugh.

*Emotional.*

He steers the light craft around a series of narrow canals that weave like capillaries between the organs of Central, the gargantuan cloudscrapers that loom over the old city.

Artificial light cuts through a slit in the concrete structures and I catch sight of our faces – Hartman, Ernie, Mother Kadi and myself. Staring out with guilty eyes. The words 'WARNING – EXTREMELY DANGEROUS' are plastered over mine as I'm the only one they don't have. The one they want to make people scared of, make people hate.

Eve's beautiful face appears next on the screen before the gap closes and we sail onward.

'Nearly there,' Saunders reassures me, obviously sensing my concern at being so exposed.

We pass boats, cruisers mostly, the permanent dwellings of people who have no tie to a particular location. They come and go as they please, some with as many as a few thousand people on board, sailing the floods to wherever they desire. Wherever is safe.

'In there,' Saunders says, pointing to a triangular spike of glass and metal pointing up from the flood to the sky. It's totally dwarfed by the new buildings of Central but towers over anything I've ever seen from the city BE.

'What is this place?' I ask, as we drift inside the skeletal structure's steel ribs.

'Just a ghost from another time,' he replies.

He pulls up at a roughly made dock inside. 'Don't worry, it's empty,' he says, as he helps me out of our boat.

I follow him as he walks a path he's obviously

walked before. Through deserted rooms with cubicles and fossils of a life we left behind. Computers and telephones sit on desks that were once worked at. Saunders takes me to a stairwell.

'That's a long way,' I remark, at the winding steps that disappear above.

'It's worth it,' he assures me.

When we reach the summit of this man-made mountain, I'm speechless. I step to the glass and see the city sprawling in front of us.

'Beautiful, right?' Saunders says, looking out with me at the water that reflects the twinkling lights from the windows of surrounding cloudscrapers.

'If you squint, you can pretend they're stars,' he says. He's right.

'It's the best view you're gonna get of the city without being seen. Most people's attention is on the EPO Tower right now. The last thing anyone cares about is a bunch of nobodies loitering around a dead building from the past.' Saunders points at the mountainous monstrosity that is the EPO Tower spanning most of the horizon and disappearing into the clouds, 'She'll be pretty safe here, so long as it's cleared with the scout team.'

'She?' I ask.

He looks at me. 'Well, you didn't think I was bringing you up here on a romantic date, did you?'

'Eve can't come here,' I say. 'It's too dangerous for her. She's got to stay below, for her own good.'

'For her own good? *This* is for her own good. The view, the city, the height are what she's used to. A bit of familiarity is exactly what she needs right now. There's no place like home, Bram, and like it or not, *that* was her home.' He taps his finger on the glass at the EPO Tower.

I stare at him in disbelief, letting him feel my concern. 'That was not a home,' I say, calm and slow. 'That was a prison.'

'And the Deep is different because . . . ?' he fires back, sliding his finger down the glass to the half-submerged clock face, the entrance to the Deep.

'Because she's safe there. Until the dust settles and we figure out what the hell we're going to do next,' I say.

'Well, that's convenient for you, isn't it? You and your little obsession,' he snaps.

'Obsession?'

'Oh, please, we all know what's been going on. We're not stupid, Bram. You and Eve have always been close and now the EPO aren't there to stop it you can take full advantage of her feelings. Of course she's going to be distracted by that, but you've got too close, Bram. Can you really put what's right for Eve before what's right for *you* and Eve?'

*WHAT?* I flush with anger at the suggestion. 'Is that what you think? That I'm manipulating this situation for my own – my own . . . desire?' I rage back at him.

'Hey, hey, I'm just telling you what people are saying, man, that's all.' He raises his hands and backs away.

I take a breath and look out at the city, above and below. Here I am, caught in the middle.

Is that really what people are saying, that I'm too close to Eve?

My heart sinks.

Maybe . . . maybe they're right. Of course Eve is going to gravitate towards me: I'm all she knows. I'm . . . familiar.

Like this place.

'Look, I just thought I could arrange for Eve to come up here some time, if she wanted. No one has to know. I'm in charge of who comes in and out of the Deep, don't forget. I could just show her reality, this world between the two worlds she's known.'

'Wait . . . *you* and Eve?'

He pauses. Says nothing.

He doesn't have to. I can see it.

'Oh, my God, Saunders. Is that what this is really about? This conversation is over. You know, you nearly had me with all that crap about Eve and me getting too close.'

'No, wait, Bram. It's not like that,' he protests, but of course it is.

'It's not like that? Saunders, you were the classic case of the Eve Effect. Countless pilots became obsessed with her after working with her for long periods, acting irrationally, even dangerously! You were totally infatuated with her in there. It's why you were locked up. We were told you'd been executed, for crying out loud! I thought your time out here had calmed those feelings.'

'Well, maybe it's time to look in a mirror, my friend,' he replies.

The words bounce off me.

I'm immune to them now.

I know what Eve and I have.

'Take me back,' I order.

The return journey to the Deep is silent. The gentle splash of water lapping against the black boat provides the only soundtrack to the awkwardness in the air.

I shrug it off and use the time to take in the surroundings, the city. It's not often I get to see it without someone chasing me. It feels so open, compared to the close walls of the Deep. Here the air is cool and wet, and the spray of the river on my face is a welcome wake-up call.

Saunders's motive was wrong, but his plan ... Maybe it's time Eve saw the world I revealed to her.

# 25

# Michael

The Cardinal leads the way quickly from the cell to the lift. Inside he is silent but his eyes are on me, saying a thousand things.

I root my feet to the floor, trying to appear strong as I escort him and whatever he removed from Hartman to the place they're all being so damn mysterious about.

We ascend. Fast.

'Are we going to the Dome?' I ask.

'No,' the Cardinal answers bluntly.

'It's Turner. You have a name?'

'You may refer to me as Cardinal,' he replies.

It's like that then.

The lift stops and I hear Miss Silva's voice repeat in my head — *If anyone tries to stop you, shoot them on my authority.* I place my hand on my weapon as the circular door swishes open and pray no one stops us.

*YOU HAVE ARRIVED AT THE DOME,*
the automated voice says.

I scan the area and step out into the space before the Gate, the entrance into what was once Eve's world.

'Well? I thought you said we weren't coming here . . .' I stop as I don't sense any movement behind me. I turn to see the Cardinal still inside the spherical lift.

'If you are coming with me, you must remain inside,' he explains.

'What's going on?' I ask.

He doesn't answer.

I don't have any choice but to step back into the lift.

'Turner?' a voice calls, before I'm fully in the sphere.

*Shit!*

'Hey! Turner, wait up!' It's Guard Reynolds.

There's always a Final Guard on patrol at night.

The Cardinal lunges for the gun on my belt. The move catches me totally off guard and he's armed in a second, pointing the barrel at me.

'If he sees me, he must be killed,' the Cardinal replies.

'Wait! He's a Final Guard. Like me,' I whisper.

'Then you'd better deal with the situation or I will. You heard Miss Silva,' he says, as Reynolds's footsteps get louder in the corridor.

I step out of the lift before he sees the Cardinal.

'Hey!' Reynolds chirps, walking from the Gate a few yards away. 'What are you doing up here?'

'I was going to ask you the same thing,' I reply, trying to sound casual as he comes towards me.

'Ah, I'm on night duty. Gotta keep it up, even if Her Highness has left the building.' He shrugs. 'It's gone six, though, so I'm just about done. All the weapons have been checked and replaced in the stores. The Gate looks tight. The Dome is empty. I'll ride down with you.'

'No!' I blurt.

I can feel the presence of the Cardinal in the lift behind me, Reynolds just a few steps away from receiving my bullet.

'No?' he repeats.

'Actually, there's something you can do for me,' I say.

'You feeling okay, Turner? You're sweating.'

'Yeah, it's just been one of those nights,' I say, wiping my brow. 'Look, I need you to do another sweep of the Dome. You saw what Miss Silva did to the pilots and I don't want to end up like Squad H,' I say, improvising as best I can. 'We can't afford to be slack now.'

Reynolds squints suspiciously at me. 'Okay . . . but I've already done the rounds. It's a ghost town in there,' he says.

I pause.

'. . . Better safe than sorry, though. You've got me doubting myself.' Reynolds turns on the spot and heads back through the Gate.

'Thanks, I owe you.'

'Don't sweat it. You're the boss now, remember!' he calls back.

I return to the lift and allow the door to close.

The Cardinal flips my weapon around. 'My apologies.

226

We cannot be too careful,' he says, offering my gun back to me.

I take it and, in a swift move, drive the butt into his nose.

He falls back into the lift wall.

'Never touch my gun again,' I say, as he nurses his bleeding nose. The adrenalin rushes around my body and I fight to keep it under control.

*That was stupid, Turner.* But Ketch always said that at the start of a new relationship someone always grabs the other by the balls and I'd been feeling this guy tugging for a while.

Still, it was bloody stupid.

*DESTINATION?* the automated voice asks.

'Eraeon,' the Cardinal says clearly, then wipes away the blood with the sleeve of his white robe.

'Excuse me, where?' I ask, but the lift interrupts with an unusual jolt.

Are we turning? The ball seems to be spinning on its axis.

I didn't know they could do that.

After a turn of 180 degrees the door slides open again but this time it reveals a new corridor leading away from the Gate, stretching far out in a long, straight line.

I've never seen this place and, as a member of the Final Guard, I'm having difficulty comprehending that. We're trained to know every possible way in and out of the Tower — lifts, vents, air ducts, cooling systems, doors, anything. It's a vital part of our training, to allow us to protect Eve in the most efficient way.

So how is this even here?

More importantly, where does it go?

The Cardinal exits swiftly and I follow to the far end of the corridor. Its black walls give nothing away. This place is all purpose and no design.

Neither of us speaks until a few minutes later when we reach another lift.

'Where now? We're already at the top,' I ask, knowing we can't go any higher.

'To go down, first you must go up,' he says, sounding like a bad riddle.

'Well, I'm glad we're back on speaking terms but that makes absolutely no sense.'

'Get inside,' he replies flatly.

I step in and the door closes. No voice asks for our desired destination. It just starts descending rapidly.

Through the glass sphere I see nothing but black as we plummet through this impossibly large building.

'You won't need that now,' the Cardinal says, looking at the gun still clenched in my fist.

'I'll be the judge of that,' I respond, leaving it exactly where it is.

The lift slows to a soft stop and the door slides open, allowing a familiar voice to pour inside.

'I don't care if it was an emergency. Unscheduled movements in or out are always, *always*, to go through me. It's the whole point of having security.'

'Ketch?' I push past the Cardinal into whatever this cavernous place is.

'Mikey?' My brother's face is turning white, like he's seen a ghost. 'What the hell are you doing here?'

'Me? Why are *you* here? *How* are you here? Where even *is* here?' I shout, needing some answers.

'Is there a problem?' The Cardinal steps in.

'Problem? Yeah, I'll tell you the problem. Miss Silva put me in charge of escorting you to some mystery place I've never heard of, almost killing my friend on the way, and now my brother is here! I seem to be the only one who doesn't know what the hell is going on!' I feel all the stress of the night running out of me.

'You two are . . . ?'

'Brothers, yes, Cardinal.' Ketch confirms the obvious.

'Miss Silva instructed your brother to escort us.'

Ketch's eyes widen. *'Inside?'* he asks.

'Just to the border,' the Cardinal says firmly.

'What is it? What's inside?' I ask Ketch.

'I can't tell you that,' he says, raising an eyebrow at me.

'Then what are *you* doing here?' I ask, pushing him away to get a better look at him. 'You're all healed up and didn't think of paying me a visit?'

He pulls me aside, away from listening ears. The Cardinal instinctively moves closer, wanting to know what's said.

'A moment, please, Cardinal. It's family. You're

clear to enter when you're ready.' My brother holds up a hand with an authority that is impossible to disobey. It's why he's the best at what he does.

'Look, it's complicated.' He pulls me closer. 'I told you I'd been offered a new job and this is it. They said they'd fix me up if I took it, so here I am. They needed me on duty a little earlier than expected. The border isn't operational yet and someone needs to monitor anything going in and out.'

I pull up his shirt revealing his bandaged wounds. 'And you're fit to do that? You nearly died and now you're back already?'

'Well, Dr Wells is working on something big in there and things are moving fast, apparently, so someone's gotta man the gate out here. Someone he trusts.'

'So, what's this new job, then? Doorman?' I scoff.

'Sort of, smartass.' He smacks me around the back of my head, like when we were kids. 'It's border control.'

He leads me forward to show me the gate.

My mouth hangs open.

'Yeah, that was my First Response too.' He laughs.

I stare at the enormous entrance, only half constructed in places. Black marble floor as clear as a mirror, large information kiosks, walls lined with reali-TV monitors, it's an entirely new entrance hall within the Tower. The gate itself is a circular opening leading into somewhere larger that I can't see, but the metallic rim of the entrance is ornately engraved, nothing like anything else I've ever seen inside the EPO Tower.

The Cardinal approaches the entrance where multiple unmanned gates wait. It makes me aware that we are the only people here. It's like a ghost town of tomorrow.

'What is this place?' I ask, as Ketch leads me across the polished floor.

'You're in the core of the Tower, the heart of the mountain. This is, or will be, the entrance to Eraeon,' he says, with mock grandeur.

'Eraeon?'

'I don't know, Wells came up with it. *Era* and *aeon* or something. Whatever it is, it's beyond classified.'

'Hello, may I help you?' says a voice.

A *female* voice.

I have to double-take at the beautiful woman standing at a kiosk before us.

'It's okay, Stephanie, he's with me,' Ketch replies. 'My little brother.'

'Oh, you must be Guard Turner of the Final Guard. Ketch has told me so much about you,' she says, with her perfect red lips.

'About me?' I hear myself repeat, like a doofus. 'Wait, are you *the* Stephanie?'

She nods with a proud smile. I stare in amazement at the perfect projection of a person in front of me. Thousands of light particles creating something so real you'd never tell the difference between her and a real woman.

'Whoa, I always wanted to meet you when you ran the main entrance but I heard they switched you off.'

'Switched off?' She frowns, feigning offence.

Ketch wallops me over the head again. 'She's still a person, you idiot. Just because she's a projection doesn't mean she's software you can power down. Real feelings, real emotions . . .' Ketch explains.

'And more real than any woman you'll ever have,' she fires at Ketch, and winks at me. 'And it's *Projectant*, not projection. It's okay – it's hard for you physical folk to wrap your heads around,' Stephanie teases, flashing a smile that would be perfect if it weren't for the tiny speck of red lipstick on her tooth.

In my peripheral vision I catch sight of the Cardinal walking towards the gates of Eraeon.

'What's it scanning him for? Weapons?' I ask, watching him pass through some sort of automated body-scanning machine before the gate. Beams of light waves pass over his body before allowing him through.

'No, no, it's a Matterscan.' Stephanie giggles at my ignorance.

'To check that they're real,' Ketch says.

'Real?' I ask.

'*Matter*,' Stephanie corrects my brother. 'The scan assesses whether you are of organic origins or . . .'

She stops, realizing I'm having trouble keeping up.

'I am made of light. You are matter. Both may exist within Eraeon but it is easy to confuse the two, so we must keep track.'

'You mean there's more like you in there?' I ask.

She's silent. I see her perfect eyes glance at Ketch.

'I think it's time you got back to your own world.' She winks again, and Ketch turns me away from the gates of Eraeon.

'Look, the less you know about this the better. I've got a feeling Wells is up to something big, bad and ugly,' my brother warns. I look back to see the Cardinal disappear through the gate, taking whatever was left of Hartman with him into that new world. I shudder at the thought of what might go on in there.

'Then what the hell are you doing here?' I ask.

'I had no choice. I could let them heal me and be reassigned here or be retired, leave the Tower behind and rot away with my injuries out there,' he explains.

'Don't give me that bullshit. You just couldn't resist finding out more about – about – What the hell is it called again?'

'Eraeon.'

'Yeah. That. You're a sucker for anything top secret,' I say.

'Just promise you'll keep your mouth shut and won't try coming back. Family or not, orders are orders.'

'Brother, I never want to see this place again,' I say, although something in the pit of my stomach tells me this isn't the last time I'll see the gates of . . . Ah, damn, what the hell is it called again?

# 26

# Eve

I've devoured every single piece of information held within the box Saunders gave me. I've watched every video on loop, read and reread articles and interviews. I've looked at photographs of me at every developmental stage, taking on every obstacle thrown in my way. I've tried to see any hint of sadness behind my eyes. I don't think I can. I was fully immersed in that life. I *was* happy.

I've had to stop watching because it made me desperate to be there – with my mother and father in that room, running around my beautiful garden with Mother Nina. Or simply sitting somewhere, blissfully unaware and not having to question every little thing I see and hear. My heart has swelled, and as a result I feel more crushed than before. All that footage, those words, those pretty pictures – that world has gone. My life is very different now, but I'm determined to turn it into the one I want.

'Chubs!' I call, leaping to open the door as I hear his heavy boots clomping past.

'Eve?' He looks half asleep and dazed.

'Anything?'

'Nothing from outside.' He sighs. 'It's unnerving.'

I'd have to agree. At least if they were attacking us in some way we'd know what we were dealing with. Their stillness has led to our imaginations taking over. I'm sure I'm not the only one envisaging Vivian blasting her way through the city to find me.

'Has anyone in the Deep come up with anything fruitful?'

'A way of getting in?' he asks.

I nod.

'A few of the men helped build the Tower so they're comparing what they know with the info you've given to see if there's anything we've missed in the past.'

'Literally looking for loose screws?'

'Yeah,' he says plainly. 'We've got another guy who worked in the kitchen with his mum. They're looking into waste disposal.'

'Everything's worth investigating,' I say. 'Let's call for a meeting in the morning. They can report their findings then.'

I want to get moving now. It feels like we've been down here for weeks, although it's hard to tell when we're constantly underground, away from any natural daylight.

'Absolutely.' Chubs nods, giving a slightly embarrassing bow as he starts backing away.

'Where are you off to now?' I ask.

He shrugs. 'Told Bram I'd meet him for something to eat.'

'I'll come too!' I call, backing into my room to put on my boots. I sigh as I close the door and lean on its frame. I take a deep breath and think of my dad, someone I feel even more connected to, thanks to Saunders's gift. The thought of us being together makes me feel stronger. I need to channel that energy and focus on a plan.

But then there's Bram.

The last time he was in my room with me alone was when Saunders had left. We'd spent hours together that day. We've hardly seen each other since. It could be in my mind, but I've felt he's been yearning to get away while I've been longing to have him close to me. My worry is that he's freaked out or been spooked over our relationship, and instead of talking to me about it he's backing off and avoiding me.

I hastily put on my boots, wanting to get to the dinner hall before Bram can be given the heads up and leaves. I make for the door and start walking, aware of my feet stomping as I go. I walk down the corridors, of which there are plenty. I walk through the common areas, past people singing and tapping out rhythms with their feet. Past people laughing while playing cards, couples kissing and snuggling, or shouting and scuffling. Love and hate providing ways to pass the time.

Walking into the dining hall, I spot Chubs and Bram whispering to each other. Bram looks annoyed while Chubs holds up his hands in protest.

'I'm off,' I overhear Bram say, as I get closer, only he spins on his heels and knocks straight into me.

'Shit,' he whispers, grabbing hold of my arm and stopping me falling.

'Going somewhere?' I ask.

'Yeah, I've just got to –' He stops, his lips buttoning.

'Sit down,' I murmur, grabbing an empty table and pulling out a chair for him to join me.

'Erm . . .' He looks from me to Chubs.

'I'll go get us some grub,' Chubs says, patting his mate on the back before wandering off.

Air fills Bram's lungs as he slowly sits down.

'Out with it.'

'What?' he says, his smile unable to hide his discomfort.

'Why do you keep running off?'

'I don't,' he replies.

'Want to answer that one again?' I prod.

He forces a laugh and shrugs.

'It's okay. I get it. You're over it,' I say, managing to block out any emotion that's lingering in my throat.

'Over *you*?' Bram asks, his voice high-pitched.

'It's too much. I'm too much,' I say, nodding at my own statement.

'I'd say.' Bram smiles, looking exhausted as he rubs his palms over his head. My head whips around in his direction. 'I'm joking. You're not,' he adds, placing his hands inches from mine on the table.

'What's this about?'

'You're asking me that question?' he replies. 'I'm not the one marching around ordering people to sit.'

'I didn't . . .' I stop, unsure how the tables have turned and I'm now having to defend *my* actions. 'I need to do *something*,' I say, frustration shooting out of me.

'I forget you're used to a daily routine,' he notes. 'Folk down here don't need that. They make do.'

'Well, I'm different,' I snap.

'Eve, calm down.'

'I am calm,' I shoot back.

I look up and see his concerned eyes staring back at me.

I feel like an animal that's been plucked from its natural habitat and put into a cage. Although right now the cage is my own mind.

'It will be okay,' he whispers, leaning towards me.

'That's a lovely sentiment, but we don't know it will, do we?' I challenge. I know I'm being difficult but I'm unable to snap myself out of this mood.

'What do you want me to say?' he asks. 'That it won't be? That, no matter what happens, there will be some casualties? That your dad, Hartman and the Mothers might all be dead by the time we get there? That Vivian's going to find a way to drag you back into that Tower?'

'No.' My chest tightens.

'Well, then . . .'

'I feel so anxious, Bram,' I say, feeling my body soften as the words are released. 'The waiting, the uncertainty . . .'

'We're all feeling like that. It's not all on you any more, Eve. The load is not just yours to carry,' he says, placing his hand over mine.

'But it is,' I say, exasperated.

'Talk to me, Eve. It's me . . .' he says gently.

I look into his beautiful brown eyes. 'I want all this to be over so that life can start . . . but I'm worried about what that future looks like and who will be in it.' The words come out as a whisper. I haven't been brave enough to admit this before, even to myself.

He listens. 'It's as though they have all the power and I've got none of the control – just like when I was in there.' I shift in my seat. 'I thought it would all be so simple. This is so hard. It feels like I'm playing games with my own head. I'm closer to the real world than ever, but in some ways I feel even further away from it than I ever was before . . . and you've been distant,' I say.

'Huh?' He looks perplexed. 'When?'

My mind scrambles to find examples, but fails. Suddenly it all seems pathetic. 'It was more a feeling . . .'

'Yeah . . . What was that you were saying about your mind playing games?' He tuts, sighing to himself. 'Okay, okay . . . It's not all in your head.'

'It's not?' I ask, aware of the panic rising once more.

'This hasn't gone unnoticed,' he says, his hands moving away from mine and gesturing between the two of us.

'Saunders?' I guess. Even after he apologized he's been hot and cold with me. There seems to be something going on there, something bothering him, so it's not too difficult to imagine him having an issue with something I'm doing.

'And others,' says Bram, his eyes giving a little roll. 'I haven't wanted to ruffle feathers. Make anyone jealous. There are too many people here with too much time to think.'

'Glad I'm not the only one,' I mutter.

'Yeah, but they're deluded . . .' he says, a flicker of something unreadable, yet unpleasant, passing across his face.

'How so?' I ask.

'You really don't want to know,' he says. 'How would you like to get out of here?'

'And go where? Is it safe? I thought it wasn't safe, that I was pushing my luck before?' The questions tumble out. Bram is presenting me with a chance to break out of this place and suddenly I'm scared to do so.

'I know somewhere we could go. We could do things properly . . .' he says, his eyes soft and inviting. 'We could call it a date.'

I stare back at him, aware that he's stopped breathing, waiting for me to reply. I smile. 'I thought we were waiting for a war to start,' I tease.

'That's going to happen no matter where we are,' he replies. 'You said you needed a break.'

'You're such a gentleman,' I say mockingly, thinking back to the stories Mother Nina used to tell me of the time before. She was always so disappointed that I wouldn't get to experience the romance of it all. 'A date,' I say, enjoying how the word sounds on my tongue.

# 27

# Michael

'Man, it's tiring doing nothing,' Reynolds says, as we walk with our Final Guard comrades to the dorms after another Eve-less day.

'I know. We should at least be out there looking. Right?' Hernandez adds.

I get a nudge in the back.

'You awake, boss?' Franklin asks. 'Got any words of wisdom for your crew?'

I shake my head.

'Nice,' he scoffs. 'I guess that's the human race done for then.'

'She's alive. I know that,' I say.

'Oh, got a *feeling*, have you?' he teases. 'Maybe a connection opened up between you when you got intimate in the lift.'

I don't rise to it. There's nothing else to do in here

but gossip and fight these days. I can cope with the gossip but not the fighting. Not after what I've seen lately.

'So, what the hell was that about the other night?' Reynolds asks, as we turn into the corridor that contains our living quarters.

'Excuse me?' I reply a little nervously. I've been dreading Reynolds asking me about our encounter outside the Gate to the Dome. A few seconds' difference and the Cardinal would have killed him with my gun.

'Why were you up at the Dome in the early hours? Don't give me that crap about playing it safe for Wells. You know there's nothing to guard in the Dome right now.'

'Look, I just couldn't sleep and wanted to make sure we weren't letting things slip in Eve's absence,' I say. I think that's passable as an answer. I hope.

'And that's very wise, Turner. Miss Silva is pleased with your dedication.' The voice stops me dead in my tracks.

'Dr Wells?' I whisper, seeing him waiting outside the door to my room, cleaning his thin glasses on his cardigan.

'Final Guard – attention!' I command and the unit stops and salutes.

'At ease, guards. I'm here for Turner,' he says, and I can almost feel the relief wash over the squad. Everyone has been on edge since the mass execution of the pilots, and we all know that if Eve doesn't show her face soon, the EPO will have no further need for any of us.

'Sir?' I say.

'Follow me, Turner. You have unfinished business,' he says, and walks towards me, splitting the Final Guard down the middle, like a ship breaking through the tide.

The looks that hit me from my colleagues as they get beyond Wells's eyeline are of total confusion and concern.

I try to respond with my own confused look but I'm not sure I convey it clearly enough before I have to turn and follow.

The lift ride with him is intense. Silent. The man manages to make a ride in the fastest vertical-motion vehicle in the world feel like it takes eternity.

*DETENTION LEVEL. HAVE A GOOD EVENING, DR WELLS*, the automated voice says.

I follow him down the now familiar concrete corridor towards the traitors' cells.

'Any decision on a sentence for Mother Kadi and the old man?' I ask casually, trying to break the ice while remaining professional.

'Miss Silva will make that call,' he says.

I want to ask him about Miss Silva and Hartman's execution. Is this man caught in the same trap, too tangled in Vivian Silva's web to escape? Or is he just as much a part of this as she is? It's on the tip of my tongue when I notice him looking at me over the top of his spectacles, as though he's staring into my inner workings.

'Turner, you are only permitted to know what Miss Silva allows you to know. We are all here to assist her in ensuring the survival of our species, and sometimes doing what's right for the people of the future means doing what's wrong for the people of now.'

I nod. It's like he read my mind. Sounds like Miss Silva has him more brainwashed than anyone.

'You are here because you have shown that you understand that. Unlike many others.'

I do understand. That doesn't mean I agree but being made aware of my compliance comes with a side order of shame.

He continues towards the cells and a fresh brew of anxiety bubbles up in my stomach. 'Last time I was here two men died.'

'The time before that it was four,' he replies, as though he's simply stating a fact. 'Tonight you will see quite the opposite.'

We turn on to the cell block.

The opposite? What the hell does that mean? Why does everyone talk in riddles in this place?

Ahead of us I see the two masked security soldiers standing with their backs to the glass wall of the cell that was once Hartman's as though they are guarding it.

Wells approaches and they step aside as he places

his hand on the glass. It responds instantly, allowing him total access to the cell's control options, more than I've ever been granted. A glimpse of the power Miss Silva has given this man.

He instructs the cell to open and the invisible seal in the transparent wall reveals the open door. He gestures for me to step inside first and once he follows the unbreakable glass reseals itself.

His soldiers fall back into place on the other side of the wall and for a moment I'm relieved. That's one less threat to worry about.

'*Privacy*,' he says clearly, and the transparent wall frosts over instantly, making it impossible for anyone outside to see in.

And the relief disappears.

'Sir, I don't mean to speak out of turn but may I ask what unfinished business we have here?' I ask.

'That's what I like about you, Turner. You don't beat around the bush. Always straight to the heart of the issue. It's unfinished business with Hartman.'

My heart thuds. 'Hartman, sir?'

He holds up a small transparent disc, like the ones that stored the minds of the pilots.

'Hartman.' He rubs his thumb over the surface and, reaching into his back-trouser pocket, he pulls out a piece of flexible, rubber-like material. He unrolls it to reveal a flat pad about the size of a dinner plate.

'What is that?' I ask.

'Not *what*, but *who*.' He smiles as he kneels down to place the pad on the spot where Hartman died.

'That looks close enough,' he remarks, leaning back, better to judge the positioning. Then he inserts the clear disc into a perfectly sized slit on the side of the pad and steps back to watch.

The lifeless pad illuminates, turning from matte grey to glowing brilliant white.

'Emanate,' Wells says, firm and clear.

Words suddenly burst into existence before us – *WELLS INNOVATIONS* appears floating in mid-air – as clear and as solid as if they were carved out of stone.

'What you are about to see is the result of my life's work,' Wells says. 'There have been many failures. Too many. But with the help of Miss Silva I have been able to realize my vision.'

I stay silent.

What the hell is he about to show me?

'When he wakes up he will be confused. For us, days have passed since his death but it will feel instantaneous for him and his mind will not comprehend the time lag.'

'Hold on, who are you talking about? Who's waking up?' I ask, totally confused.

'Hartman,' Dr Wells says, with a slight smile.

I stare at him. 'Sir, Hartman is dead.'

'Physically, yes. Our bodies are weak, poorly designed. They are nothing more than vessels for the true essence of our existence – our thoughts. Hartman's thoughts don't require skin or bone or blood, they just require a new vehicle with which to communicate them.'

'And that's what this is?' I ask, nodding at the device.

'Precisely. Think of that pad as a sort of three-dimensional printer of light, creating a way for us all to continue to communicate with those who are no longer physically available. Particularly useful when someone dies before they give you an important piece of information.'

*No longer physically available?* I've not heard death described like that before.

'Wait, sir, how is a recording of Hartman going to give us his thoughts?' I ask.

'Not a recording, not a simulation, real thoughts from Hartman's own mind,' he says, pointing to the pad containing the clear disc.

'You mean, like Stephanie, a Projectant?' The words sound crazy as they leave my lips.

'Very good.' He nods. 'As far as Hartman is aware, he did not die. In a few moments his consciousness will experience coming around from blacking out, just as he did before, triggering the emulated network of synapses – thoughts – to work just as they would if he were alive. It will be Hartman's mind, thinking, working and, hopefully, cooperating.'

I blink slowly.

Mind totally blown.

'I know it's a lot to understand. It will be for him too, which is why you are here. To ease the transition from matter to Projectant. The closer the environment is to the last one the mind experienced, the more likely the mind is to accept.'

'Look, sir, I'm not going to lie, but this is all a bit much for me to deal with right now.'

'You have no alternative, Turner. Now that the doctor is no longer with us, and Miss Silva is occupied with finding Eve, you are an anchor point, a physical link between his existence before and now. When he wakes he will expect you to be here. You are a necessary part of this and will do as I say, or I'm afraid Vivian will not be as understanding as she has been thus far.'

My heart sinks.

I know what that really means. Is that what Miss Silva really wants for me? Dead, like the pilots, like Hartman?

'Now, forget the way the last questioning ended. When he appears we are still there, on that day, ready for another round.'

'What about Miss Silva? What about Dr Chaudhury? Won't he notice they're missing and you're here?' I ask. I'm subconsciously avoiding the spot on the floor where he died.

'He will be disoriented and unless we draw attention to it he won't question uncertain memories. His mind will want to cling to the reality with which it is presented. You and me. Here and now. The consistency of you being present will be enough, providing you play your part.'

My heart starts to beat fast.

My head starts to pound.

He's actually bringing someone back from the dead. Someone *I* killed.

He turns to the light-pad and readies himself.

'Wake up,' Wells instructs, strong and clear. More like a command for a piece of software than a request of a person.

The floating words suddenly glow brighter until it's impossible to look directly at them. They fill the whole room with white light and I shield my eyes. Then the light disappears, and in the middle of the room a body has formed.

I see him right before my very eyes, in the exact position he was in when he died, wearing the same prison overalls and suspended by cuffs that are no longer there.

'Hartman, can you hear me?' Dr Wells asks.

He coughs and splutters, gasping for air. His image is so vivid, so perfect, it's as though I could reach out and touch him. He doesn't glow like he's made of light. I see now how Holly would have appeared to Eve in the Dome and get it. It's impossible to see the difference between this and the real Hartman, and as far as this Projectant knows he *is* the real Hartman.

'You blacked out momentarily, Hartman, but you are

back with Guard Turner and me now,' Wells informs him, while he regains a regular breathing rhythm.

'Where . . . where am I?' he asks, glancing around the room.

'Your cell. You've been detained for your traitorous actions that resulted in Eve, the saviour, being kidnapped from the Dome and you are going to tell us all you know about the Freevers, their plans, location and anything else that Bram told you.'

I can't take my eyes off Hartman.

It's crazy.

He's there – like, actually there! Moving and talking and breathing and existing . . . except he isn't existing, really.

What the hell is going on?

'I feel strange,' Hartman mumbles.

I look at Wells, who subtly nods at me, as though this is normal behaviour. Like any of this could ever be classed as normal.

'You have been through a lot, Hartman. Resisting is useless. I will not stop until I have what you know,' Wells says in his calm, eerie tone that has almost an undertone of pleasure.

I see Hartman reflected in Wells's glasses and the glistening in his eyes, like the wonder of a little boy seeing something incredible for the first time.

'Hartman. Do as he says,' I interrupt.

Hartman stares at me and I see Wells's head twitch in my peripheral vision. Obviously taken aback. I'm here to be seen, not heard, but I'll be damned if I stand by and let him go through whatever hell Wells has planned for him. I killed him once to put him out of his misery. How do you kill a beam of energy?

'Go on, Turner, don't leave it there,' Wells says, giving me the floor.

Me and my big mouth.

How can I help Hartman but keep my cover? Eve must remain my priority. Our loyalty must be to her, always.

'Bram and Eve would never forgive themselves if they knew what you were going through . . . for them. This is not what they are fighting for, Hartman, and you've served them better than anyone ever would.' My words are sincere. He's been through enough. More than even he knows.

'But if the time has come to put yourself first, know that they will not blame you for doing so,' I say, trying to ease the burden he must be feeling.

Wells raises an eyebrow in agreement, obviously missing the true motivation behind my words. I don't wish to help him: I wish to help Hartman.

'Whatever . . . you are doing to me, it will never be enough to make me betray my friends,' he rasps, still thinking he's bound by his invisible restraints.

'Very well.' Wells sighs. '*REST.*'

The moment Wells speaks the command Hartman freezes. Totally motionless. It's like looking at a perfect statue of him.

'He cannot hear or see us for the moment,' Wells explains. 'I have paused all neurons running to and from his synapses. He is essentially frozen in time until I say otherwise.'

He reaches into his pocket and pulls out a small holo-pad. He taps it and a three-dimensional image appears above it, floating in his palm.

'What's that?' I ask, unsure if I really want to know the answer.

'How do you torture a Projectant?' He returns my question with his own.

I shrug.

'Information,' he says matter-of-factly. 'Now we are dealing with a mind, we have more tools at our disposal. We are not restricted to showing images or implanting memories. Using all the information from the pilots, I can have Hartman experience the event in real time from every vantage point simultaneously.'

I stare at him, trying to pass off my disgust as confusion.

'Imagine being able to feel the sensation of hearing all of Beethoven's nine symphonies simultaneously.'

'Or four deaths,' I reply.

He nods.

This is unethical madness and I cannot bear to be part of torturing this lost soul again. I have to do something.

There is a sudden thud.

Wells turns to the frosted-glass wall where the

silhouette of a soldier is tapping it with the butt of his rifle.

'Hold this,' Wells says, handing me the holo-pad. He places his hand on the cell wall and, at his request, the door appears.

'Sir, he's here,' the security guard says urgently.

'Now?' Wells fires furiously.

'Yes, sir. I've had him detained and –'

'Not here.' Wells cuts him off, obviously wanting to keep this information secret. 'I'll see him, now.'

Wells turns back to me. 'Turner, we're not done. I won't be long,' he says, and places his hand on the other side of the frosted-glass wall. The door reseals instantly, trapping me inside.

'Wait!' I scream. 'Dr Wells!'

I see his dark shadow disappear, flanked by his two soldiers.

I'm alone.

I turn back to the motionless body floating in the middle of the cell and a chill runs down my back. Trapped with the thoughts of a man I killed.

I look at the holo-pad in my hand. No use tampering with it: Wells would know.

If only I could speak to Hartman, help him understand what the hell is going on. Or maybe he could help me understand, I don't know.

Could I do it? Un-pause him?

What would the command be?

'Unfreeze,' I bark.

Nothing.

'Un-pause,' I try, but again nothing. Hartman is totally still.

What would Wells use? I think back over the commands so far.

'Wake up!' Nope. I guess he's already awake. But something else that would humanize him, perhaps. Something to give a Projectant a sense of authenticity?

'Hartman, breathe,' I say.

His head snaps to me, standing where Wells was a few moments ago. His chest starts rising and falling rapidly.

'How did you do that? Where's Wells?' he asks, and I realize he would have perceived Wells to disappear in the blink of an eye.

'He's gone for a moment, Hartman. I'll try to explain everything but I need you to listen and to trust me. We don't have much time.'

# 28

# Michael

How do you tell someone you killed them?

'I feel strange. Confused,' Hartman says.

'Yes, you will,' I say, as calmly as I can, 'I'm sure you'll be feeling many side effects.'

'Side effects?' He looks at me.

A shiver runs down my spine.

How is he not real? The projection is perfect.

'Hartman,' I say, preparing him and myself, 'Wells has done something to you that is . . . hard to explain. This will be difficult for you to comprehend, but it's important you know the truth.'

'Try me. The week I'm having, nothing is going to surprise me,' he says, spitting on the floor. I follow the glob of saliva as the pad projects its trajectory on to the floor of the cell.

*Incredible.*

'Well?'

Okay, I've got to do this.

'You're dead,' I say.

Just like that. Blunt. Honest.

'And I killed you,' I add.

Hartman blinks at me.

'I'm sorry.'

'Is this a joke?'

'I wish it was. You were being tortured.'

'Was?' He coughs.

'Well, yes, you still are, but . . . it's different now. I felt the most humane thing to do, the kindest thing for you, was to end it.'

'You either don't know the definition of killing someone or you did a terrible job because I'm still here!' he says, looking down at himself.

'Yes, that's the second part of this riddle, Hartman. You are here, but not physically. I'm just a guard so I don't know the science but this is your mind talking. Your body is just one of those Projectants.'

Hartman's skin tightens around his face at the mention of the word. He stares down at his hands. His feet. His body. 'Impossible. You're mistaken.'

I say nothing and let him have a moment to study himself.

'Where are the cuffs?' he asks, realizing he's not being restrained.

'They were on your body, your real body,' I explain, stepping closer to him, hoping to show some sincerity in my eyes.

'Come closer,' he says quickly, a little panic in his voice. He raises his hand towards my face and I instinctively back away.

He keeps his hand there and looks at me.

I step forward and offer my hand in return.

He takes it in a handshake.

'You're full of shit.' He sighs, relieved. 'I feel. I feel you. You had me going for a second, though. Is this one of Wells's new tactics? You'll have to try harder.'

'Look now,' I tell him, and he looks down as I squeeze the fuzz of energy until my hand disappears within his, passing straight through the projection of what should be solid.

He chokes on the air. Gagging. Retching. Heaving.

'Whoa, okay, calm, stay calm,' I say, as he collapses to the floor. 'I know it's difficult. I don't understand the first thing about this shit!' His image flickers and distorts as though his mind is turning on itself.

'How . . . how . . . can this be . . . possible?'

'I don't know!' I say. 'When you died he had someone come up and . . . I dunno . . . scan your head or something. He's got a whole secret place he's built within the Dome, and whatever they got from your brain they took there. The next thing I know you're back in front of me as if nothing happened.'

Hartman sits and takes a few deep breaths to calm

himself. 'I can still feel it . . . the air . . . in my lungs,' he says, as he brings his hands up in front of his face to study them. He sees the light-pad he's sitting on. 'Is that it?' he asks.

'That's some sort of projection thing, I guess,' I reply.

'He had us test these with Holly a while back.' He sighs. 'Portable tiles capable of manipulating light waves. He'd planned to redesign the whole Tower with these, allowing Holly or any of his projections access to anywhere they please.'

'Why didn't he?' I ask, as he runs his finger over the edge of his light source.

'I guess Silva vetoed it. It was unnecessary. The Holly projectors were sufficient for what Eve required.'

'I guess Eve isn't Wells's priority any more.'

'I'm not sure she ever was,' Hartman replies, his lip quivering. 'So what's he doing in this new place you mentioned?' he asks.

'I don't know yet but I have a man who can help.'

'And you trust him?'

'He's my brother.'

'And you trust him?' he repeats.

'With my life. I already owe it to him. His loyalty is with Eve,' I say.

'Yet he works for the EPO.'

'So did you,' I fire back.

He nods in acceptance.

'Do you think there's more of . . .' I pause, unsure how to finish the question.

'More what? *Things* like me?' he asks, waving at the pad of white he's sitting on.

'People. Not things, Hartman,' I correct. 'If there are more *Projectants*, or whatever you call them, down there, then he's messing with people's lives.'

'You have to find Bram before Wells does,' Hartman commands.

'Where?' I ask.

He pauses.

I can see every part of what's left of him trying to resist giving away his friends.

'Hartman, there's no time to doubt me now,' I say.

He looks at the light-pad once more and sighs his artificial breath.

'They have a place. It's hidden in the old city under the flood. It's . . .'

'SLEEP,' Wells commands from the open glass wall behind me and Hartman's image disappears instantly into the light-pad.

'No!' I scream.

Wells stares at me.

'He was about to tell me, sir,' I say honestly, leaving out the part that I had no intention of revealing that information to Wells.

'No need. Circumstances have changed and that information has now been given to us from a reliable source on the outside.'

'Who?' I ask, desperate to know who gave them up.

'One of their own,' Wells says, bending down and

removing Hartman's clear disc from the pad and placing it inside the leather pouch alongside Squad H.

A small part of me finds comfort in that he's at least with his fellow pilots in some way.

'Ready your team, Turner. Today is the day Eve returns home,' he says, then leaves me in the empty cell.

# 29

# Eve

'Time to wake up,' he whispers in my ear, his hot breath tickling my neck.

I roll over, my fingers running through his hair. My arms reach around his neck and pull him towards me. 'I'm awake,' I croak, as our lips cushion together.

He pulls away, softly chuckles. 'We need to go,' he says. 'Come on, before everyone else wakes up. Unless you don't want to go out any more?' he teases.

'Our date!' I sing, scrambling out of the bed and throwing on my clothes – a variety of black garments to keep me hidden in the shadows.

'Wear this,' he says, chucking a heavy woollen coat in my direction. Also black.

'Really?'

'You'll thank me.' He looks in the bag he's carrying, then starts patting his pockets and searching the floor around him, making sure he has everything we might need.

I reluctantly push my arms into the coat's sleeves, trying not to gag at the stench of the fabric. Being down here in the Deep, it's hard to remember the last time I smelled something nice and inviting.

When we're dressed and Bram has checked the contents of his bag once more, we leave the room, being as quiet as possible while walking along the corridors and past rooms containing sleeping Freevers. It's eerily quiet, considering there are so many of us living down here. We make it to the capsule unseen. To my surprise, Saunders isn't here, but Bram is unfazed as he locks us in and starts pulling levers. We barely talk as it travels skywards and delivers us outside.

It's cold, but in the thick of night I take a moment to stand in the dark, my eyes closed as I breathe in the fresh air and marvel at how different it feels as it travels down my throat and hits my lungs. I wonder if I'll ever stand outside like this without feeling euphoric. I hope not.

'Come on,' Bram hisses from somewhere below.

I snap out of the moment. I look down to the water and see him sitting in a rubber boat. Taking his hand, I climb in, grabbing on to the side and crouching low – careful not to wobble it too much.

I grab the blanket by my feet and wrap it around my shoulders and head. I'm hidden, but I can still see what's going on.

With one push, we're drifting down the river. Bram guides us in the right direction with the oars, bouncing us away from other vessels and pulling the boat through the water with long strokes, helping us to pick up speed. When we can no longer see the opening we've come from, he starts the engine.

In the darkness it's impossible to see the murky brown of the water. Instead, as it reflects its surroundings, it feels almost magical. Others might see the towering buildings, shattered glass and derelict structures as threatening, but to me they're fascinating.

I guess that's hardly surprising because I wasn't here to see their world crumble and fall apart. To me, this is a place to marvel at. To the people down here, it's their reality, their past, their lives.

'Move to the right,' Bram whispers, leaning over me and grabbing hold of a piece of sodden fabric hanging from above. 'Hold on.'

The boat screeches and jolts as it collides with a wall.

'Sorry,' Bram says, tying us securely to the building we bumped into.

I look up at the skyscraper towering above us. Floodlights from surrounding buildings bounce off its glass panels, highlighting its uniqueness. It's not rectangular, or made of the same grey material as others I've seen. Nor does it look like it was thrown up as a matter of urgency. Time and care were taken over its spectacular design, with glass shards protruding into the sky.

'Watch yourself,' Bram says, climbing on to a platform and leaning back to help me out.

I take his hand and step up to join him, then follow him through the huge hole in the side of the building. Back on steady ground, Bram marches through the tall room we've arrived in. I'm not so quick to move. Instead I try to absorb it all. People must've worked here, I think, as I take in the rows of desks and chairs that would once have been occupied by hundreds of employees.

I'm drawn to a photograph hanging beside one station. Four faces beam back at me: a man, a woman and two children – boys, of course. Which one used to stand on this spot? Were they a close family? Did they live long, happy lives? I wonder what happened to them. I pocket the photo and drag myself away. If Bram weren't here, I would be going through every cupboard to unlock more details of a life I know nothing about. *Next time*, I think, as I jog towards Bram, who is waiting for me.

'Let's take our time with this,' he says, when I arrive, nodding at a huge staircase.

All I see is the challenge. I haven't done much by way of fitness down in the Deep. This is the most appealing sight I've seen in a while.

'And we're going all the way to the top?' I question.

'Yep.' He nods.

'Race you!' I shout, running to the first step, grabbing the handrail and leaping up the rest.

'That's not fair,' snorts Bram from below. Within seconds I hear his heavy boots collide with the floor.

Laughter echoes around the stairwell as we set off. There's the thrill of being chased and of wanting to win. And I do. Desperately.

My body responds well to the sudden exertion, but becomes heavy the further up I go. I push through, not wanting to stop, enjoying the opportunity to feel my muscles being put to work.

When I reach the top my legs are burning and my heart is beating so forcefully in my chest that I fear it might actually pop out. I win but don't have enough air in my lungs to declare it. I hunch over to catch my breath, delighted with what my body has achieved.

'Worth it?' Bram asks, annoyingly sounding less breathless.

'Amazing.' I chuckle.

'That's not what I'm talking about.'

With my hand still on my chest, I pull myself up. My jaw drops as my eyes widen. A view. A spot where I can take in the city – and it's all around me: I can pace the entire floor for a complete, uninterrupted view of Central.

'Wait. Is it real?'

'Absolutely.'

I press my hands and forehead against the cool glass. Life. Real life. An unedited view of Central in all its murky, wet, broken glory. The brilliant city, with the gargantuan Tower right in the middle. It might demand attention, but the beauty is in its surroundings.

'I wonder what I would've made of all this if they'd allowed me to see it. I still would've loved it,' I say, with certainty. 'What were they so scared of?'

'I used to think they just wanted to show you an idyllic world. Their Utopia,' Bram says, coming to stand next to me. 'If you were happy and content there, you were less likely to ask questions. But it wasn't only about keeping you in. It was there to keep others out.'

I gasp as a fiery light shines across Bram's face, and illuminates the rest of the space around us. I shield my eyes and look to see the sun rising in the distance. A thin sliver of sky on the horizon is glowing a dazzling orange, lighting the bottom of the stormy clouds hovering over Central, which are threatening to burst and splutter.

Without tearing my eyes away, I slide my arms around Bram's waist and pull him closer, breathing him in – not just his smell but all of him. My whole body relaxes as I bask in the delicious sunlight. How I wish this perfect moment could last for ever. That things could just freeze and leave me here for eternity.

'Do you wish you'd never gone up there?' I ask, nodding towards the Tower.

'I didn't have a choice,' he says softly. 'But I'm glad I did.'

'You joined me in my cage and made it your own.'

He squeezes me a little tighter.

With our heads bowed together, I find myself thinking back to the video I saw of my mother and father sitting in that hospital corridor.

'I really do love you,' I say, pulling away to see his face.

A smile slowly spreads, even though I can tell he's trying to suppress it. 'You're not so bad yourself,' he says, moving his arms around my back and pulling me into his warm body. 'I love you too.'

I sigh, enjoying the pause, the peace and the feeling of being exactly where I want to be.

There's a flash of light in the distance.

'What was that?' I say, jabbing at the glass.

'What?' Bram asks, rummaging through his bag and pulling out a device that he holds to his eyes.

I don't need to reply because he, too, is looking when the second explosion of light occurs.

'Fuck,' he mutters, his voice so grave I know it could mean only one thing.

The Deep.

# 30

# Bram

The explosion is powerful and purposeful. Part of me hoped the flashes were just gas explosions, or parts of the old city giving way, as they do from time to time, but my eyes are already trained in the right direction and as another flash erupts it leaves no doubt for either of us that the Deep is under attack.

A plume of smoke gathers and rises from our home a few miles away, yet I feel it as though we were down there with everyone.

Our safe space is gone.

'It's them, but the explosions must be ours. The EPO would never put your life at risk,' I say, not taking my eyes off the base of the black cloud as EPO drones swarm and circle through the thick smoke.

'Then we need to help them fight!' Eve says, turning her back on the view.

I grab her arm as she tries to run and pull her to my side. 'Are you insane? You are the only reason they're there. If we go back, it's game over. Vivian wins. You'll be taken back to the Tower!'

She raises an eyebrow as if to say, *That's exactly where I want to go.*

'This is on *their* terms, not yours. Getting caught now is not going to save your dad,' I add.

She thinks about it and I see the frustration, the anger boil inside her. There's nothing we can do.

'We have to do something, Bram, I can't hide up here while they suffer for me. We –' She stops. Realization flashes on her face. 'If you get taken back, they'll –'

I nod.

*They'll kill me.*

Without doubt, and she knows it's true. After everything I've done, the uprising I've helped craft and execute, once they have Eve, I'm just trouble they won't let happen again.

I sense her will to leave fade. If I weren't with her, I know she'd be running to fight alongside the Freevers in the Deep right now.

Am I being selfish? Do I just want to stay here to protect myself?

'That's not why I want to stay, though, Eve. If helping them is what you want, I'm right with you,' I say, my own heart pulling me towards my new family. The urge to help them is powerful but not as powerful as the instinct to protect Eve.

Another explosion blasts away my doubts as the shockwave ripples down the river, sending deafening vibrations up this ruin.

It's far from the solid, unbreakable fortress of the EPO Tower but this is the safest place for Eve right now.

She sighs and settles on staying put, turning back to the attack with a heavy heart.

'Who is it?' she asks, looking through the glass at the shattered entrance to the Deep, just visible in a sliver between the cloudscrapers.

I unclip the ocular scope from my belt, stare down the single eyepiece and enlarge the image to see black smoke pouring out through the shattered clock face, which now bears a fresh wound. At the small dock a large EPO carrier ebbs on the rising floodwater as squads of First Response troops fall out into the world we thought was undetectable.

'First Response are inside.' I point out the ant-like figures piling into the Deep, many of them equipped with dive tanks and masks.

How did they know where we were?

'Will they kill them?' Eve asks.

'If they think you're inside, they won't use lethal force. It's too risky. They'll arrest and detain anyone they find,' I say, reassuring myself as much as Eve.

A few moments later the smoke starts to thin and three Interceptors appear in the air, circling like birds of prey over food they're about to devour. One craft lowers to the dock and two Final Guard officers step out. The empty Interceptor automatically rises into the air to continue to monitor the area.

'Final Guard are going in,' I say, as the first armed men step through the clock and enter our world.

'Final Guard?' she repeats.

'*Your* guards. You've never heard them called that? They were your personal security force in the Dome. The ones who escorted you anywhere and everywhere.'

'Ketch?' she says, with an air of obvious fondness.

I nod, and she takes my scope to see for herself. I realize she's looking for him. 'Ketch isn't there now, Eve. Even if he survived the battle at the sanctuary when we rescued your father, I doubt he'd be returning to service.'

She doesn't reply. I suddenly realize the connection she must have had with him as one of the few people, other than the Mothers, who had direct contact with her. Even I saw Eve only through Holly's eyes, but Ketch and she really saw each other, face to face.

'He was always kind to me,' she says.

'He was one of the good ones.'

'I hope he's still alive,' she murmurs.

'I do too. I don't blame him for what went down at the sanctuary. We were both doing what we felt was right for you,' I say, and she shoots me a look.

'Well, that makes me feel much better,' she fires, and looks back at the Deep through my ocular scope, giving her a magnified view of the explosion site.

'How did they find us, Bram?' she says, snapping me back to the moment.

'I don't know. After all this time the chances of them just stumbling upon us are so slim.'

'What are you saying?'

'That it's more likely someone sold you out than the EPO just chanced upon our location,' I say.

'But who? I can't imagine any of them —'

'Eve, the EPO are persuasive, powerful,' I interrupt. 'Even those willing to die for you can have their heads turned if they're offered enough. These men are sworn to lay their lives down for you, but when that moment becomes real, how many of them would see it through if another option was presented to them?'

'I don't want anyone to die for me. For anyone,' Eve says, with a sadness that breaks my heart.

I point out of the window to where First Response officers are dragging resisting Freevers from the Deep.

Eve watches through the scope as her new army is escorted into the waiting ship, a detention vessel.

'Oh, Chubs . . .' She sighs.

I lean on the glass, blocking the reflections with my hand to get a clearer view. The figures on the dock scuffle and resist the officers.

'Just go, Chubs. Just go with them . . .' I mutter under my breath.

'Where will they take them?' Eve asks.

'Detention Level. There's essentially a whole prison in the Tower.'

'A prison?'

'Eve, that Tower is bigger than some cities. Look at it.' I tap at the juggernaut beyond the smoke. 'It has everything inside to sustain a functioning society. You could live many lifetimes in there and never need to leave. They'll be held there first for questioning.'

'Just questioning?' she says.

'Vivian isn't going to kill anyone who might know where we are,' I reassure her.

'You're sure?'

I nod.

She returns to the view of the Deep, of the people being captured instead of her. I try to imagine what it must be like for Eve: to have lived so unaware for so long and then be awakened to a new world, a complicated, cold, hard world. If the weight of knowing that the future of human life on Earth is dependent on you wasn't heavy enough, the thought of people losing their lives for your freedom must be crushing.

'Michael,' she whispers.

I follow her line of sight and see a second Interceptor on the dock, and another Final Guard.

'Let me see.' I hold out my hand but she keeps staring down the sight. 'Eve?'

'Sorry,' she says, as though I've woken her from a daydream, and hands it over.

I recognize him instantly, and not only is he there, he's giving commands, calling to the First Response officers on the dock, sending the drones to set a perimeter. So, he's commander now. Someone must have friends in high places . . .

*Friends in high places.* The thought stirs a memory. My dad was always *that* for me. No matter what I did and how hard I denied it, being the son of the infamous Dr Wells gave me special privileges – never from the man himself, of course, but those around me.

Michael has to have some influence in there or he'd be gone, not calling the shots.

'So what do we do now?' Eve asks.

'We wait. There's nowhere else to go yet. Until we have a better option, this is your safest bet.'

Eve looks around the empty room, the summit of an abandoned glass mountain. A few moments ago this was a haven. I'd offered her a breath of air from the Deep and now all she wants is to be back down there fighting for it.

'We can't stay here long. Once they know I'm not there they'll come searching and if someone gave us up before . . .'

'No one knows we're here. It's why we snuck out this morning.'

'You're sure?' she asks.

I place a comforting hand on her back.

She sighs and closes her eyes, then opens them, takes the scope from my hand and places it back on her eye.

'Bram, it's Saunders,' she says, staring intently at the Deep. She passes the sight to me.

'First Response have him.' I note the uniforms of the two soldiers struggling to keep Saunders still.

'He's resisting them. Just go!' she says. They pause on the dock with Saunders on his knees. 'Aren't they taking him with the other Freevers? Why have they stopped?' Eve asks.

'I'm not sure.'

# 31

# Michael

Thick, damp air sticks in my throat as the brassy sphere depressurizes and we step into this sunken hideaway.

Guard Franklin and the Murphys take the lead and head along the corridor that stretches in front of us.

'First Response have cleared the halls. We have no visual on Eve. Repeat, no visual.' Reynolds's voice crackles in my earpiece.

It stinks down here but that's not surprising, considering how old the place must be. I pull down my visor to get some clean air, and its display artificially illuminates the dark corridor, allowing me to see more than the naked eye would.

I step through thick watertight seals between rooms and catch sight of some of the original wooden walls. Impressive.

Gunshots ring out ahead.

'Non-lethals only!' I order.

'It's them, not us,' Reynolds says in my earpiece.

There's a sudden boom. The ripples of a pulse of energy.

*That's us*, I think. The blast would have been enough to floor anyone in the surrounding vicinity.

I pick up the pace, glancing into every room we pass.

Shit, this place is big.

'They said these rooms were clear. There's a small group barricaded into one of the larger chambers,' Hernandez says, looking back to see why I'm not hot on their heels.

'I'm not leaving any stone unturned. If Eve is here, we'll find her,' I say, my heart beating hard beneath the blast-proof body armour.

Each room is different. Messy. Old.

Another round of bullets: the sound of resistance up ahead.

Hernandez and Murphy E. pause where this hall-way ends and a water-seal separates it from the next.

'What are you waiting for? Let's move!' I say, trying to get past.

'First Response haven't cleared it, sir,' Murphy says.

'Reynolds will give us the okay,' Hernandez adds.

'I don't give a shit if the whole damn Freever army is still down here. We're here for Eve. We don't know if they have another exit, but time is on our side. Let's go,' I say. It's bad enough having to wait for another unit to sweep the place before us. If she's here, I have to get to her first.

'But, sir, the informant said that was the only way in or out,' Hernandez says, pointing back to the sphere.

'I don't trust that ex-EPO traitor any more than I trust any of the men firing at us. Now, move on. That's an order.' I push through.

Location mapping on my display pulls information from our bio-tags, showing me the Final Guards' position. Hernandez and Murphy follow me.

I don't trust anyone else around her now. Freever, EPO, it's all the same. My loyalty is with Eve.

We pass room after room: no people inside, just weapons, stolen EPO tech, holo-maps, books, living quarters, kitchens . . . It's a maze.

My visor displays every room tracked by any soldier in this place they call the Deep, creating an ever-expanding visual map in the periphery of my display.

My earpiece suddenly crackles.

'Turner, I think you'd better see this,' Hernandez says. His location pings as a red dot on the map. 'I think she was here,' he adds.

My heart leaps.

Adrenalin explodes into my leg muscles and I sprint as fast as I can through the sunken labyrinth until I practically fall into a grand room and find Hernandez at the foot of a large, unmade bed.

'What have you found?' I pant, out of breath from the sprint.

He picks up a pile of clothes and throws it to me. Among the wet material in my hands I find a black hoody.

'It's hers,' I say instantly, recognizing the item of EPO-issue clothing.

'I thought so,' he replies. We were both there that night, giving chase through the Dome, watching her jump from our world into this one. It's impossible to forget what she was wearing – all black, running trainers, trousers, hoody, not her usual attire.

She was prepared to leave.

'That's not all,' he says, picking up a pair of male boxer shorts with the barrel of his weapon. 'I see only one bed . . .'

My blood boils. I know it's totally irrational but the idea of Eve sharing a bed with him, with Bram . . . Dr Wells's own flesh and blood . . .

I try to shake away the mental image. Who the hell am I to judge them, to be jealous of him? After everything I did.

I want to hit myself.

*Focus, Turner!*

'Keep searching. They were here and they might still be close.' I kick over the bedside table, its contents spilling over the damp floor.

'Sir, we have all remaining Freevers in custody, no sign of –'

'Eve or Bram.' I finish the sentence, interrupting Reynolds's voice in my earpiece.

'Correct, sir. We have a complete floor plan of this

building now, and no signs of life that aren't already accounted for.'

I sigh.

This was it. This was going to be my chance to redeem myself for what I did. To bring her back to safety at least.

*Safety.*

Who am I kidding? Wells and Vivian aren't safe. Everyone wants Eve for their own gain. Saving the human race is starting to seem so far down the to-do list that I'm not even sure it's on the agenda any more.

So, where the hell does that leave us? What do I do if we find her? We were ordered to come out here so fast I've not had time to formulate any sort of plan. If I take her back, am I betraying her? If I leave her out here, is she safe with Bram? Alone?

Maybe –

'Turner!' Reynolds shouts, snapping me back to the moment, his voice in the room now, rather than in my earpiece.

'Sorry, I was thinking. What is it?' I ask.

'It's the informant, sir. He says he has some new details he's willing to share,' Reynolds says.

'Where is that lying bastard?' I snap, walking towards Reynolds. 'Take me to him.'


'You treacherous little shit,' I bark at the pathetic-looking man, as I step outside, through the clock face and on to their makeshift dock.

'I swear they should have been here!' he replies, grovelling on his knees with his cuffed hands in the air, using his arms to wipe away tears as they run down his big nose.

'It's not me you need to explain that to, it's Miss Silva,' I say, nodding to the Final Guards to take him.

The Murphy twins hoist him by his arms and march him towards our ship as it bobs on the rough river.

'No, please, don't take me back yet! My deal only guarantees my safety if Eve is brought back alive!' he wails, as they drag him away from me. 'If you take me back without her, Miss Silva will kill me!'

'You should have considered that before giving up your friends, Saunders. But I guess you've always put yourself first. It's how you ended up down here in the first place.' I wave my hand for him to be taken but he fights it.

A panicked man with no other options is powerful. He slips an arm free and breaks Murphy E.'s nose. He swipes his leg under Murphy F., bringing him to the ground hard, and goes to leap into the water – but I'm there too fast.

The charge of my Pacify Glove sends a shock through his body, making it as rigid as a plank of wood. He hits the deck, unable to move.

'You can't keep running, Saunders,' I say, leaning over and pulling his stiff frame around to face me while the Murphy twins regain themselves a few feet away.

'They *were* here, I swear,' he snarls, through clenched teeth.

'I know. We found their clothes,' I say.

'There's only one other place they can be. They'll be there together.' He struggles.

My heart almost stops.

He didn't mention any other possible location earlier. If Eve is there, EPO doesn't know.

My thoughts fire around my head, like a battle between right and wrong, EPO and Freever, me and Bram . . .

'Tell me now,' I whisper, checking the twins are still out of earshot.

'I c-can take you. I can lead you there n-now,' Saunders stammers, the symptoms of having been pacified still affecting him.

'Tell me right now or you're going back to Miss Silva,' I hiss, letting my eyes show him that I'm not bluffing.

He pauses.

Reluctant to do it but he's out of options and he knows it.

His eyes break contact with mine and move to a point over my shoulder.

I turn my head and follow his line of sight. Through the overbearing cloudscrapers surrounding us, it lands on a distinctive spike, sticking out from the flood, like a great shard of broken glass.

'Up there?' I whisper urgently, turning back to him.

'Yes, and if we hurry we can –' I stop him with a second charge from my Glove, which passes through his already weak body. He blacks out before he can inform anyone else.

'For Eve,' I whisper into his ear, just before the Murphy twins hoist his unconscious body off the deck.

'Put him on the ship. Separate him from the rest of the Freevers. Let's get them all to the Tower ASAP,' I order.

'Yes, sir,' they reply in unison, and I find myself alone momentarily on the dock.

I stand with my back to the enormous hands of the clock and stare out at the broken triangular skeleton of the building. Another relic of the world we left behind.

An energy pulses around my veins at the thought of being so close to her, potentially looking at the building she's in. Then I remember that if she's there so is he. Just the two of them together. The saviour, and the son of a psychopath.

# 32

# Michael

Saunders wakes, startled and confused. He stumbles to his feet and shields his eyes from the cold lights that focus on him.

'Where . . . am I?' he croaks.

'Welcome home, Saunders,' Vivian says, her voice echoing from the cold concrete of the stark room.

'Miss Silva,' Saunders gasps, standing to attention instinctively.

She steps forward, her presence automatically demanding obedience. There's not a hair out of place as the light casts sharp shadows on her angular features.

She walks past us, the Final Guard, as we line the wall behind her, standing to attention. Alert and nervous.

The last time we were all together a lot of people died.

'For the benefit of everyone here, would you please explain the reason for your last visit? It's not every day a convicted fugitive returns to the place they escaped from, begging to be let back in.'

Saunders takes a breath that catches in his throat.

'Can you remember what you said to me?' she asks, in a disarmingly calm tone.

'Yes, Miss Silva,' Saunders says.

'Then please remind me.'

'I . . . I came here with an offer.'

'Go on.'

'Eve's location in return for full amnesty for my crimes against the organization.'

There is a silence.

Miss Silva stops walking as if she were letting that information hang in the air.

When Wells told me that a *reliable source* had disclosed Eve's location, *one of her own*, I found it hard to believe. Even more so when I discovered it was Saunders. He was totally in awe of Eve, infatuated with her. What the hell could have turned him?

'I would grant your freedom and pardon you of your treasonous crimes in return for you giving up the Freever stronghold, where you claim Eve has been living,' she clarifies.

'Yes, Miss Silva,' he says, fear clearly audible in his throat.

'I must say, I was surprised that you of all people would come forward and betray Eve. You had freedom, the safety of these so-called Freevers, and now you had your precious Eve back. It made me wonder why you would turn your back on all that. You must have had very powerful motivation, Saunders.'

Saunders says nothing, just drops his head.

'Why the silence all of a sudden? It doesn't suit you. We all know what Eve meant to you. After all, your feelings for her were the very reason you were imprisoned in the first place. Could it be that those same feelings would turn you from her apostle to her Judas?' The truth slices through him, like a knife. His torso shakes as he tries to suppress the emotions.

'I imagine that your reunion wasn't as special for her as it was for you,' she continues.

'Yes.'

'I bet she struggled to remember you, barely a blip in her distant memory, a forgotten grain of sand at the bottom of an ocean.'

'Yes,' he snaps, and I see satisfaction on Miss Silva's pale face.

'But she remembered Bram,' she says slowly.

Saunders's fingers roll into tight fists.

'That must have been difficult.'

'She's not the same person she was. He's corrupted her. She's safer in here, away from him. This is where she belongs,' he cries, still trying to justify his betrayal.

'Jealousy,' Miss Silva hisses.

'Yes,' Saunders confesses. 'It is.'

Part of me feels sorry for him. I mean, I'd be a hypocrite to judge someone for acting irrationally around Eve, but selling out your friends, Eve's entire defence? He's totally lost himself and it will be the Freevers who pay the price.

Miss Silva paces the room again. 'Now, I understand we raided the location you revealed to us, and while we managed to detain many of your so-called Freever comrades, unfortunately Eve was nowhere to be found.'

'Yes, that's true but –'

Miss Silva stops him. 'The days of you playing both sides of the board in this game are over, Saunders.'

'Please, Miss Silva . . . I know where they are,' he begs. 'I tried to tell Guard Turner before he pacified me. If we move fast, they might still be there . . .'

Vivian turns to me.

'Is this true, Turner? Did he reveal a second location to you?' she asks.

I gulp. Here we go.

'Yes, Miss Silva. He claimed he knew of another location where the saviour and the fugitive *might possibly* be,' I say, bending the truth, 'but having seen the extent of the Freevers' armoury and operation in the place they call the Deep, I deemed it too dangerous to go on another wild-goose chase at the request of this traitor.'

Miss Silva is silent, her mind processing this new information.

'You were right to be cautious of Saunders, but this second location needs to be dealt with immediately after we have finished here.' She shoots me a stern look.

'Yes, Miss Silva,' I reply, and subtly take a deep, calming breath.

'Miss Silva, if we'd gone straight to the other location we could have had them! It's Turner you should blame for Eve not being here right now, not me,' Saunders says.

'If Eve and Bram are still in Central, they will not get far. The most famous person in history and her kidnapper? It seems to me that Bram would stay put, and if that turns out to be the location you gave to Turner, we will find them,' Miss Silva concludes.

'And my amnesty?' Saunders asks.

Miss Silva takes a breath and lets the moment hold. She looks at Saunders with an expression that can only be described as somewhere between disappointment and sympathy.

'Turner. Would you do the honours?' she says, not even raising her eyes to meet mine.

I step forward, breaking the Final Guard line-up, and cross the room. The look on Saunders's face as I pass is of pure fear.

Poor bastard doesn't have a clue, but it's about to get a whole lot worse.

I place my hand on the frosted glass on the opposite wall from the guards, and my options are displayed.

I look to Miss Silva for confirmation.

'Thank you, Turner,' she says.

I take a breath and hit the glowing circle with the word *Privacy* inside it, causing the entire glass wall to demist, revealing the cell within, allowing Saunders to see its occupants and them to see him.

'What the . . .' Saunders chokes, as his fellow Freevers stare out at him. He falls to his knees, covering his face with his hands, unable to look at them. Some cry silently at his betrayal. Others scream and pound the glass, the cell keeping their sounds muted.

'Yes, Saunders. In case you were wondering, they heard every word you just said,' Miss Silva confirms.

'I'm sorry.' He sobs. 'I'm so sorry.'

I can barely look the Freevers in the eye. I might not have given up their location but my position in the EPO, the uniform I'm wearing and everything it represents, it's all a betrayal to them and, right now, they are fighting for the cause I believe in: Eve.

In their presence I feel useless, passive. I'm carrying out the orders of an organization I don't believe in for people I don't trust.

Thinking about it, I'm not sure who's worse, Saunders or me. At least he's true to himself. Acts on his beliefs while half of me is still obeying the orders of someone I no longer support.

In a really messed-up way, I'm a little jealous.

'Is there anything you wish to say to the people you betrayed?' Miss Silva asks.

Saunders sobs uncontrollably on the floor outside the cell containing his friends, his family. With the harsh beam falling on him like a spotlight, he's centre stage and all eyes are on him.

'I'm sorry,' he chokes out. 'I know that's not enough. It will never be enough. I'm sorry. Please . . . what are you going to do to them?'

His words are shot through with uncontrolled emotion, the guilt, the remorse instantly taking over his shaking body.

'You betrayed Eve once, letting your feelings overcome reason. You had a lucky escape that time, thanks to the people in front of you . . .' Miss Silva says, pacing at the edge of the pool of light. 'If it hadn't been for the rebels' raid on the building years ago, you would have wasted away in your cell. They gave you a life, albeit one of treason and betrayal, but you were free – yet you still came back, betraying Eve once again. Why?'

He breaks down further under the stare of the Freevers through the glass, unable to give Miss Silva any sort of answer.

I've never seen anyone so utterly broken.

'Saunders, you are guilty of treason, of putting the life of the saviour in direct harm and betraying the oath you swore to the EPO. Your sentence is death,' Miss Silva says in a plain, unemotional tone. 'Turner,' she calls.

Not me, please, not me.

'Please carry out the sentence,' Miss Silva orders.

I look at Saunders, trembling, in tears on the floor. He slowly pulls himself to his knees, to face me.

'Please. No. Please.' He sobs, clutching at my boots, desperate for a forgiveness that will never come. His mouth moves but words fail to come out as he reaches for Miss Silva, so overcome with the weight of what is about to happen that he can't even beg for his own life.

'Commander Turner!' Miss Silva repeats, snapping me into the reality that I now face.

I reach to my belt to retrieve my gun and my hand brushes past the Pacify Glove. I unclip that instead and slip my hand inside it.

I slide my thumb over the small sensor, removing the safety lock and selecting the highest charge. A small haptic warning inside the glove informs me of the danger and I ignore it as I take up position behind him.

'Any last words?' I ask.

Saunders sniffs and splutters with fear as he pulls himself together and softly mutters, 'I'm sorry,' to the window of watchers.

Few turn away as I place my open hand on the side of Saunders's head and administer the fatal shock that relieves him of his guilt.

It's quick. His muscles spasm and contort violently before the thud of his body hitting the floor echoes through the Detention Level, followed by dead silence.

I crouch over his still body and check his pulse.

'It's done,' I inform Miss Silva.

She just nods.

'Miss Silva, I shall lead a team to the location Saunders gave me and, if they are there, I'll personally see to it that Eve and Bram are returned to the Tower,' I say, causing the Freevers to protest within their muted cell.

'Eve is the only directive. Bram is acceptable dead or alive,' she replies coldly, before exiting without a second glance at Saunders's body on the floor.

I take a moment to breathe. That's the second life I've taken for the EPO.

I take a look at the stunned Freevers in their cell. I want to call out to them, to scream to them that I'm with them. I might be on this side of the glass, but if their loyalty is to Eve, my heart is right in there with them.

I feel a fire inside that I've not felt before, a desire to do the right thing, regardless of the consequences. I need to find Eve before anyone else does.

The three-dimensional map of the city slowly rotates in front of us, the real-time image still replicating the light smoke billowing from the Deep.

My heart is pounding as I point out the building to the watching eyes of First Response and the Final Guard.

'From there they'll have a clear view of the Deep. Do you think they'll know?' Franklin asks, running his fingers nervously through his wavy hair.

'After the noise we made today, yes. I think half of Central knows,' Reynolds replies.

'We are to use non-lethal force only. Some live rounds were fired this morning and that's a risk we cannot take. I want Eve-lock on all weapons,' I instruct. The safety precaution is not automatic outside the perimeter of the Tower.

There's an audible groan at being made to switch their weapons so that they won't fire in Eve's direction. If she's standing close to Bram, they won't fire at all.

'We're not dealing with the threat of the Freever army now. This is Bram and Eve,' I remind them. 'Non-lethals. Are we clear?'

'Yes, sir!' they reluctantly reply.

I step to the wall and wave my hand across it, causing the realiTV screen to wake. The view is displayed as crystal clear as if we were staring out of a window. Dark storm clouds obscure the skyline, as they do every single day, hiding all but the very tallest of cloudscrapers from sight. Nothing comes close to our level in the Tower.

'Highlight skyline,' I command, and the realiTV traces the outline of the buildings through the smog and cloud.

'That one?' Hernandez asks, pointing to the box-shaped building I showed them on the map.

I nod and feel the adrenalin pump inside me. The rush of a lie.

Hernandez taps the square skyscraper of the old city.

'First Response, you are to secure and search the building and allow Final Guard to handle the recovery,' I order.

'Yes, sir,' they reply.

'Dismissed,' I call, and the dozen First Response officers hurriedly fall out.

No one wants to miss the chance of returning the saviour to the EPO. It would be a historic moment among the ever-expanding list of recent historic moments.

Except I already know it won't happen.

Not if I can help it.

The noise level rises as people suit up and check weapons around me. I use the moment to familiarize myself discreetly with the *real* location Saunders gave me – the pointed spike of a building adjacent to the square relic to which I've sent these men.

Close enough for me to slip away unnoticed? I hope so.

*What the hell are you doing, Turner?*

It's too late to turn back now.

# 33

# Eve

I'm startled awake by the sound of a boot scraping along the floor and echoing up the stairwell. I don't know when I fell asleep or what time it is, but it's getting dark outside. The day is over. We should've been getting ready to leave. The fact we're still here might mean we're trapped with no way out, and I think one jump off a tower is enough to last me a lifetime. I don't want to do it again.

'Bram,' I hiss, leaping to my feet, but he's heard the noise too and is glaring at the opening, gently rocking with his fists clenched. I can tell by the puffiness of his face that he's also been asleep, and that this arrival has caught him off guard too. The realization leaves me feeling uneasy.

'Who knows we're here?' I ask.

'No one,' he mouths, glancing at me with a frown.

We stay frozen in silence as we listen for more signs of an intruder. I don't breathe.

We saw the Freevers being captured: either one of them has escaped, or the EPO have found us, or someone else happens to like this spot too.

'It's just me, Eve. I'm not going to hurt you.'

I recognize the voice. It transports me back to the Tower, back to the lift and into that lab. Fear floods me at the memory of all that's come before, and the anticipation of what's to come now that one of them is here.

Then I remember.

It's him.

Seeing his face outside the Deep and having the two worlds collide was a shock, but I wasn't horrified by the sight of him. Far from it. After meeting so many strangers in the Deep, it was comforting to see someone familiar, especially him. He's seen so much of what I have. So much of the torment. I flash back to the moments when he could've hurt me but didn't, and the moments he's shown me kindness and understanding. I'm not scared of him.

'Michael?' Even I can hear the relief in my voice. I know he isn't here to hurt me.

'What the –' Bram leaps to his feet as Michael walks into the room with both of his hands high in the air, showing us he isn't holding a weapon. He isn't a threat.

Bram charges towards him.

'Bram!' I shout, but it falls on deaf ears. He rams

into Michael, causing them both to crash into the wall behind him with a thud. They pull apart yet come back together within seconds, adrenalin pumping through them as they fight.

Bram jabs Michael in the jaw with his fist, causing him to utter a guttural sound before he falls backwards and stumbles to the ground. Michael responds by taking out Bram's legs with one sweep from his own. Another thump of a body finding the floor. They roll across it, grunting as they grab hold of each other's clothing.

I hear a hoarse voice yelling at them to stop. It takes me a few seconds to realize that it's mine. They're completely oblivious. They've zoned out, or rather zoned in, their attention only on each other.

'I said stop it!' I scream, leaping forward, deciding the only way to stop them before they do serious damage is to step in. They aren't the only ones trained to fight, I remind myself.

Michael is clearly on his own. We need to hear him out and use what he knows, not bludgeon him to death or waste precious time and energy attempting to do so.

I grab Bram's arm to stop him delivering another punch to Michael's shoulder. The second my hands are on him I realize I should've spoken, should've warned him that I was entering their space, should've let him know that I wasn't another member of the EPO here to give Michael backup. I should've let him know that it was me.

I've judged it wrongly.

Bram drops his grip on Michael and spins on the spot, throwing his arm out into the air with the weight of his whole body behind it.

I let go of his arm and feel myself fly a few feet off the floor.

Bram goes to grab me, but he doesn't manage to get me before my back slams into the glass window. The pain is instant, but I manage to land on my feet. I stand upright, defiant, glaring at both Bram and Michael, who look at me in horror.

'Eve, I'm so sorry!' says Bram, starting towards me.

'Are you okay?' asks Michael.

'Enough!' I hiss, pointing between the two of them as I try to ignore my aching bones. I do not want either of them fussing over me right now.

'What's he doing here?' Bram's breathing is laboured as he scowls across at Michael. 'He's one of *them*.'

'I'm not!' Michael protests.

'Your actions say otherwise. We saw what you did down there. This is a pretty good viewing spot,' snarls Bram.

'It's not what it looked like,' urges Michael, glancing from Bram to me, pleading, 'Eve, you know I'm not here to hurt you. Either of you.'

'Like you could,' mutters Bram.

Michael doesn't take the bait.

'Why are you here, then?' I ask.

'To warn you.' He stands a little straighter. 'You aren't safe here. They know where you are.'

'How?' asks Bram.

'Saunders.'

Oh.

'The bastard!' shouts Bram, the back of his fist pounding on the wall. Then he's pacing the floor. 'I should've known he couldn't be trusted. Where is he now? That backstabbing traitor. Sitting alongside Vivian and my dad, I bet. Their new little pet. I'll kill him. What a piece of shit –'

'He's dead,' cuts in Michael.

There's an eerie silence.

I think of Saunders, of his Holly, and feel guilty that he was ever brought into this life with me. He would've been so young. Can he really be blamed for his behaviour when his version of reality was as warped as my own?

'He promised them *you*,' Michael explains. 'He failed to deliver.'

'And you haven't done the same?' I ask, needing to check.

'I never would.'

I nod, knowing he's speaking the truth. I've not doubted his actions from the moment he embraced me in that lift as my world fell apart. It was wrong and against every protocol and rule, but he treated me like a human who'd had her heart broken. He held me together and showed me compassion.

I look at Bram, aware of the guilt that stirs.

Too much has happened.

'Saunders, man . . .' Bram groans, his head in his hands.

We're silent for a few minutes as we process the loss. He did a hideous thing, but he was still someone we cared for.

'Is my father still alive?' I ask quietly, gripping hold of the scar on my wrist, the only real connection I have with him, terrified of the answer.

Michael nods but breaks eye contact.

I'm relieved and fearful all at once.

'If Saunders gave us up, how come you're the only one here?' Bram asks suspiciously.

'Bram, I trust –'

'Come with me,' Michael interrupts, leading us around the viewing platform to the other side of the building. Before we can turn a corner he holds out an arm to stop us. He peers around the end of the wall, then turns back to us. 'Take a look for yourselves. I gave them false information, told them the wrong location. Figured Saunders isn't around to correct them.' He flinches, realizing what he's said. 'This might just buy you enough time to get away, now that they're busy looking elsewhere. That's why I'm here. To tell you to leave. Go west to the closest peak. Not north,' he adds to Bram sternly.

'Why not?'

'It's overcrowded and unsafe up there. But west should be fine. Gentler folk wanting an easier life . . . They'll be kind and fair. They'll keep you safe.'

I slide my face out from behind the wall. The

building opposite is alive with commotion as a group of guards scale the tower. Their weapons are poised and ready as they enter rooms, upturning tables and furniture as they go, looking everywhere in the hope of finding me.

'I don't need more time to run or to be hidden by more strangers,' I say decisively, turning back to both Bram and Michael. 'Look at them. There is no way I will ever be allowed to leave Central. Or find a way of leaving that doesn't mean I'll spend a lifetime constantly looking over my shoulder.'

Michael stares at me, perplexed.

'That's not freedom,' I explain. 'Going back into that Tower and fighting has always been the only way of truly being free. Otherwise nothing changes. They'll never stop looking for me.'

'Eve, there is no fight,' says Michael softly. 'They have all of your army. You only have the people standing here.'

'You?' Bram frowns. 'As if we'd ever –'

'Really? You still don't trust me?'

'Why would I?'

'It's safer if you leave,' Michael says to me.

'I've tried telling her but she won't listen,' Bram explains, as though I'm not there. 'Why do you think she's still in Central?'

'Her father?'

'Bingo.'

'The longer she avoids that place, the longer he

stays alive. They know he's the one person who is no use to them dead. She has to go. Eve, you have to go.' It's almost as though he's begging. He doesn't want this personal mission of his to have been for nothing.

'She won't.'

'I can't,' I explain, feeling crushed as I say it.

'Not even for him? For Bram?' Michael frowns, turning to look at me, his eyes wide and full of fire. 'Eve, they'll take you back, you know that. But they'll also kill him.'

'She knows that too . . .' I hear Bram say, his voice indifferent, even though it's his life on the line.

'But she doesn't know how. She hasn't seen the torture that goes on in there, the things they've ordered, the hideous crimes they've committed. Made me commit.' His eyes, filled with pain, are back on me. 'They'll do all that and more to him, Eve. They won't just pick up a gun and shoot him, and they'll leave you wishing they had. They'll take over his mind, make him experience the most hideous, unspeakable things – the horror they'll do to him, Eve. You will not be able to live with that.'

'Looks like she'll have to,' says Bram gravely, as a blinding light burns through the side of the building, putting us in clear view of the vehicle that's hovering outside.

We've been found.

It's too late.

I've led Bram to his death.

# 34

# Bram

The Interceptor's headlights illuminate the room with dazzling white shards of light that pierce the windows and slice through the tense air until they find our faces.

There is no hiding.

Michael instinctively grabs his weapon and aims it at my chest before the occupants of the Interceptor, looming dangerously close on the other side of the glass, can properly analyse the situation.

He widens his eyes subtly at me before directing them out of the window at the Interceptor.

'I've found them! Sending location now,' he says, pressing transmit on the radio connected to his earpiece, informing his team in the building opposite. 'Repeat, I have found the fugitives.'

The noise traffic that follows in his earpiece is

audible even from a couple of metres away. Across the river, through the windows of the adjacent building, a frantic lightshow of torches illuminates the glass as his fellow officers turn towards our position, trying to catch a glimpse of us.

'Hit me,' Michael hisses at me, through clenched teeth.

'What?' I ask.

'Just do it. We gotta make it look like I'm trying to bring you in or they'll think I'm helping you. I can't help you in the Tower if I'm arrested.'

He's right. I know he's right. We're going back to the EPO one way or another, and without him free we're two soldiers against an army. We need someone on the inside.

We need him.

I clench my fist but before I even think about taking a swing there is a dull thud and Michael hits the floor hard. Eve is standing over him, rubbing her reddened knuckles.

She shoots me a look. 'What are you waiting for?' she asks.

I'm suddenly swept off my feet as Michael swings his foot around from his position on the floor. I smack into the cold surface and before I can get up he's on top of me, using his weight to pin me down.

'When they arrive, don't resist. Our orders are to bring you in dead or alive,' he warns me.

This information stokes the fire inside me and I

use it to roll him off me. We both throw convincing punches but clear enough to allow the other to block.

I take a step backwards and my back finds a solid support beam of the building. Michael pins me against it and gives two light jabs to my ribs, hard enough to hurt like hell but not enough to cause any damage.

Eve leaps on to his back, getting him into a hold that counters his weight and brings us both to the floor again, but before either of us can find our feet the large window explodes inwards, with a blast of energy from the Interceptor, and a guard jumps into the building.

'Reynolds! It's Eve,' Michael shouts, his voice deep and rough from the adrenalin.

Reynolds, the other guard, spreads his fingers. Static electricity sparks between them as he steps towards me, coming to Michael's aid.

'No, I have him under control. Restrain her,' Michael orders, but before Reynolds can make a move Eve is upon him, planting a firm elbow directly into his solar plexus that brings him lurching forward, followed by a quick upwards jab to his arm so the Pacify Glove grazes his face, just enough for the electric charge to remove consciousness.

He collapses in a heap.

'Jesus, Eve,' Michael says, as she crouches to check that he's breathing.

'Don't move!' a new voice commands, as the erratic stomping of heavy boots fills the tip of this building.

'Stay down,' Michael says, twisting my arm into a hold.

From my position on the floor I quickly count two dozen soldiers as they burst into view but come to an abrupt halt at the sight before them.

Eve rises slowly, standing over the guard's unconscious body, illuminated by the spotlights of the hovering vehicle through the broken window, causing a silence to fall over the room. We are surrounded by armed men sent to capture us, with no escape, no chance to fight, yet an almost divine stillness has fallen upon our hunters, the entire squad utterly entranced by her presence. Too scared to restrain her, too stunned even to approach.

This is not the first time these men have seen Eve in the flesh – many of the Final Guard will have been present when escorting her within the Dome – but something about her is different. As though she has gained a new strength now that we are away from the EPO Tower, and for all of us here, standing in the shadow of Eve, it's clear where the power truly lies.

'Sir . . . what shall we do?' one of the soldiers asks.

'Restrain the fugitive,' Michael says, lifting me off the floor and shoving me over to his men to cuff my wrists.

'. . . And the saviour?' the soldier asks.

'It's just Eve,' Eve says.

The soldier averts his eyes when they meet hers. 'Sorry, Eve.' He cowers.

'Keep your cuffs. I'll walk,' she says defiantly, as she takes the first few steps towards the troops.

The crowd parts, allowing Eve to walk through it, like a drop of oil falling through water.

'Well? Are you taking us back or not?' she says from the door.

The men quickly fall in at her side, escorting her into the dark stairwell and down through the spine of this dilapidated building.

Michael follows closely behind her, his watchful eyes acting as her protector rather than captor, though it appears no one else knows that.

Good.

Two Final Guards jab me in the back.

'Walk, traitor,' they snap, the barrels of a gun pointing at me.

*Dead or alive.* The words repeat in my head.

Is that what Miss Silva and my father think of me now? My time inside the Tower will be limited. Whatever we have to do to save Eve's father and get the hell out, we have to do it fast.

I feel my spirit drop as though the task ahead is physically weighing me down. Suddenly it seems impossible.

It *is* impossible.

'Psst!' a voice hisses from behind to get my attention. 'Me and my bro have a little bet going. How did you do it? Huh? How did you manage to break back in, you crazy bastard?' asks the guard with his gun aimed at my back as we walk.

I remain silent.

'Oh, come on. You got nothing to lose by telling us. I mean, not like you'll ever pull off that shit again,' he says, gesturing arrogantly to the dozens of armed men escorting us to the EPO.

'I don't need to break in again. This time you're taking us,' I say, shutting him up.

I'm shoved onwards as we descend towards the EPO vessel waiting on the water. I take a breath and prepare myself to return to the Tower.

The fight isn't over yet.

## 35

# Eve

Peripheral vision is interesting. I seem to have spent a lifetime looking at the men before me out of the corner of my eye, piecing images together to make them one whole being. I've always thought them to be rigid, stiff and devoid of personality – but looking around the boat, taking in their excited, nervous, relieved expressions, their sweaty bodies and reddened cheeks, I see how wrong I was. This security team, Vivian's soldiers, they're just people. People with emotions. People who have been used.

Like me.

Even though we are no longer in the Dome, even though the EPO aren't here to ensure we follow protocols, I'm aware that many of them still think it's forbidden to look in my direction. Hardly surprising when they've had that order drilled into them for years.

But they're curious. I spot the occasional glance. Reynolds, the poor guy I took down, looks sheepish in the corner – shifting in his seat when my eyes meet his.

A powerful energy surrounds us. I'm on high alert – although it's difficult to say whether it's because I'm now a prisoner returning to my cage, because there's hope of being reunited with my dad, or because flooring Michael and Reynolds has given me a surge of adrenalin.

Fight or flight? There was no choice. No matter Bram's preference or Michael's grave warning. In no lifetime would I have run. This was always going to be the outcome.

Michael is glued to my side while giving orders, telling the other men to stay vigilant for subsequent attacks – not likely when they have our people – to prepare the Tower for our arrival, and to ensure everyone is ready for the awaiting crowds, apparently unpredictable in their behaviour.

All the while I notice Michael's little finger gently tapping against his thigh. It's a telling movement. He's nervous. I wonder fleetingly if my presence has set him on edge, but quickly quash the thought. This isn't about the lift, or any other encounter we've had before. This is about survival.

I wonder what he's seen that's swayed his allegiance. Perhaps the sight of the lab in the Tower and all the horrors they perform in there was enough . . . I want to ask him. There's so much I don't know about Michael, like what took him to the Tower in the first place, how old he is or anything of even the slightest significance – yet despite all that I feel reassured by him. It's comforting to know that he's standing with us.

He twitches, listening to his earpiece. He sighs, making an effort to stand tall and wide.

'Come,' he says, his voice gruff as he gestures for me to get up and walk.

'Where?'

'Get up, Eve,' he says, his voice devoid of all the emotion he showed before.

I do as he says and walk through the boat.

'You. Behind me,' he orders, as we pass Bram, his wrists still in cuffs as I see him start to shuffle into formation.

Michael directs me outside on to the metallic armoured decking of the boat. My heart races as I spot our destination. The Tower is gargantuan, imposing and threatening – more so than I remember it – now that we're so close.

Images of my old room flash through my mind. My bed, that view, the Drop, the garden – the Mothers. A longing stirs in a way I hadn't anticipated. I've been telling myself it was all a lie, yet I know it was real. It was the life I lived, and now I pine for the comfort, safety and love they gave me. It existed, and it pains me that I have so much love for a place that has caused me such pain and heartache. A place I will never truly escape because, no matter how hard I try, they've stamped their blueprint on my heart and shaped how I see the world.

As we fall into the shadow of the Tower, as the buildings surrounding us grow more cluttered, as I become aware of the presence of civilians who scuttle around us, a light flashes down on me from above.

'The saviour has been found!' a voice booms all around us, causing my body to stiffen. Vivian. 'Attention, all citizens, the saviour has been found! She is alive. She is safe. She is returning.' Even without seeing her face, I know how smug she looked while she delivered those words.

Noise erupts up ahead as more figures gather in the darkness. I am back in the spotlight. The EPO's trophy girl.

'Argh!' Bram cries out behind me.

I turn to see him on the floor, grabbing his shoulder as a couple of the men hover over him menacingly.

'Leave him!' I order.

They look up sheepishly, their eyes flicking to Michael before they do as I say and retreat. It occurs to me that, although the public think Bram kidnapped me, the men on this boat know that I went willingly. Many of them saw us up there. They must know I went of my own accord . . . yet they're still happy to take me back. It's what I want, of course it is, but they don't know my motive. As far as they're aware, I've been captured and they're taking me back under Vivian's orders. Are we all so easily led? So quick to do as we're told, regardless of what we see with our own eyes, or what we think is right?

My mind wanders to my home at the top of the Tower, and the state it's in. Have they got rid of everything now the pretence has gone? Is it dark and empty now that the screens have been turned off and the Mothers have no one to look after? Will they ever forgive me for leaving?

The thought of how I've disappointed them causes an unsettling feeling in my stomach. There are people in there who must hate me for what I've done. They must feel betrayed.

I take a deep breath and try to shake away the thoughts. I'm not planning to be in there for long, and I hope I'll make those women proud by claiming back what is rightfully mine.

Ours.

When the boat moors at a dock, Michael quietly orders me off. I refuse his offer of help and clamber on to solid ground independently, taking care not to wobble and appear weak. I know she'll be watching, and I will not give her the satisfaction.

A sea of bodies awaits, as men and a few scattered women stand with their heads bowed, lining a long pathway leading all the way to the Tower. The route is lit by little beads of light they cradle in their hands, creating the illusion of stars in the sky. If it weren't leading me back into my past, I'd almost think it was pretty.

When Helena threw me on to her back and stormed through this crowd with me, it sounded angry, aggressive and hostile. It is not now, and my arrival is not greeted with euphoria as it was in the Deep.

It's still, it's quiet, it's sombre – as though relief, regret and despair swirl around us all.

The lost girl has returned, but at what price?

Sobs are heard. Shoulders bob up and down.

I push my chin an inch into the air and walk through the parted crowd. There must be thousands of people surrounding us, yet I can hear the thump of my boots as I go.

As I pass, the crowd dips to its knees, the people holding the lights above their heads, like an offering. For what, I do not know.

Her harsh voice slices through the silence.

'We have also caught the traitor,' she practically shrieks. 'See him scurrying behind Eve. He will be punished in due course. He has betrayed us all. He must be punished.'

The crowd twitches. Her words are an invitation – an invitation to seize the person who took their saviour. To seize Bram.

I stop walking, causing Michael to stumble in surprise.

'Keep going,' he hisses, his body leaning into mine.

I turn to him. His face implores me to get to the entrance quickly, but I know that if I keep walking I'll have no control over what happens behind me. Judging by the sounds of confusion echoing among the people around us, the next few seconds are crucial between them deciding to keep the peace they've created or take out their fear and panic on Bram. If it turns to the latter, he won't make it through those doors alive.

I shake my head and walk past Michael towards Bram, who's being dragged by two of the guards. When they see me walking towards them, they release their hold, causing him to drop to the ground. He spins on the spot and stands, looking panicked, as he stares at the wary crowd.

'Go and get him, Eve,' shouts an angry voice. 'You throw the first punch! Make him pay!'

I stop a few feet away from Bram and wait for the crowd to quieten. They seem to be anticipating the next few moments as much as I am.

I do not throw a punch. Instead, I reach out, and take his cuffed hands in mine.

A collective gasp spreads around us as the crowd understands.

He did not force me to leave. I willingly left *with* him.

I turn so that we're both facing the Tower, and I start walking.

With my love by my side.

I take in the faces around me. I smile and nod my thanks. I try to be everything they should want me to be – kind, approachable, forgiving, driven and strong. With each step I take, I feel those things – because I am them. Love swirls, love conquers, love changes the tide. Love for them, their love for me, and love for myself. I never realized how much self-worth could be created by the love of strangers, and each part of this journey has taught me of my own strength and resilience. The people in the Tower, Vivian and her minions, made me think I was weak and undeserving, but the truth is finally starting to dawn. It's been awoken, and I will not revert. I will not go back to sleep.

I hold on to Bram, flanked by Michael and his team, as we make our way to the end of the throng, and to the ginormous steel arches of the entrance.

'This is it,' Bram mutters.

Before life stops, before I'm swallowed by the Tower and have to live with whatever comes next, I turn back to the crowd, back to life beyond the walls they built for me. I give one last wave, one last smile. Closing my eyes, I fill my lungs with one last intake of real air, reminding myself that I am no one's prisoner. I have come here to fight for freedom – for my own, and for that of those they've taken.

I've always brushed off the title they bestowed upon me: 'the saviour of the human race' left me feeling overwhelmed. Maybe I'm not here to save us from the future but from the present. Perhaps coming here, reclaiming my body and my worth, is where this all begins.

I step inside.

# 36

# Bram

The sterile sting of the air fills me with memories as we enter the EPO Tower, replacing the watching eyes of the outsiders with more watching eyes inside.

'Thanks,' I mutter to Eve, as the doors seal behind us.

'It's not over yet,' she whispers back.

Through gaps between the heads of our captors I glimpse Michael up ahead. He beckons Eve forward, and the guards part to let her through.

'Go with him,' I whisper.

'I'm not going anywhere without you.'

'Look, we need him. Let's not make things any more difficult for him than they already are. Just play along for now. It's all protocol anyway. Vivian wants you to be seen and we need her to know that Michael is still hers.' I nod towards him and Eve understands. She squeezes my hand before joining him, taking the lead as he continues to escort his apparent prize through the vast entrance hall with every single employee seemingly on pause, stunned at the unnatural sight of a butterfly returning to its cocoon.

A slow trickle of applause begins as we walk across the concrete. People follow like sheep, and after a few seconds a deafening clapping of hands echoes all around us. People reach out to shake Michael's hand, congratulating him, as if he's a hunter parading his trophy, but guards from behind push them back, keeping them away from Eve. They bow and nod in acceptance.

I make eye contact with a few EPO employees and something in their stares is off. They appear to be pleased she's back, pleased with the efforts of the Final Guard, but what's going on behind those eyes? I get the feeling that not all of them are thrilled to see their saviour return to this prison.

Michael follows a glowing yellow strip that appears on the floor before him. The orders of the Final Guard always cut across the concrete leading them to wherever Vivian wants them.

I steal a look at the arsenal of weapons each Final Guard officer is armed with and come to the conclusion that we're totally fucked, unless Michael has some brilliant secret plan that he's not made us aware of yet. He's our only hope now.

Do I trust him? No.

Do I have a choice? No.

Breaking back in here once and getting Eve out,

even with the element of total surprise, was 99.9 per cent going to fail. We got lucky. Being brought back inside wearing cuffs with every man and his gun ready to take me down? We've no chance without Michael.

We need you, Michael.

You'd better not be screwing us.

If he is, I'm dead, and Eve is Vivian's prisoner once again.

We pause for a moment as the lift arrives. The doors open and I'm shoved inside.

Michael grabs my cuffs and drags me to the wall, leaving me at a spot furthest from Eve.

'Detention Level,' he announces, as he takes his place at Eve's side and the doors swish shut.

'Not the Dome?' I ask.

'Silence, traitor,' he barks.

Well, I guess he's got to keep up appearances.

'I want to go to the Dome,' Eve says.

Funny how he doesn't dare to shut her up.

'Not yet. Our orders are to escort you both to Detention Level,' he explains to Eve, with a tone of respect that none of the guards disputes. Something about the atmosphere is strange. These men would die for Eve, and their actions in the deserted building made it clear that she has an unspoken authority over them, yet here we are with them sentencing her to a life they know she doesn't wish to live.

The lift stops and the doors open to reveal the long,

cold corridor of the prison within this prison. I see the men in the lift exchange the quickest of glances.

Something's going on.

Something that has them on edge.

It's either really bad or they don't know what's going to happen next either. Both options sound equally concerning.

I've not been in the Detention Level before, but if I hadn't managed to escape from the Tower this is where I would have spent the last of my days. Perhaps it was inevitable that I would end up here. My destiny.

Eve steps out first, following the glowing strip of Michael's order along the floor but he quickly follows and retakes the lead, perhaps not wanting Vivian to see that he isn't in control of the situation.

His men already know that to be true.

He leads us around to the cells where long walls of impenetrable glass allow us to see into the empty cages. I used to think this place was for the truly evil, those who wished to destroy any hope of a future for our species. Now I see it's somewhere for Vivian to hide people she deems to be a danger to her plan. Whatever it may be.

The group halts so abruptly that I almost walk into the armoured back of the guard in front of me.

I crane my neck and see that Eve has stopped. Michael turns to guide her on but she doesn't move.

I stretch a little more and see why.

The glass cell to her left isn't empty. In fact, it's so full that I can hardly see the walls.

It's them. The Freevers. Everyone captured in the raid on the Deep is here, squeezed into this cell, like a herd of cows being led to the slaughter.

They all see us. They see Eve and I can almost hear their hearts breaking through the wall of their prison.

Everything we worked for is over. Everything we went through, everything we sacrificed, the lives we lost: it was for nothing now that Eve is back inside this place.

I try to project my thoughts to them – *They haven't won yet.*

'Why are we here?' Eve asks. Her voice short and sharp.

'I don't know yet. Our orders are to deliver you and the traitor here,' Michael says impatiently.

'Deliver us to whom?' Eve asks.

Michael jumps. A soft orange glow flashes from underneath his armour coming from the tag on his chest. *The next order.*

I'm glad us pilots were never required to have those things. Of course, the old me would have done it in a heartbeat – I'd have implanted anything the EPO wanted to put into my body without question. I imagine Michael felt that way once too. I bet he's regretting it now.

He taps his vibrating chest and holds a finger to his ear to hear the instruction. His eyes flash at me.

*Shit.*

As soon as the message finishes, he walks to me and drags me across the room to the full cell.

He waves his hand over the glass and the control panel is displayed. He taps away, and a moment later the glass appears to split open, creating a temporary door.

'Inside,' he says, guiding me to the entrance.

As I'm pushed into it I see that it doesn't lead straight into the cell but to more of a holding space, a sort of airlock between the cell and the corridor. A security measure to allow prisoners to be added or removed from cells without the risk of other inmates escaping.

Michael returns to the control panel and a few taps later the glass reseals in front of me and a new opening is revealed behind.

'I'm so sorry. Are you all okay?' I say, as I stumble into the cell packed with my Freever family.

They pull me in, patting my back, rubbing my shoulders, hugging me.

'It was Saunders,' I tell them.

'We know,' Helena says, and a few of my brothers move aside to reveal her resting on the floor with her back against the wall.

'Helena, look at you. Are you all right?' I say, kneeling down beside her.

'Don't look at me like that.' She squirms.

'Like what?'

'Like I'm an old lady. There's fight in me still, you know.' She gives me a little nudge on my chin with her knuckle before letting my cuffed wrists rest in her hands, cupped in the frayed wool of her fingerless gloves.

'Well, you're the most lethal old lady I know,' I say, and she forces a laugh.

'Saunders is dead,' I tell her.

'We know that too. We all saw it happen,' Chubs says from over my shoulder. 'She wanted us to see it. He got what he deserved, though. Lying bastard. If that guard hadn't done it, I would have.' Chubs nods towards Michael and I suddenly realize he was ordered to carry out Saunders's sentence. That can't have been easy.

'What will they do with Eve now?' Helena asks, cutting straight to the point.

'I'm not sure, but I've got a feeling we're all about to find out.' I stand and face the glass wall looking out into the corridor.

'What's he doing?' Chubs asks, as Michael holds his palm to his chest.

'He's getting a new order,' I explain.

Michael's face turns pale. Whatever he's just been told to do is definitely not something he wants. He takes a breath and grasps Eve's arm.

The Freevers gasp.

'Get your hands off her!' Chubs calls, and the crowd joins in yelling profanities.

Eve doesn't fight it this time, though. She walks with him to the end of the corridor into a pool of cold white light. Michael stops in front of four cuffs on the floor. They're piled like a tower of hard steel.

He points to a spot and Eve obeys by standing in it, her best poker face presenting strength but her cheeks are pulled tight, the muscles a little tenser than usual. There's fear behind that expression but not for herself. Her eyes flash towards me and my heart skips.

*Don't worry about us*, I say, in my head. If I think it hard enough, she might hear.

Michael puts the cuffs on. One on each wrist and each ankle. He steps back to the edge of the pool of light and there is a brief stillness.

Everyone looks at everyone else.

Suddenly a thin strip of red light illuminates Eve's restraints as they are activated from some unseen source. Her arms are pulled out to the sides, her legs held tight as she's lifted from the floor by the invisible force.

'*No!*' cry the Freevers. Winces and screams of sympathy bounce off the glass holding us back.

Eve doesn't scream, though. She closes her eyes and allows the pain her restraints must be causing to settle as though she somehow numbs herself to the sensation of being suspended by her limbs.

My blood boils at seeing her treated like this. The most precious being alive and Vivian has her dangling like a piece of meat. Our fragile existence is being stretched out before us.

I see the Final Guard, lined up in formation outside

the cell, twitch uneasily as the person they are sworn to protect with their lives is displayed before them like the ultimate traitor.

Seeing Eve like this must make them wonder to whom we're traitors: she can hardly be a traitor to herself.

Again Michael jumps. Subtle light seeps through the gaps in his body armour from his chest implant.

*The next order.*

He remains calm, assuming what must be his own poker face now as he steps towards the cell opposite. I realize for the first time that this glass wall isn't transparent. It's frosted, obscuring the room's occupants from our view.

He spreads his palm and places it on the glass.

My heart beats faster: I'm desperate to discover who is waiting within.

Eve's chest rises as she takes a deep breath while the glass becomes totally clear, revealing the slumped body of an old man sitting in the single chair bolted to the centre of the cell.

'Dad . . .' I read on her trembling lips.

There is a gasp from my fellow Freevers at seeing Ernie like this.

'Is he alive?' Helena calls to no response from anyone on the outside.

A few seconds pass. Then Michael catches my eye and nods towards the display on the glass wall of Ernie's cell where his vital signs are displayed.

'He's alive,' I confirm quietly, seeing his pulse register on the glass.

As everyone's attention is directed at Ernie, Michael subtly runs his hand on the illuminated controls on the glass of our cell – the sound from the hallway is suddenly audible to us all.

'Dad!' Eve calls. 'It's me – Eve. Your Eve.'

The old man's forehead creases as he struggles to open his eyes but he manages it and a moment of disbelief flashes across his face.

'Welcome home, Eve,' a cool, calm voice says, and all heads instantly turn to face the powerful figure that has appeared at the far end of the corridor.

Vivian.

# 37

# Eve

Now that I see him I don't want to look away. Now that he is with me I don't ever want to be without him. My father. My kind, loving father, whom I've been robbed of for all these years.

This isn't the way I dreamt we'd meet again. I pictured warm embraces and shared laughter – stumbling words of forgiveness and promises never to be apart again. Instead I'm caught in a trap. Hung up to witness whatever evil has been planned for him, my army and Bram.

I don't believe this is it.

I won't let myself accept that this is where the story ends. Not for any of us. We're good people. I have to believe in our mission, or we've already failed.

I try to pull my hand from the device that's holding me in the air and cry out in pain. My strength is matched, forcing the joint from the socket before pinging it back into place.

I clamp my eyes shut and breathe through the agony.

*No*, I tell myself.

*No*, I repeat.

I will not let the people from the Deep see me like this – not when they have put so much faith in me.

I will not give the EPO the satisfaction of humiliating me in front of them, or making me look vulnerable and weak.

I will not be less than they deserve.

I look at my father and see what they've done to him. I look at the men and women I met in the Deep, at Bram, and feel my anger rise.

This is thanks to *her*. I think back to the times we used to run through the meadows, how she used to be carefree and fun, and wonder how she became so twisted and despicable. Did the power go to her head? Or was she always this way and I just failed to see it – my innocent eyes always looking for the good in people?

Look at her, flanked by her army of scared and lost men. Among them Michael, trying to keep his steely gaze now that she's back in the room. He must play his part, but it's terrifying to see the fear so visible in his eyes. If I can see it, can anyone else? Can she? Or is she so used to looking through people rather than at them that their feelings don't even register so long as they're doing as they're told?

'Are you not going to say hello?' she asks.

I stay silent.

She raises an eyebrow in reply before turning to my father's cage. 'I thought I raised her better than that. I really did, Ernie,' she says, her finger sliding down the glass between them. 'Kids.' She tuts. 'When they fall in with the wrong crowd there's just no stopping them. But they always come back eventually . . .'

My father's shoulders stoop lower, shaking with his sobs. My heart aches. How I wish I could simply scoop him up and take him far away from here. All I want is to tell him that none of this is his fault. He gave me life, and he tried to give me freedom.

Vivian glides towards me, her cold eyes on mine. When she's a few feet away she stops and stares, as though willing me to crack – to give her something to play against. I decide to bide my time and let her show her cards before acting.

'Everyone out,' she barks, turning on her heels and gesturing for the guards to go. 'Except you. You stay. You've surprised me tonight, Turner. Excellent work.'

My gaze flashes to Michael as his head dips in acknowledgement. This is what we want: we need him with us, although it terrifies me that she's singled him out. Has he really travelled this far up the ranks in such a short time? How did he manage to win her over?

The dismissed guards turn and walk away. They don't look back or show any concern for me. Traitors.

The door slams behind them, causing my body to

jerk in shock, resulting in another agonizing stretch of my limbs.

'You've never been down here, have you, Eve?' she asks. 'There's a reason for that. The Detention Level was never built for you to see. It was built *for* you, of course. It was built, like the rest of the Tower, to protect you. To keep you safe from harm. Life outside, Eve, is unpredictable. You've seen for yourself now what they have done to the world. How they have managed to ruin any good that existed before. We wanted to give you everything. We gave you Utopia.'

'You gave me a prison,' I say, through a clenched jaw.

'Ah, but it was beautiful. It's such a shame you had to go and ruin everything. If you want to act like a prisoner, then I have no choice but to treat you like one. It's for the good of the people.'

'More of your senseless shite,' shouts Helena, from the cage with the Freevers. 'You've made her a pawn in your game.'

'Helena? Is that you?' Vivian asks, turning away from me and peering through the glass. 'Oh, she's a bad one, Eve. You should see the file we have on her. She's one of the worst. Hard to calculate exactly how many people she's killed. In. Your. Honour,' she says with a deliberate slowness, punching out every word. 'You must be so thrilled to have friends like these. A mob of common criminals. Terrorists thinking they're working for the greater good, when they're the thorns on any rose we create.'

The Freevers look at her in disbelief as she attempts to rewrite their history. All the good they've been trying to do, smeared as evil. Is this how they'll be remembered?

'Still, we have you all now and can put an end to your tiresome crusade. Oh!' she says, as though she's clumsily forgotten something. 'Bram! Oh, Bram,' she says, finding him in the centre of the cage where he's been joined by Chubs and Helena. 'It appears that life outside the Tower didn't quite work out for you,' she says. 'If only you'd done as you were told and listened, rather than joining this army.'

'I didn't join them. I led them,' he says, his face full of anger. 'I led them to Ernie, and I helped facilitate Eve's escape. They followed *my* orders. So if anyone should be punished, it's me.'

'*No!*' I shout, before Vivian raises her hand, a force coming towards me and silencing me.

'How surprising,' she says, looking genuinely taken aback. 'I never realized you had anything of substance about you. Get him out,' she yaps at Michael.

'Bram, she'll kill you on the spot,' I hear Chubs warn.

'You have safety in numbers here,' adds Helena, as she grips his shoulder.

'You're one of us.'

'Stay inside.'

'You led us but didn't force us, Bram.'

The words come thick and fast as every person in that cubicle tries to make him see sense, but they fall on deaf ears. I can tell from the expression on Bram's face that he won't back down. He wants to take the punishment so that no one else suffers, but he must realize Vivian won't be so fair.

Michael's fingers swipe at the glass, causing a circle of green light to illuminate on the cell floor.

'Stand there,' he tells Bram. 'Everyone else, against the wall.' He manages to sound every bit the emotionless soldier Vivian expects him to be.

Bram obeys, stepping into the indicated spot while his cell-mates move away. The inner-glass door opens, allowing him to walk inside before resealing behind him. A second later the outer door appears in the glass wall and Michael is there to pull him out by his cuffed wrists, then drag him across to the centre of the corridor, where his ankles are restrained and tethered to a metal loop, like a dog.

As soon as Bram is out, the Freevers rush to the re-formed glass, their hands pressing against it, visibly wishing they could get to Bram and help him, just like me. All eyes are on him. All faces are shrivelled in despair as they watch him rise to his feet and turn to Vivian.

'This is all so very sweet. You clearly made a wonderful leader – look how they flock to watch. See how they already weep over your death.'

'Please, Vivian!' I can't stop the emotion hitting my voice. 'It's not him you're angry with. I'm back. I'm here! Take me. I'm the one you want!'

I pull at my arms and legs even though the pain sears through me. I have to stop her.

I knew coming back here would be a risk to Bram's life, but I never expected us to be in this situation so quickly. Or for us to be in such a powerless position. This feels so wrong.

She doesn't even flinch as I scream. Her full attention is on Bram, her head cocked to one side as though trying to read him. She glances at our friends in the cage, her face brightening at an idea. In just a few seconds Michael jumps, placing a hand on his chest. An order? He puts his finger to his ear, listening to what is being said to him in his earpiece. Whatever it is causes his eyes to widen and a shiver to run through him.

'Yes . . . Miss Silva,' he says slowly, and he nods as he makes his way back to the glass. His legs seem to have doubled in weight as it's quite an effort for him to manoeuvre himself. At first I think it's the sight of a man weighed down by his conscience, but then my doubt starts to rise. I have been duped so many times. I think of Saunders's death and of the horrors Michael confessed to having committed. He's been unable to resist Vivian's commands so far. But I hadn't expected him to carry out Bram's execution.

'Vivian, no, please. Not Bram. No one has to die for me,' I hear myself beg, but my pathetic sobs fall on deaf ears as Vivian places herself in front of Bram, the sides of her mouth lifting as she goes to speak, knowing that we're all holding our breath as we wait to hear what will happen next.

'Is there anything you wish to say to your devoted followers? Any last words?' she chimes.

I'm breathless. Even though he knew what he was putting himself up for, he must have had a flicker of hope, a plan he's not revealed yet. Something. Anything! This cannot be it.

His nostrils flare as he licks his lips. His mouth twitches as he bravely lifts his chin. He turns his face towards mine and our eyes lock. I'm taken back to when we first met – when he entered my life as my first ever Holly and became my first, and possibly only, true friend. I'm taken back to playing silly games on the Drop, to sleepovers up in my room. I'm taken back to meeting him outside the lift and our two worlds colliding properly for the first time. I'm taken back to our game with the Rubik's Cube when I could feel his hands entwining with mine even though we were floors apart. I'm taken back to our first kiss and how electrifying it was. I'm taken back to our last, and how safe that felt.

I can't help but let the tears stream down my face as the memories of us come flooding back.

'I love you,' I choke.

'Bram,' Vivian snaps. 'Last words.'

Without tearing his eyes from mine, he takes a deep breath and opens his mouth to speak.

'For Eve,' he says, his voice calm and firm.

# 38

# Bram

I close my eyes and wait for the inevitable, trying to make peace in my mind that my part of this journey is about to end and Eve will carry on alone.

Nothing happens.

My fluttering breath catches in my throat, my body surprised at being allowed one.

I'm suddenly aware of some commotion from within the Freevers' cell and open my eyes to see what the hell is going on.

A thick white vapour is flowing at their ankles and rapidly rising.

'No!' I scream, getting to my feet but my restraints hold me back. 'Vivian, no! These are good people. They were just trying to do what was best for Eve.'

My words are ignored as Vivian stands and stares into the cell and my brothers and sisters are obscured with this lethal substance, swirling its deadly finger-like wisps of air around the glass.

'Vivian, please!' Eve screams, emotion making her voice crack as tears run down her face and fall from her hanging body to the concrete.

'You asked to be punished instead of them and there is no higher form of punishment than being responsible for the deaths of your friends as you watch helplessly. Now, face the consequences of what you did, Bram. You and Eve,' Vivian says.

The shadowy figures within the cell are all but gone. The white clouds have taken them.

Something appears suddenly through the haze. A hand. It's placed purposefully on the glass, fingers spread wide and open. Not reaching out in fear or desperation but in strength.

Helena.

Another hand appears next to it. Then another. Until the glass wall is lined with this last stand of solidarity. Their faces and bodies may be gone, obscured by the clouds, but they stand to face the end together.

I raise my hand as high as the cuffs will let me and spread my palm towards them, knowing they cannot see me but hoping that on some level they understand that I'm standing beside them.

One by one the hands fall away. Fading into the white. Until soon there's nothing but a milky fog filling the entire room.

'It's over,' Michael says, his voice failing to hide his resentment at what we just witnessed.

'It's not over, though, is it?' Eve says, tears still dripping on to the floor. 'It will never be over. Not for me.' She sobs.

'No, not for you,' Vivian's voice is flat. Calm. Evil. 'But for Bram . . .'

Eve's crying pauses. 'No. Not Bram. Vivian, you have me back. You have what you want. Too many people have died for me. No more. Not Bram!' she cries.

Vivian holds up her hand to silence her.

'Putting the life of the saviour of mankind at risk is a capital offence, punishable by law. Guard Turner, the punishment is?' Vivian asks.

'Death,' Michael answers, now devoid of emotion, almost robotic.

'Death. That's correct, Turner. The three of you do seem to meet under the most extreme circumstances. Of course, this is quite the role reversal compared to the last time you were together.' Vivian waves her hand and the glass wall of the cell illuminates, displaying archive video footage.

*The lift doors open. I instantly rip Michael away from Eve and plant my fist into his jaw. He sprawls across the floor before he is arrested and dragged away.*

The footage cuts to another clip. Moments earlier, inside the lift.

'I'm not sure you would have seen this before, Bram.'

*Eve and Michael are close. He licks his lips. She looks calm as she talks to him. With no sound I can only imagine the way she's pleading for him to think about his actions.*

*His hand traces over the top of her clothes, hesitating before cupping her face and moving closer. His eyes shut, yet his face is still full of the emotion of being close to Eve – shock, delight, horror and desire.*

*They talk. They part. He unbuttons the dark khaki uniform she wears as a disguise until it falls to the floor, revealing her own dress underneath. More talking. More searching into each other's eyes. Suddenly Eve's face drops into despair. Quickly Michael holds out an arm for comfort. She walks into his embrace. She isn't forced. She accepts it almost as though she wants it.*

The footage ends.

Among all the emotion stirring through me, a distinct trace of heartache has just been added.

'Your brother begged for your life,' Vivian says, breaking the silence. 'Had Ketch not been such a vital part of our system I'd have had you executed immediately, but amid the disruption of the Potentials I couldn't accept losing the head of the Final Guard.'

'So, I endanger the most important person in the world and you just locked me up in my room, like a naughty kid,' Michael replies.

'Yes, because I soon realized the significance of this encounter. After failing to fabricate a meeting that might create chemistry with Eve and the Potentials, it happened of its own accord. Were you her captor or her saviour? The line was blurred enough and I knew it would play on Eve's mind. Physical contact, albeit pathetically small, would have a great impact on her. A connection unlike anything she could get from one of her Hollys,' she fires at me. 'I had my suspicions that this moment might be a catalyst for something bigger. And today I'm proved right.' Vivian smiles.

I see Michael glance at Eve in my peripheral vision but I can't bring myself to look at either of them yet.

'Can't you see, Turner? You brought them both here, not anyone else. *You*. It could only have been you because she trusts you.'

Vivian swipes her hand in the air and the glass screen comes alive again. This time it's all three of us.

My heart stops.

*We stand at the top of the abandoned glass skyscraper of the old city, the footage obviously taken from on board the Interceptor, judging by its shakiness. As the vehicle settles outside the glass the camera detects our faces and automatically enhances the image.*

*Michael speaks. Although it's impossible to tell what he said even an idiot would know that he's not trying to arrest us. His eyes look more like he's the one who's been caught than us.*

'She came with you because of the bond that formed after your little lift *encounter*.' Vivian's words tear right through me, as though it were itself a form of torture.

I instantly feel petty at this heartache and try to shake it away.

'I just had to sit back and not get in the way,' Vivian continues, with an air of smugness that makes me feel sick with hatred.

I notice Michael's breathing rate has increased. His shoulders rise and fall as his own emotions battle inside him. He's trying to figure out what all this means for him.

'Don't worry, Michael. It's not your fault. Women have a knack for seeing these things, for subtly influencing situations. It's why it's called *man*ipulation.'

'Enough!' I shout.

'Enough? You've had enough? Very well, let's move on then,' Vivian says, her steely calm showing a thin crack. 'Turner, now is your chance to redeem yourself, to show your true loyalty. Your chance to decide which side of the future you sit on. Their side . . .' she waves the footage away from the glass to reveal the cell and the scattering of bodies just visible through the vapour, '. . . or hers.' Vivian points at Eve.

Michael's chest vibrates and the glow from his tag illuminates his chin from beneath his collar. He places a hand on his ear to hear his order but I already know what it is.

'Would you care to share your instructions with us?' Vivian asks.

Michael looks down at the weapon on his belt. His gun. 'Miss Silva, please . . .' He shakes.

'Please? Please what? Did you really think there wouldn't be repercussions for your actions? That there wouldn't be some sort of consequence? Your failure – no, your *crime* – has in time brought Eve back to us. Now show us, once and for all, where your loyalty lies. Remove your weapon and carry out the sentence or it'll be your name next on the execution list.'

Michael can't look me in the eye as his hand lingers over the sleek black gun at his side.

I sense Vivian move close. Lingering behind me as though taunting Eve with every step she takes around us.

'There's no need to think, Turner. You're out of options,' she says quietly.

Michael pulls out the gun and aims the barrel at my head, his mind made up.

'Michael, *no!*' Eve screams.

'It won't fire so close to Eve,' Michael says, and I notice the red warning light displayed on the side of the weapon a few inches from my face.

'Consider that restriction temporarily lifted,' Vivian says. There's a subtle click and a green light replaces the red. A command only Vivian can authorize.

He's free to fire. Free to do what should already have happened.

'Michael . . . please . . .' Eve begs, hardly any energy left in her voice, but his jaw clenches. His eyes focus. The muscles in his arm tighten. I can tell it's too late and his mind is already set on pulling the trigger.

'Bram. I'm sorry,' he says, then swiftly lifts the gun over my head, aiming directly at Vivian and pulls the trigger.

# 39

# Michael

The gun fires.

I've heard of people experiencing significant events in life as though they were in slow motion. I'd always thought that was just a saying, an exaggeration, until this moment.

I can practically see the bullet leave the barrel in a flash of white and red and soar across the room towards its target, Vivian.

In that fraction of a second, my brain seems to replay every decision I've made that has brought me here.

Eve.

The lift.

My brother.

Wells.

The pilots.

Hartman.

Saunders.

But mostly Eve.

I had no choice. If I killed Bram to maintain my cover, Eve would never have trusted me and who knows what Vivian had next up her sleeve?

She has to go.

I'm not the best marksman in the world but even a baby could make this shot.

Nothing stands between us.

Vivian has no time to react, my actions were fast and unpredictable, and I'm already thinking ahead to the next step, our escape. We'll have to be fast as hell and pull off some sort of miracle but we're alone now. It'll be a few minutes before anyone discovers that Vivian is . . .

These racing thoughts vanish and I'm sucked back into the moment as the bullet reaches her chest, where the small piece of metal should pierce her skin and fatally enter her body.

But it doesn't.

What the hell?

Instead it simply glides through her image with no impact at all. As though she weren't made of flesh and bone but beams of light.

She doesn't flinch, doesn't fall, doesn't bleed. She remains exactly as she was, perfectly unharmed, despite a bullet having passed through her torso before ricocheting around the room and, by the sound of it, embedding itself in the concrete.

*She's not real.*

Vivian's eyes flicker as they stare deep into my own with a hatred I've never experienced before.

Then, suddenly, her whole body flickers, like a bulb nearing the end of its life.

Bram flinches in shock.

The particles of light that make up Vivian's image freeze and fail as she blinks in and out of existence right before our eyes.

She's there.

Then she's gone.

A flash of static appears in her place before disappearing altogether, leaving just me, Bram and . . .

'Eve! Shit! Are you okay?' I gasp across the now empty void between us, suddenly realizing she was directly behind Vivian when I pulled the trigger, suspended by her restraints.

'Yes . . . yes . . . I'm fine. It missed me,' she pants, out of breath from the shock of what just happened.

'Thank fuck for that,' Bram breathes.

'I could have killed you!'

'You didn't. I'm fine.'

'Bram, what the hell is going on?' I ask. 'Vivian was a . . . she's a —'

'Projectant. I know! I saw.' The creases on his forehead suggest he's trying to piece this together.

'Did you know?' I ask him.

'Of course I didn't!' Bram snaps.

'Okay! I just thought that Projectants were kind of your thing, you know.'

We both look up at Eve.

'Don't be ridiculous,' she replies, without us needing to ask.

A sudden burst of chaotic noise explodes into the corridor as at least thirty armed men barrel around the corner. They take aim at myself and Bram.

The game is up. In all the confusion of Vivian not being real we've missed the window to escape.

'Don't move!' a soldier screams. 'Drop your weapon, now!'

I feel the gun weigh heavy in my hand. I could turn and fire, take some of them out. Surely they wouldn't open fire with Eve so close . . .

Bram looks at me and shakes his head, then glances at his cuffed hands and Eve's restrained body.

'It's over.' He sighs.

I look at the small army that has been deployed to disarm me and realize that Bram is right. There's no fighting our way out of this now.

I throw my weapon to the ground.

'All of them,' the soldier demands.

I remove my belt, dropping the Pacify Glove and my knife on to the floor out of reach.

'Room clear,' the soldier shouts, satisfied that I'm no longer armed. Not that any weapon could help us now.

'Thank you for your cooperation,' replies a deep, collected voice. One that I recognize instantly. It's Dr Wells.

'You bastard.' Bram gets to his feet but his restraints

hold him back from the grey-haired man who has stepped forward from his human shield of soldiers.

'Nice to see you too, son,' Wells says sarcastically, as he walks towards us, stepping over my discarded weapons, and drops a set of restraints at my feet, identical to the ones Eve is being held in.

'I trust you know how to put these on,' he says.

I nod and pick them up, placing the two chunky metal rings around my ankles first, followed by each wrist.

They automatically tighten to the perfect pressure so that blood can still reach my limbs but I've no hope in hell of ever sliding out of them.

'Very good. It's a shame you didn't learn to cooperate like this a few minutes earlier and we wouldn't be in this little mess, would we?' Wells smiles.

'Where's Vivian?' Eve demands.

'It was you, wasn't it? You were piloting her. I should have known. I should have spotted it in her eyes,' Bram says, standing and pulling against the cuffs that keep him rooted to the centre of the hallway.

'Yes, you should, but you were too distracted by *her*, blinded by lust, so you failed to see what was right beneath your nose, just like the rest of the world. All they see is Eve, leaving me able to lead from the shadows.'

'No, not you. Not Wells. Vivian Silva. That's who they allowed to lead, because we trust her,' I blurt out.

'You trust her? My poor, confused boy, you've barely met her.' He almost laughs to himself.

347

'Where is she? The real Vivian?' Eve asks.

'Has she ever been real?' Bram asks, his voice sounding as though he's almost too scared to hear the answer.

'Oh, yes, she's quite real and every bit the genius you all believe her to be. Or, at least, she was once. She and I just had different visions of what the future should be . . .' Wells replies.

'So, you killed her?' Bram interrupts.

'Please, who do you think I am? I'm no monster. She's alive – or, at least, she will be again, one day. Just like the thousands of other women sleeping peacefully in their cryo-tanks below,' Wells says, his words bouncing around my head as I try to make sense of them.

Vivian. Cryo-tank. So, she's alive, just frozen.

'She's quite all right. Let's not forget that one of the main purposes of the Tower is CS – Cold Storage. I designed the facility myself when we were looking at the Projectant Program as a viable way to sustain our existence.'

'So, what happened? Vivian told you to shut the programme down and you couldn't handle the thought that maybe, just once, you might be wrong? That perhaps your insane little science project was a waste of time once Eve was born?' Bram practically screams at Wells.

It's hard to imagine that these two are father and son.

'I never needed Vivian, just her resources, her

348

influence. People respected her because she was the one who controlled *you*, Eve. My ideas were just more deserving of that respect than her morals ever were.'

'How long?' Eve stutters. 'When did you steal Vivian's life?'

Wells smiles.

'Did I ever know the real Vivian?' Eve shouts.

'Oh, you knew her, of course. The connection the two of you already had made the transition more seamless. You had no reason to question the person you trusted more than anyone else in your world.'

Eve falls limp in her restraints, sobbing silently.

I feel it too. Have I never known the true Vivian? Have we all been fooled?

'No . . . it can't be true,' Eve whispers.

'Whether you believe it or not is of no concern to me now. Things have changed,' Wells says, as he steps towards Eve, putting his face uncomfortably close to hers.

'Living in the shadow of a woman you sentenced to a life in a metal tank. You think that's power? That's cowardice,' Bram shouts.

'Power? I never needed power, just the illusion of it,' Wells bites back, and swipes across the air with his hand. In an instant the entire squad of soldiers aiming their weapons at us vanishes.

'You bastard,' I whisper, feeling the restraints weigh down on my arms and legs. He made me cuff myself under the threat of that firing squad when, in fact, he waltzed in here alone.

'It's amazing what you can do when people don't question the reality of their surroundings. Reality is merely acceptance of the world around us. Isn't that right, Eve?'

# 40

# Eve

I look back at him blankly. I've spent the past few weeks wondering how much of my life was a lie, yet I'm shocked I didn't see through this one.

I knew about the Hollys instantly – they were children. Girls my age. If there were others like me, I wouldn't have been locked away in the first place. But why would I have questioned Vivian? Why would I have suspected an adult to be another of their creations? I had no reason to doubt what I was presented with.

I can't help but review my conversations and run-ins with Vivian. All the time I was talking to this man. Bram's father.

'You'll never get away with this!' Bram shouts.

Dr Wells steps towards the glass and peers inside, his eyes squinting as though trying to see the fallen

Freevers clearly. When he looks back at Bram his face is maniacally gleeful. 'Look around you, son. I think you'll find I already have.'

I look at the floor and see the crushed shell of the bullet. It hit my cuff with such speed it almost yanked my arm out of its socket. As I turn my attention back on myself, away from the horror of Dr Wells, I realize the cuffs aren't holding me with as much force as they were previously. My movements aren't matched with as much resistance. Looking up at my left hand, I notice the damage caused by the bullet is clearly visible. A crack has appeared from one side of the cuff to the other.

A weak link.

My heart races as I focus again on Dr Wells. There's a possibility this isn't going to be as straightforward as he hopes, but first I need answers and this might be my only chance to get them.

'I'm not the only one you've lied to,' I say, the thought comforting and horrifying at once: I'm not the only gullible person here, but it's difficult to figure out how far the web of lies has been spun. 'Have we all simply played our part?'

'Been played, more like ... *Dad*.' Bram's voice is thick with sarcasm.

Dr Wells doesn't wince at his son's words. He doesn't even look at Bram. It's as though he doesn't exist. For years I've dreamt of having a living relative at my side, to be able to go through life knowing

I have a deep connection with someone and feel like I belong. But blood isn't enough.

I can remember the day Bram told me about his relationship with his dad. The pain and resentment were apparent – I could see them even when he was talking through his Holly. He called Dr Wells controlling, which I batted away with some romantic notion of a parent's love. It's shocking to see that he was right to feel as he did. The man standing before us has not been swept away with love for his child. Instead he has treated him as a pawn. Just one more piece to use in his game.

I glance at my own dad and see he's moved from his slumped position. He's picked himself up and has moved towards the glass. It occurs to me that Bram simply got unlucky with his father. I know mine would do anything for me.

'What happens now?' I ask. 'Killing seems to come easily to you. You have no conscience. I imagine you'll have no qualms about killing Michael and your own son to prevent them from interfering further. Then what's it to be for me? How am I going to be used next?' I manage to calm my breathing and get my words out clearly. 'Will we be keeping up your façade? Am I going to be meeting your third Potential? Or are you going to pump me full of drugs and make me a part of your Frankenstein experiments upstairs?' The anger in my voice doesn't match the queasiness I'm feeling inside at the memory of that lab.

His laughter cuts through my thoughts, allowing me to see a glimpse of Vivian.

'Oh, Eve. Even now you don't quite get it, do you?' He chuckles. 'I've never cared for any of that. You and your spawn heroically attempting to save us from extinction is merely the stuff of fantasists. It was never going to work, but I've had to play along, of course I have. You're their *saviour*,' he mocks.

'But I'm a small cog,' I say, remembering how Vivian once worded it to me.

'Clever girl,' he says, with a grin, as though my understanding has made him giddy. 'Although, the way I see the future panning out, you're barely even a cog.'

'Big statement for a little man disguising himself as a powerful woman,' mutters Bram.

Dr Wells turns to Bram, his chest steadily rising and falling as he takes him in. 'Bram was right earlier. I had been looking at alternatives for our future that didn't depend on the arrival of a *girl*,' he says, the word causing his lips to curl. 'For decades we've been plagued with fertility issues – even before females were wiped out people were struggling to conceive. There have been flaws in natural science, so it was time to move things on with the help of modern science. To make a way of living that didn't depend on something as precarious and fragile as the human body. There is no need to prolong the existence of life for future generations, but rather maintain the existence of those already living.'

'So after us there is no more?' I ask, trying to understand.

'There's plenty more.' He beams, throwing his arms wide. 'You've seen the world beyond these walls now, Eve. You've seen what humans have done to it. How they've destroyed it with their greed and wars. Life on this planet is not sustainable. It's crumbling away and has become inhospitable. No one should be born into that world,' he says, with a passion that is almost alluring. 'I can offer everyone an alternative. Their own Utopia.'

'By sticking them in a Dome and planting a few trees?' I say.

'By taking them away from their bodies and giving them a world they can't destroy? No waste, no destruction. No limitations. Without our bodies, our minds and our thoughts can live for ever.'

'If it's so wonderful, why didn't Vivian go for it?' I ask.

'She couldn't see what I could,' he says.

'She rejected it,' Bram states.

'So I rejected her!' he replies without a trace of remorse for what he has done to her and whoever else has stood in his way. 'She was a coward, afraid to be bold and discover a better option. But *you* – you, I kept,' he says, pointing his finger at me.

'Why?'

'I might be callous but you were only a baby, and an important one for the watching eyes of the world.'

'How touching,' I say drily.

'Don't settle for that shit,' shouts Bram. 'Your age had nothing to do with it. He doesn't have a heart. He's a psychopath. Eve, you were too valuable to kill because without you he and his insane ideas would've been kicked out of this building years ago.'

'And there's that,' Wells concedes, with a nod of agreement. Taking a deep breath, he paces the room, slowly meandering around the three of us. 'I needed the people out there to watch you grow, fall in love with you and believe in everything we're doing here. You living in the Tower made them trust us. I needed them to believe in the wonder of your existence as much as you did. The Eve illusion brings hope to a nation – no, a *generation* – gagging to find faith and purpose.'

'So, I'm the Trojan Horse? An offering?'

'Hardly, but good to know you enjoyed your history lessons. The Mothers would've been pleased to know that,' he says, before bringing his hand to his lips. 'It seems I'm dropping revelations all over the place. They just keep spilling. Yes, Eve. Your loyal team here have dispersed. No longer living the high life, as it were . . . Collateral damage for your little stunt. A shame. And all because of you.'

'Ignore him, Eve,' Bram calls.

It's too late for that. My heart is breaking at the thought of what he's done to them and where they might be now. My carers. My friends. My mothers. All put in danger because of me.

But I never wanted any of this.

'I was happy to keep Vivian's vision ticking over,' Wells continues, his words carelessly stampeding through my torment. 'I knew it would eventually fail and I just had to bide my time. Vivian's elaborate set-up here was the perfect façade for me to develop my own vision, my own answer to the extinction threat. When the time was right I would be ready.'

Dr Wells walks around the room as he tells us more, relieved to share his project – or perhaps it's meant as an extra form of torture for the three of us to see how we've helped him achieve his goal. We came back, and now we're here for his victory dance.

'The EPO were clever. They built the Tower. Set it up to be a self-sustainable city, a safe fortress on Earth to protect the last remaining members of the human race from the harsh environment of our destructive planet. If you were ever going to repopulate Earth, it was going to start inside this tower. An Ark in the flood.'

'But you've never wanted it for that,' says Michael, who has been quietly listening.

'Not in the same way others did,' he says. 'I was giving them a solution to the epidemic. I told them it was temporary. A solution to preserve the body and use the mind while we discovered a cure for the gender drought.'

'Do you remember the trails that used to go out, Michael?' Bram asks, as though recalling a funny memory from school. 'It was an animation. A fluffy cloud being taken from a person's brain while the body drifted into a huge canister – separated while some upbeat jig of a song played underneath. Then a computer-generated image of a young woman popped up on screen, sounding serene as she gave the sales pitch.'

'"Freeze your physical body and allow your con-sciousness, your mind, to live without restriction,"' Michael says, with ease, making me wonder how many times these words have been heard. '"When the time comes your Projectant-self will unfreeze your physical body, and allow you to reproduce and repopulate the Earth once again."'

In the silence that follows, I imagine the homes this was played into, thinking of the people sitting on their sofas and taking comfort from the idea while cuddled up to their loved ones. 'How many people signed up?'

'Enough for there to be floors' worth of people floating in Cold Storage,' says Bram.

'It was a success, and continues to thrive,' states Wells. 'It's only the beginning of the tale, of course. Once inhabitants begin seeing what we're offering no one wants to return. Our thoughts can take us much further than our bodies,' he explains, patting his chest. 'If anything, these decaying prisons of bones and flesh hold us back from our full potential. Our minds, our thoughts are what have made us so powerful. We've created a world too advanced for Earth. No,' he says, shaking his head vigorously. 'Thought is the essence of humanity, the anchor of our brilliance. *That* is what's worth saving, and now we can live as thought for ever. Through my work I've found a way for our immortal minds to interact.' Dr Wells grins. 'Vivian believed in you, Eve, but even their saviour can't offer anyone a forever existence. My Projectants can.'

'It's barbaric,' says Michael, his nose screwed up in disgust.

'Oh, I agree. The things *you* have done have been quite barbaric,' nods Wells, walking up to him and jabbing him in the chest. 'Do you remember Hartman, Bram?' he asks, innocently looking over his shoulder.

Michael's face falls, speechlessly turning to Bram, who is making sense of what he's hearing, desperately looking from his father to Michael. The look of horror on Michael's face confirms his fears. Bram's best friend is no more – and, by the sound of it, Michael played a significant part in his death.

Bram is unable to stop his anger flaring. He attempts to plunge forward. His cuffs stop him. I can imagine the pain searing through his body as he repeatedly yanks at his limbs, his shoulders and chest fighting for freedom. He's aching to get to Michael or Dr Wells – wanting someone to feel his pain.

I do.

# 41

# Eve

'I was shocked too, Bram,' Dr Wells says sympathetically, while placing a hand over Michael's shoulder, his firm grip causing his knuckles to go white. 'I'd like to say it was peaceful, but sadly it was quite a horrific event. I can replay it, if you like,' he offers, raising a hand in the same way Vivian did.

'Don't,' pleads Michael.

'No,' adds Bram, unable to look at either of them.

Dr Wells rolls his eyes. 'I understand. It's not easy to accept who we truly are. Or how our decisions alter our paths and that of those around us.'

'I haven't been allowed a single decision in my whole life,' I remind him.

'Oh, but you have. If you'd carried on with it all, I was happy to let you be. You could've met your match while the world watched, had your little ceremony and then eventually failed to bear a child. I would've allowed you to wither away up there while their interest waned. It would've made no difference to my plans.'

'I wouldn't have failed,' I argue. I'd like to think I would've given the world what it so longed for. That I still will – in my own time and on my own terms.

'You are an anomaly,' he says dismissively. 'Don't fret, you have still played your part in the survival of our species. If it weren't for your birth, none of this would've been possible.'

'Because you auctioned her off to the highest bidder to fund your crusade,' states Bram, his contempt for his father growing. 'Where'd the Potentials come from, Dad? The sons of rich investors? Random men with their own agenda? No wonder Diego found his way in.'

A memory of that man's hands around Mother Nina's neck flashes before me.

'He could've killed her!' argues Michael.

Not an ounce of expression passes across Dr Wells's face.

'Did you care about me at all? About any of us?' I ask, the question strangled in my throat as I remember that my life has been in his hands the whole time.

'I don't care for sentiment.' He shrugs. 'But you've been good for ensuring the EPO retains its power in today's world, and that power made my work possible.'

Laughter spills out of me. I can't contain it, even though I know nothing about this situation is funny. This despicable man has made a mockery of us all: he's played us, made each and every one of us disposable, as though our own dreams, feelings and thoughts are inferior to his ambition.

'Good until now,' I remind him. Until now I've been his homing device, his beacon of light giving comfort to everyone out there, but now I'm his biggest threat.

'You have become a liability,' he concedes. 'I certainly can't let you leave.'

'The truth must stay here within the Tower.'

'The *truth* is that I'm offering more than you ever will, and spouting your nonsense will simply hinder their final chance of happiness.'

'The truth is that you're a narcissistic bastard,' shoots Bram.

'Must've got that mouth from his mother,' Dr Wells says, his voice monotone and unfeeling. 'As fascinating as this is, I have things to be getting on with, so let's get this over with, shall we? Actually, while we're all here,' he says, stopping next to me and turning to face Bram and Michael, 'Eve, it's no secret that these two fools have fallen for you. The last girl standing and they both thought they had a chance.' He snorts. 'Why don't you enlighten us? Looking at them both – if I were to let you choose – who would have been your match? They're both useless to me now. Without you around to amuse, manipulate or protect, they're surplus to requirements. I have no need or desire to have them living in the building yet, for obvious reasons, neither can leave.' As he talks, his words rushed and careless, he takes a gun from his belt and dangles it by his side. 'Which one would you keep?'

Is this a game? A trick? Might he spare the person I choose? My heart instantly goes to say Bram, but my head stops me.

Bram. I've already put him in so much danger.

I might only just have met Dr Wells, but with his love of games, I wouldn't be surprised if he kills whoever I pick. I wouldn't give him the satisfaction. Neither would I disrespect Bram or Michael in that way. Regardless of love, they've both risked their lives to protect me.

'Neither.'

'Hear that?' cackles Dr Wells. 'You really are surplus to everyone's requirements. Such a shame.'

He takes a breath, glancing down at his gun as he prepares to lift it. His hand lingers over it. I watch the hesitation, the briefest flicker of regret, of sorrow, and know exactly who he plans to take aim at.

As he looks up, his hand starts moving through the air, the gun going to target his victim, I yank my arm with as much force as I can muster. The cuff cracks open. One arm free, then the other, the open restraints seeming to automatically disengage the others. One foot loose, then free, then the other. I fly through the air, my body tensing as I leap on to Dr Wells. My body collides with his just as his finger pulls the trigger and the sound of a single gunshot echoes across the room.

# 42

# Bram

Pain slashes across my biceps, like a hot knife slicing through butter. The high-pitched zing of the bullet, rushing past so close to my head, deafens me momentarily and I lose my breath.

I wince and fall to the floor.

But I'm alive.

I shake off the burning pain in my arm and try to ignore the warmth of the blood collecting in deep red blotches on my jumpsuit against the cold of my goose-pimpled skin.

'Eve!' Michael screams, bringing my hearing back into focus.

I look up and see her restraints lying on the floor.

*The bullet!* I suddenly realize. When Michael shot through Vivian's projection Eve was directly behind. It must have hit her cuffs.

'Eve, watch out!' Michael screams again, tugging at the restraints on his own wrists, which root him to the spot.

Too close to take another shot at me, my father swings the gun at her head but she ducks out of the way. She lands a kick in his ribs and, with the sound of cracking bone, he stumbles back into the solid glass of Ernie's cell.

The old man musters the energy to pound on the wall by my father's head, causing him to turn, and, for a moment, he and Ernie are eye to eye, Eve's father and mine, face to face yet worlds apart: one giving his life for his daughter, the other trying to take the life of his son.

Eve's attack is swift. Her moves are well practised, precise and loaded with adrenalin. With nowhere to go, her jab to his jaw and a kick to the knee land perfectly but the threat of the gun in his hand is still very real.

He tries to raise it but Eve swings again. The glasses fly from my father's wrinkled face as he ducks just in time to avoid her fist. He counters suddenly with a sharp shove to her chest and she stumbles backwards.

The gap between them is what he needs.

He raises the gun and takes aim at her, but her speed is her strength. Faster and more agile even than his mind, she adjusts her weight and throws herself back towards him, closing the gap between herself and the barrel of his gun without hesitation, then dropping to her knees at the last moment and sliding across the concrete until she connects with his legs, taking him down.

Another shot rings out but the bullet bores itself into the concrete ceiling, releasing a cloud of grey powder and dust on to us.

I feel totally helpless.

I *am* totally helpless, as is Michael.

All we can do is watch as my father scrambles back to his feet, wisps of his grey hair poking out in all directions, making him look every bit the crazed psychopathic murderer that he actually is.

'Eve, look out!' Michael calls again as my father's gun-wielding arm swings up for another attempt but she's lost momentarily in the watching eyes of her father through the glass of his cell.

The trigger is pulled.

My stomach flips and my breath catches in my throat.

The shot misses.

Just.

There is an ear-splitting crack of the bullet connecting with the impenetrable wall of Ernie's cell and rebounding in a shower of sparks as it ricochets around us, causing us instinctively to cover our heads.

I look up just in time to see a fierce, determined, jaw-set Eve throw a series of punches and blocks, kicks and throws that totally overwhelm my father.

He's on the back foot, swinging pathetically in any

direction he can while Eve lands a fist on his nose, a side-palm to his throat, and a final kick to his chest that brings his feet off the floor and sends him falling backwards into the wall, his gun spinning away from him.

Eve spots it, and while he clutches his bruised throat trying to catch his breath, she picks it up and takes aim.

'Do it,' I say, without thinking.

Eve hesitates.

'Don't think, Eve, just pull the trigger,' Michael shouts.

My father turns and slides himself backwards across the floor, one hand clutching his broken rib in obvious pain.

'She won't, Michael. She's not a killer like you.' He spits blood on the floor.

The gun fires without warning and the wall next to my father's head explodes into pieces of crumbled concrete, leaving behind a fresh bullet-hole.

'You don't have the first idea who I am or what I'm capable of,' Eve says, re-aiming the gun at his head. 'Now, release their cuffs.'

My father slowly reaches his shaking hand into the inside pocket of his now dust-covered jacket and pulls out a spherical remote. He presses down firmly with his thumb and the red strip of lights on our cuffs turn green as they loosen and click open.

Michael shakes his off before me and is at Eve's side.

'The gun, Eve,' he says, holding out his hand for the weapon.

'No, get my father out of there.' Her voice is firm and decisive. She's in control.

Michael obeys, rushing to the cell and placing his hand on the glass. The control panel illuminates, giving him access, and in a few moments the cell door appears and opens.

'My Eve . . .' Ernie's voice cracks as he stumbles out into the corridor, looking frailer than I've ever seen him.

'Dad.' Eve sobs as they fall into each other's arms.

They have no more words for each other. Ernie holds his daughter's face in his palm and examines her like a precious, fragile object. Her eyes return the admiration and love.

In the moment, I take my eyes off my father, distracted by the reunion. He doesn't miss a beat.

He throws himself across the corridor in a split second, ignoring the injuries he sustained from Eve, slamming his hand on to the red emergency button on the control panel still illuminated on the glass of Ernie's cell.

I push past Michael and lunge after him, stretching out with all my strength as the entrance to the cell begins to close, going into emergency lockdown, but he slips inside through the shrinking gap in the glass wall.

I slam against the sealed cell wall and pound my fist against it.

'Open it!' I scream at Michael over the deafening siren that's now wailing throughout the Detention Level, accompanied by red lighting to indicate an emergency.

'I can't now. He's triggered an emergency, the cells are totally sealed,' he replies.

'You coward!' I roar at the glass. 'You're just going to hide in there and let everyone else do your dirty work for you. I guess hiding is all you've ever done.'

He replies with a splutter of laughter.

'What the hell is funny?' I yell at my father.

Michael suddenly clutches his chest, his tag buzzing frantically beneath his clothes.

Lines suddenly illuminate on the floor.

I look at my father and spot a device clutched in his fist, sending orders to the Final Guard.

'We've got to go, now! They'll be coming for us, look,' Michael shouts over the deafening alarm, pointing to the orange-yellow line tracing from his position to my father. 'He's called for the guards to come here.'

'Go where? You won't make it out of this building alive, especially not with him.' My father points at Ernie, while laughing through the pain of his injuries at the helplessness of our situation.

'I've done it twice. I can do it again,' I say, pulling Ernie's arm over my shoulder. I head towards the lift. 'Let's go, now!'

Eve follows, helping Ernie on his injured side, but Michael stops.

'Michael?' Eve calls.

He bends down and picks something up from the floor. A brown leather case. The sort of old-fashioned style for which my father had an affinity.

'Turner, they don't belong to you.' My dad coughs, his tone suddenly changing as he watches Michael scoop up some transparent discs that have scattered across the floor and return them to the case.

'They don't belong to you either,' Michael replies, slipping the leather case into his pocket and running to join us.

'You won't get out alive!' my father screams at us.

'We're not going *out* . . .' Michael speaks quietly to us as we reach the lift. 'Come with me.'

# 43

# Michael

I repeatedly wave my hand across the sensor to call the damn lift.

'Where the hell is it?' I can't stand still.

'Eve. You came back, silly child. Leave me – I'll only slow you down. I came here so you could escape and have the life you deserve,' Ernie says, the sight of Eve's face obviously easing the pain he's in.

'How could I live out there if I let you die in here?' She smiles.

'I tried telling her but she's as stubborn as you,' Bram jokes.

'What's the point in saving the world if I can't save my own father?' Eve says as the lift arrives.

'Give me the gun,' I say, and Eve hands it over. The door swishes open, and I aim inside, half expecting it to be full of my fellow soldiers, the Final Guard, but instead we're face to face with the two security soldiers who have shadowed Wells for the last few weeks.

We catch them both off guard and I shoot instantly. It hits one in the shoulder and he's kicked back into the wall from the impact.

The other soldier launches at me, the familiar fizz of energy from the Pacify Glove on his approaching open hand sending a surge of adrenalin through my veins. I swerve to miss his lunge.

Bram appears from nowhere, ignoring the gunshot wound to his arm, and tackles him back into the lift, slamming the other man's powerful body into his injured partner.

A flash of static charge lights up the lift as the live Glove connects with the other soldier, rendering them both unconscious on the floor.

'Idiots.' I step inside and disengage the Glove. 'That's why these things are for Final Guards only. They'll be out cold for hours. Get in,' I tell Eve and Ernie.

'The Dome,' I instruct the lift.

'What?' Eve says in disbelief.

'Are you insane? We'll never get out from up there. Not again,' Bram adds.

'I'm not jumping again!' Eve says, her grip on her father tightening.

'No, we can't go to the Dome. We wouldn't even make it through the Gate,' I agree, and Bram nods, remembering the security measures in place to stop anyone getting in. 'I know one place we can go. It's a long shot but it's the only option we've got now. Plus, your dear old father won't see this coming. At least, not until we're inside,' I say, as the lift rushes up a few hundred floors.

'Inside?' Bram looks at Eve, obviously not liking my plan.

'Look, I know you don't trust me. I get it. I wouldn't trust me either. In fact, it's probably a good idea you don't trust anyone, Eve,' I say, staring into her eyes, 'but, right now, it's either follow me or we all die.'

'I trust you, Michael,' Eve says, reaching out a hand to me.

I take it, in shock at the gesture.

'We all have to trust each other now. We're all we have,' Eve says, and I get the sense it's aimed more at Bram than me.

'Tell that to Hartman,' Bram snaps.

I pull out the leather pouch, open it and find the disc with Hartman's name.

'You can tell him yourself when we get there,' I say, holding it out for Bram to take.

He examines it and reads his ex-partner's name engraved into the toughened glass.

'What is that?' Eve asks.

'I've seen these before. Projectants?' Bram asks.

I nod.

'So, he's really gone.'

'Physically, yes. It was all I could do to save him

from torture,' I explain, 'but I've seen him in that thing. He can come back. They all can.'

I hand Bram the leather case and let him see inside. He thumbs through the contents. 'No . . .' he gasps, reading the names of his fellow pilots on the transparent discs that store their minds.

'I'm sorry.' I place my hand on Bram's shoulder, as he processes the news that so many of his friends are dead.

'You're right.' He closes the case. 'We're all we've got now. We're in this together and we have to trust each other.'

'Deal,' I say. 'Then you'd better trust me that shit could be about to hit the fan.'

The lift comes to a stop.

'Are we there?' Eve asks.

'No,' I reply.

*'This is an emergency announcement.'* It's Vivian's voice over the Tower's emergency broadcast system. *'Traitors have infiltrated the Tower and are attempting to escape with your saviour. Please remain where you are and do not approach them. They are armed and extremely dangerous. The Tower is on complete lockdown until they are detained.'*

My chest suddenly vibrates.

'Shit!' I reach for the knife on my belt.

'What is it?' Eve asks.

'This tag, it can track me and –'

*The burst of energy is like nothing I've ever felt. My limbs go rigid. My teeth grind against each other so hard I can feel them start to crack in my jaw.*

'Michael!' Eve screams from somewhere, but all I see is white.

*Palpitations increase to a rate like I've never felt. My heart can't handle the shocks being emitted by the tag in my chest, designed to incapacitate any member of the Final Guard who disobeys orders.*

*The white turns to grey.*

*Grey turns to black.*

*The high-pitched ring flatlines and dies.*

I sit bolt upright, gasping for air.

'Easy, easy. You're back,' says a voice, with forced calm.

'Who the ... Eve?' I breathe, trying to piece it all back together.

I stare down at my bleeding chest and follow the trail to the flashing piece of metal that continues to zap out little sparks of electricity on the floor.

'I had to cut it out. Did the best I could. It's not too deep but keep pressure on it.' Bram places my own hand on my chest and pushes down. 'Now get up; we're moving!' He offers my knife back and a hand up from the floor of the lift.

'Won't the guards be in the Dome when the doors open?' Eve asks, hoisting her father's injured arm back over her shoulder, ready to carry him into battle.

'Wait!' Bram bends down and starts stripping the uniforms off the unconscious soldiers.

'Put the other one on,' he says. 'If we bump into any unwanted guests, they'll think we're these two escorting the saviour and her father.'

'Escorting us where?' Ernie asks.

'Anywhere, wherever they want to believe, I don't care, but it might buy us a few minutes before they figure it out,' Bram says, already zipping up the new uniform over his tired jumpsuit.

I wince as I put the other on and Bram hands me the visor, his own already pulled down, hiding his face.

'The bodies!' Ernie says. He might be old but he doesn't miss a trick.

'Slide them up against that side,' I say.

YOU HAVE ARRIVED AT THE DOME, the lift instructs, as we prop the unconscious pair just out of sight of anyone who might be outside the door as it swishes open, revealing a dozen stunned eyes.

Shit!

The entire Final Guard are there.

They take one look at us and raise their weapons.

Bram instinctively steps in front of Eve, shielding her from any fire.

'Stand down!' he commands.

The guards don't. Reynolds, Franklin, Hernandez, the twins, they're all there, confused and alert. A bad combo.

I clear my throat and pray this works.

'You're too late.' I'm trying to sound as unlike me as possible.

'Too late? Who the hell do you think you –'

I cut Reynolds off by raising my open palm, just as

the man who wore this suit before me did just a few moments ago.

'We have the saviour and her father in our custody and are escorting them now on Dr Wells's orders,' Bram says. 'Anyone who intervenes will face the same fate as the pilots.'

Oh, he's good.

They hesitate, looking at our uniforms. Then at Eve and Ernie, who look appropriately nervous. Not that they'd need to act that.

'Stand down, gentlemen, and you might want to think about running some emergency drills to speed up your response time in future.' I wave my hand over the panel, calling for the door to close on my friends.

'That was too close . . .' Eve whispers once the door clicks into place.

'We're not clear yet,' I reply.

Here goes nothing . . .

'Eraeon,' I command, without wasting another moment.

The lift obeys my instruction and starts to turn on itself.

I sigh in relief and lift my mask to breathe.

'What the hell is Eraeon?' Bram asks.

'Not what, where,' I correct.

'Okay, *where* the hell is Eraeon?'

'You won't believe me,' I reply, and the doors open on to the long corridor.

'Quickly, go!' I drag myself to one side and let them exit the lift first.

'What are you doing?' Bram asks, looking back at me standing just outside the door.

'Flood level,' I instruct clearly with my face still inside, hoping my voice and the weight of the two unconscious soldiers stuffed against the wall are enough to fool it into thinking that it's still occupied.

The door starts to close and I step back and listen to it descend from the outside.

'They'll track my tag and think we're going down. Might buy us a little time,' I explain.

'Good thinking,' Bram replies. 'Now where are we going?'

I lead the way to the end of the long, straight corridor to the second lift.

We don't speak once we're inside. The silence of not being chased is almost worse than footsteps and gunshots.

Almost.

Our nervous glances at each other confirm that we're all in this until the end now. There's no way back for any of us. My days of questioning which side of the fence I should be on seem like a lifetime ago.

We descend rapidly, silently, through the core of this mammoth building and it strikes me suddenly that I might never see the outside again.

My head feels light. Maybe it's the blood loss from the fresh wound on my chest or the air pressure changing as we descend. Or maybe it's not that at all. There are butterflies in my stomach that aren't like the intense ones you get when someone is shooting at you. These feel different, almost exciting, new, and come with a sense of doing something worthwhile. Of doing the right thing. For once.

The lift stops, the cue for Bram and me to pull down our stolen visors once again.

The door slides open silently, revealing a single broad figure, waiting with his gun aimed into the lift.

'Whoa, don't shoot! It's me!' I jump, showing my face.

Ketch drops his weapon as he spots Eve behind me, his eyes widening in disbelief. 'Brother, what the hell have you done?'

# 44

# Eve

It's a relief to see his face staring back at us, even if he does look mortified and confused.

His words ring in my ears and I see the likeness between the two of them instantly. Brothers. I had no idea. I sincerely hope their family bond is a little less breakable than that of Bram and his father.

'It's okay, Ketch,' I say, passing the weight of my father to Bram in the hope of reassuring him. We need his help and quickly. Who knows how long we've got before they manage to find us again?

With my hands in the air, I step towards the man I've always trusted with my life, and show him I'm unharmed. 'He's not done anything. He's helping me.'

'That right?' he asks Michael, his brows creasing as his eyes dart across us all, trying to read the situation.

I look back at the rest of my party to see what he's

seeing and find a group of roughed-up, bedraggled men – one elderly and in urgent need of care, one shot in the arm and the other bleeding from his chest. It's not surprising Ketch looks troubled by our arrival – we're hardly bringing peace and harmony with us. 'It's not as bad as it might've been,' I offer.

'And that's an understatement,' adds Michael, as he drops his visor to the floor with a thump. We all flinch, still jittery and unnerved.

'You shouldn't have come back,' Ketch says, visibly uncomfortable as he glances around us. 'You shouldn't even know about this place, Mikey.'

'I didn't have much choi–' tries Michael.

'And you shouldn't have brought her down here!' Ketch aims at Michael, while pointing at me.

'Ketch!' I gasp, stung by his coldness.

'I'm sorry, Eve, but you shouldn't be here,' he says, his eyes fixed to the floor.

'And where *should* I be, Ketch?' I challenge. 'The Dome was a prison, the Deep a hideout. Is there anywhere I can just be free?'

I'm grateful to see his cheeks turn a slight shade of pink.

'This is our only option,' says Michael, helping Bram with my father as the pair become wobbly on their feet. 'You would not believe the things we've seen. I'm losing my mind wondering what's real around here. Wells has been playing everyone. Nearly killed us too. *All* of us!'

'Even Eve? What happened?' Ketch asks, curiosity

getting the better of him as his chest puffs out. I'm relieved to see that, despite what he might've conveyed, he still cares.

'My dad is a psychopath, that's what,' says Bram, drawing my attention to his pale face and lost expression. I can't imagine what's going through his head right now. To be disowned by your father is one thing: to have him direct a bullet towards your skull is quite another.

'You are the only thing I'm certain of right now,' declares Michael, looking at his brother. 'We're family. You're the only one I trust with this – with her. There's no way we'd make it out, and even if we did, the crowds would overwhelm us. This is the only place I thought we could go. It's so unplanned that it might just catch Wells off guard. You've gotta let us in.'

'What do you think this place is?'

'An opportunity,' Michael replies, without missing a beat.

'Mikey . . .' Ketch says, looking fraught.

'Listen to your gut and tell me I'm wrong,' Michael says, placing a palm on Ketch's shoulder and the other below his ribs.

'Ketch,' I whisper, forcing him to look up at me, suddenly realizing he's acting out of fear for my safety rather than annoyance at my being here. 'Thank you for keeping me safe all these years. If I listen to *my* gut,' I say, echoing Michael's words, 'it tells me I've been lucky to have you. You have been devoted, and I believe your actions have been for *me*, not blindly for the good of Vivian and the EPO . . .'

'And, brother, you were right on that,' Michael says, making me think of the horrors we've been forced to see. 'You were right!' he repeats, punching the words to give them more weight.

'We should get a move on,' urges Bram.

'You know that once you're in there I can't come and help you, that you're on your own,' Ketch warns, leaving us all to stare at him blankly.

I've come here not knowing what's inside, but blindly followed the word of others.

'There's no other way,' Michael says, his jaw tensing. 'I need this one last act of loyalty, Ketch . . . For Eve.'

Ketch meets his brother's gaze and sighs, nodding slowly. He understands.

'You've got to be quick.' He exhales, turning and guiding us further into the vast room.

We follow him, my father's shoes squeaking as he's dragged across the shiny black floor by Bram and Michael – despite their own injuries.

Only now do I take in where we are, and I'm stunned at the vastness of the space around us, of the detail and grandeur of this place, which exists inside the Tower. I think of the Dome, and then of the little 'outside' hideaway they created for me, and realize this shouldn't come as such a shock.

'Is this my dad's work?' Bram asks, matching my disbelief.

'Well, it's not Vivian's,' Michael replies flatly.

'What is this place for?' I ask, trying to make sense of what I'm seeing.

'If I'm honest, I'm not entirely sure.'

'What?' asks Bram, stopping in his tracks. He repositions my father, who lifts his head questioningly at Michael.

'Look, all I know is it's our only hope of making it through the night, let alone anything else, and every minute more that we're alive is a small victory,' Michael says.

'You've brought Eve here on a hunch?' Bram frowns, getting angrier. 'Who knows what might be through there?'

'Exactly. Who knows?' Michael is clearly doing his best to keep his voice calm. This isn't the time for an internal dispute. 'The only thing we know for certain is that anywhere else is instant death. For all of us. Remember, your father doesn't need her any more.'

Bram's head whips round to me, his eyes filling with sadness. Before, it was his life on the line, but now I'm in just as much danger.

'You should've gone without me, Eve,' whimpers my father, his body curling in pain. 'You would've had more of a chance without me slowing you down. This is my fault.'

'Stop it!' I tell him, running towards him and placing my hand on his cheek.

'I've let you down,' he argues, his words breaking

my heart. I wonder how long he'll berate himself over something that wasn't his decision to make.

'You could never . . .'

'We have guests!' sings a voice, causing Ketch to groan and the rest of us to jump.

'Stephanie,' he replies hurriedly. 'They were just –'

'Eve!' she interrupts, her beautiful face turning to look at me, clearly intrigued. Such perfection. She reminds me of Holly, her expression knowing and innocent all at once. Although she's different somehow. Her expectant gaze makes me stand a little taller, appear a little stronger. She breaks eye contact and moves on to the other members of our group. 'Bram Wells, Michael Turner and Ernest Warren,' she says, a smile spreading across her red lips. 'Please come with me to our VIP entrance to avoid congestion.'

I look around at the stark area surrounding us and back at Stephanie.

'Thanks,' says Michael, shuffling behind her to encourage us all to follow suit.

Despite his reservations, Bram does as he's told. We all do.

Whatever this place is, they're expecting it to be busy, I think, as we pass multiple help points and check-in desks. We bypass those and head straight towards the circular entrance.

'Please come forward one by one, go into the cylinder, and stop on the gold mark,' Stephanie instructs, stopping us just a few metres away from our final destination. 'Here you will be scanned from head to toe.'

'Why?' Bram demands.

'Protocol,' she replies. 'The gates to Eraeon won't open without us knowing what you are.'

Bram shoots a questioning look towards Ketch and Michael, but Stephanie continues to speak. 'It's important to know how much light and matter are entering.'

'It's fine,' insists Ketch. 'Once it knows you're matter it'll hover over your heart for a few seconds for further clarification. It needs to know you're real, nothing more. It's just population control. Stand there, get scanned and get going. This is taking far too long, Mikey,' he says, with urgency and a quick glance behind us.

'Go,' I tell them. 'Can you stand, Dad?'

'Only for a second or two,' he grunts.

'We'll go either side of you,' Michael says, carefully placing him against Bram so that he can go through and be ready to receive him on the other side.

Ketch manoeuvres himself so that he's on the opposite side of the glass cylinder.

I watch as Michael stands on the gold spot. Once he's still, a bright beam of light moves from the top of his head down to the bottom of his heavy-duty boots. The data is then transmitted on to the glass panel between him and Ketch, showing the outline of his frame and the location of his organs.

Satisfied, the beam then pings back up to his chest,

lingering for a second before a beep sounds and a red beacon light appears to locate his heart on the image before him. He is declared as matter – which I find comforting after today's events – and encouraged to walk through.

'Your turn, Ernest Warren,' Stephanie encourages, while Bram carefully helps him into the cylinder.

A beam of light, a satisfied bleep, a glowing red light.

Matter.

Michael catches him once he's cleared for entry, the two of them lingering under the circular arch.

'Bram Wells.' Stephanie smiles, her hand gesturing him forward.

'I'm surprised you're still alive,' Ketch says to Bram, an air of something unpleasant in his voice.

'Family connections,' Bram says, his voice raspy and tired. He starts to make his way through, but stops himself and turns back. 'I'm sorry,' he says, looking straight at Ketch. 'I didn't want any of that to happen. We just . . . it just . . . got out of hand. We . . .' He stops, choked on his own words.

Their eyes remain locked as they take each other in.

'Thank you,' Ketch eventually says. 'You'd better go and help Ernie . . .'

Bram nods, his face still shadowed with regret, and steps on to the gold spot.

A beam of light, a satisfied bleep, a glowing red light.

Matter. He glances at me with a relieved smile before stepping away.

'Eve,' invites Stephanie.

I step inside, looking towards the three men waiting for me on the other side.

A beam of light.

A beam of light.

Two beeps.

No beacon.

'What?' I hear myself whimper, looking up to Ketch.

'One second.' He frowns, going to a pad beside him and punching at it so that it repeats the process.

'Do we have time for this?' shouts Michael, becoming impatient as he and Bram struggle with Ernie.

'Yes,' croaks Ketch, staring intently at the screen.

'Can't you override it and let her through?' Bram shouts.

'Wait!' Ketch replies. 'This'll take a second.'

There's a commotion from across the hall as we hear shouting and feet stamping along the floor.

'Take him through!' I demand to Michael and Bram, holding my father. 'Don't waste time.'

They're hesitant, but as the machine starts moving again they do as I say, walking through the archway and down the corridor beyond.

A beam of light.

A beam of light.

Two beeps.

A beacon of light hovering over my heart.

Matter.

Relieved, because I was almost starting to doubt my own existence, I look through the glass to Ketch. However, his eyes are fixed elsewhere in complete bewilderment. Intrigued, I follow his gaze. And there it is, a second flash of red hovering a foot lower than the first.

There's a second heartbeat.

A *second* heartbeat.

I'm speechless. Breathless.

'Eve,' Ketch whispers.

Looking up I find a face full of bewilderment and hope staring back at me.

'Is that –' I'm trying to process what I think I'm seeing.

'You have to go. Now,' Ketch says in shock.

My head bops around, my whole body having turned to jelly.

'Quickly.'

I do as he says, wobbling as I place one foot in front of the other towards a new world.

A world I'm not prepared for.

A world in which I'm pregnant.

*To be continued . . .*

# Acknowledgements

Firstly, let's start with a massive thanks to you, the reader. If you're reading this then we imagine you've already read the first book in the trilogy, which hopefully means you enjoyed that book enough to read this one. HURRAH! Hopefully your nose will be getting stuck into the third book of the saga when that arrives too.

A huge thanks to our incredible teams at Michael Joseph and Penguin Random House Children's for continuing to gel into one big supergroup to tackle a co-written book by two busy authors. Our thanks goes out to Tom Weldon, Francesca Dow and Louise Moore for giving us our amazing troop of talented humans; Rebecca Hilsdon, Maxine Hitchcock, Natalie Doherty and Amanda Punter for their superb editorial input; Hazel Orme for putting us through our paces with the copy-edit; Emma Henderson for tackling the page proofs; Lee Motley and Jacqui McDonough for designing the cover; Ellie Hughes, Ella Watkins, Harriet Venn and Sophia Dryden for ensuring people know about the book; Claire Bush, Jennifer Breslin and Michelle Nathan for encouraging people to read the book; Christina Ellicott and Geraldine McBride for kindly asking shops to sell the book; Chantal Noel, Zosia Knopp and their teams for ensuring the book is translated and read in lots of different countries around the world; Alice Mottram for making the book an actual tangible thing; and to anyone in the office who has had to listen to any of this lot going on about this series for the last four and a half years . . . one book to go!

Massive thanks to our brilliant agents Stephanie Thwaites and Hannah Ferguson, managers Fletcher and Happy Entertainment, Rebecca Burton, Claire Dundas, Angela Walter and all the team at YM&U, and Kaz Gill.

A big shout out to both our families who've kept asking when this book is out so they can read the next instalment – they've really piled on the pressure. We couldn't do what we do without their support, love and laughter.

Lastly, our boys – Buzz, Buddy and Max. We are so lucky to call you ours.

*By Giovanna Fletcher*

Billy and Me
You're the One that I Want
Always with Love
Dream a Little Dream
Some Kind of Wonderful

SHORT STORIES
Christmas with Billy and Me
Dream a Little Christmas Dream

NON-FICTION
Happy Mum, Happy Baby
Letters on Motherhood

*By Tom Fletcher*

FOR CHILDREN
The Christmasaurus
The Creakers
The Danger Gang

Brain Freeze
(written specially for World Book Day 2018)

FOR YOUNGER READERS
There's a Monster in Your Book
There's a Dragon in Your Book
There's an Alien in Your Book
There's a Superhero in Your Book
There's a Witch in Your Book

WRITTEN WITH DOUGIE POYNTER,
FOR YOUNGER READERS
The Dinosaur that Pooped Christmas
The Dinosaur that Pooped a Planet!
The Dinosaur that Pooped the Past!

The Dinosaur that Pooped the Bed!
The Dinosaur that Pooped a Rainbow!
The Dinosaur that Pooped Daddy!
The Dinosaur that Pooped a Lot!
(written specially for World Book Day 2015)
The Dinosaur that Pooped a Princess
The Dinosaur that Pooped a Pirate